Daring to Fall

Also by T. J. Kline

Hidden Falls
Daring to Fall
Making the Play

Healing Harts Novels
Heart's Desire
Taking Heart
Close to Heart
Wild at Heart
Change of Heart

Rodeo Novels
Rodeo Queen
The Cowboy and the Angel
Learning the Ropes
Runaway Cowboy

Daring to Fall

A HIDDEN FALLS NOVEL

T. J. KLINE

AVONIMPULSE
An Imprint of HarperCollinsPublishers

*To my family and friends, I can't thank you
enough for joining me on this journey.*

Excerpt from *Making the Play* copyright © 2016 by Tina Klinesmith.

DARING TO FALL. Copyright © 2017 by Tina Klinesmith. All
rights reserved. Printed in the United States of America. No part
of this book may be used or reproduced in any manner what-
soever without written permission except in the case of brief
quotations embodied in critical articles and reviews. For information, address HarperCollins Publishers, 195 Broadway, New
York, NY 10007.

Digital Edition JANUARY 2017 ISBN: 9780062651822
Print Edition ISBN: 9780062651839

10 9 8 7 6 5 4 3 2 1

Chapter One

"HEY, BEN, I have a favor to ask."

Ben McQuaid rolled his eyes skyward. Of course, his brother Andrew needed another favor. Lately, Ben seemed to be the one *doing* the favors more often than receiving any. But, that's what brothers did for one another, right? And with six siblings, most of them younger, that added up to be a lot of favors.

"Make it quick, I'm on my way into the fire station for my shift."

"Good, because this is more of an official call than a favor anyway. I need you to head down to the Quinn place on Mosquito Road. Apparently, there's a cat stuck in a tree. It seems stupid to call it in to the firehouse and drag the engine out for a cat. See? I'm actually doing *you* a favor and saving you all that cleaning and polishing you have to do just for driving a truck out of the garage."

They'd be cleaning the engine anyway. Plus, without an engine, Ben had no ladder to get up the tree. "So, what you're suggesting is that I shimmy up the tree the way I did when we were ten to get the football you and Grant would get stuck."

Andrew's chuckle sounded through the receiver. "Pretty much. Look, the call just came in from dispatch and you've got to drive by there on your way into town anyway. No sense in making it an official call."

There was nothing about this that was a *favor* for Ben. "What's wrong, is there an apple fritter with your name on it? This way you save yourself the effort of having to fill out another police report, right?" Andrew wasn't fooling him.

"There's that too." Ben heard Andrew address someone else in the background. "Hey, I have to run. There's a domestic dispute at the winery. You got this, right?"

"Yeah, I'll take care of it," Ben said with a sigh.

"Thanks. I owe you one."

"One?" Ben muttered to himself as the receiver disconnected in his ear and he took the turn off onto Mosquito Road. "You owe me more than that."

He wasn't looking forward to this. Hollister Quinn was one of those old guys who spoke his mind, loudly and often. He'd been the first in line to protest the latest upgrades being done to spruce up their small foothill town. Said he liked it rustic, the way it'd been for years and that it should stay that way. However, now that there was talk about Hidden Falls trying to become more of a tourist attraction along the way to Tahoe, an idea that would bring higher profits for local businesses which, in turn, kept the town thriving, Quinn was complaining even more. A visit with Quinn, even to retrieve a kitten, was sure to bring a lengthy lecture about how the people of Hidden Falls were selling out. Ben rubbed the knots of tension already building at the back of his neck.

Pulling into the circular driveway in front of the Quinn house, he maneuvered his pickup between several other vehicles, none of which were Hollister's. A crowd was already gathered under one of the tall pines in the front yard.

"Great," the old man complained as Ben edged closer to the chaos. "Please, tell me you're here to do something productive, not just here to gawk like everyone else. I need someone to get that damn thing outta my tree." He pointed to where a tabby kitten yowled loudly from a high branch on the tree.

Ben squinted, following the old man's gaze. "Are you sure that's a cat? It doesn't look—"

"What else would it be?" Quinn rolled his eyes before glaring at Ben and shoving him toward the godawful howling the cat in the tree was making. "Do your job, fireman, and get that thing down." He turned away, muttering something about the woman running the animal sanctuary down the road but Ben didn't quite catch it and he wasn't about to risk having the old man rip him a new one again.

"Sure thing, Mr. Quinn," Ben agreed, wondering again why he'd wanted to be a firefighter. Sweating it out with the cattle on his parents' ranch sounded a hell of a lot better right now than climbing a tree to get the shit clawed out of him by a frightened kitten.

He glanced around at the large group of neighbors that had come to watch, curious at the interest for a simple kitten stuck in a tree. It wasn't a big enough deal to warrant this sort of hullabaloo. The kitten yowled louder and Ben had just lifted his foot onto the ladder Quinn had left braced against the side of the tree when Ellie Quinn, the old man's daughter, hurried to his side.

"Ben, I'm sorry. I tried to get my dad to just leave the poor thing alone, but you know how he is." She shot him a coy smile and her eyelashes fluttered.

Ellie was a nice woman. The same age as his younger sister and obviously interested in him. She was sweet, kind to everyone she met, a member of the local women's shelter planning committee and generous to a fault. In fact, she was exactly what he wanted in a woman, plus she had a "girl next door" quality that made her adorable. His mother had been trying to set them up for months, reminding him that he should be giving her grandchildren before she was too old to enjoy them. The problem was, Ben wasn't attracted to Ellie at all. He wanted to be, but every time he was around her, there was no stirring in him, no warm fuzzies like he'd had with other women. Nothing to get a rise out of him, so to speak, at all. It was almost like he *wanted* to continually find himself getting screwed over by crazy women. "Don't worry about it, Ellie," he said, waving a hand in her direction and looking up the tree. "I'll just get this guy down and he'll take off back home." Ben wasn't nearly as confident about his ability to get the cat down as he sounded but Ellie was sweet. He couldn't blame her for her cantankerous father.

She cocked her head and gave him a confused look. "Oh. Um, okay."

Putting one foot over the other as he climbed the ladder, trying to ignore the jeers and shouts from below, Ben pulled himself into a fork in the tree, hanging his legs over the branch as he straddled it. He could barely see the spotted fluffy coat of the kitten but, from what he could see, it was definitely young. He'd never understand how a stupid animal could get itself into a tree but couldn't get back out. Then again, it wasn't like people didn't get themselves into some pretty precarious positions they couldn't figure their way out of.

Tucking his feet under him so he was squatting on the limb, grateful for the heavy tread of his work boots, Ben reach for a thick branch to his right, using it to swing him to the V beside where the cat was hiding. The gasp from the onlookers below nearly made him laugh. Sure, falling would be painful but the fifteen-foot landing into mulch couldn't hurt any more than the second story floor of an old farmhouse collapsing from under him during a call and dropping him into the concrete basement below. Those two fractured ribs had hurt like hell.

Straddling the second branch, he watched the kitten for a moment. The poor animal was scared out of its mind. Its big blue eyes were round with fear and, from this vantage point, he could see that it was a matted mess. Tiny claws clung to the rippled bark of the tree and he wondered how he was possibly going to convince the frightened animal to let go without his very vulnerable bare arm replacing the tree trunk under its claws.

"Here, kitty," he called quietly. The cat turned toward him and he saw the unmistakable black tufts over the kitten's ears. It turned away again, edging out onto the branch and he saw the stubby tail.

Holy crap, that is not a cat. It's a freakin' bobcat kitten.

"Shit," he muttered. "That damn brother of mine owes me *big* time."

EMMA JORDAN PAUSED at the doorway of the reinforced chain link gate that separated her from the nearly one hundred and fifty pounds of pacing lithe mountain lion to eye the truck heading down her long driveway. The cat chuffed at her, making the noise of pleasure deep in his throat, rubbing his face along the fence line. "Okay, Buster, I'll be right back with your breakfast."

Interrupting the animals' feeding schedule was something she rarely did, especially with the animals that couldn't be rehabilitated and released back into the wild. They needed routine but visitors at feeding time was an even worse prospect than a grouchy cougar. She hurried back to the old golf cart and headed for the front gate. Sierra Tracks Animal Sanctuary wasn't open for visitors any longer, not since her father had suddenly changed his policy and stopped his educational programs after his first stroke a year ago, complaining he just couldn't keep up. It was probably better that he'd slowed down, but it had hurt the facilities bottom line, putting them into the red for the first time. It was one of the things she intended to change now that she'd been thrust into taking over after his death, but she lacked the manpower to give tours for now. Until she could find some more funding, it would have to wait. Just one more in a long list of changes she wanted make now that she'd become the director of Sierra Tracks.

Emma jumped out of the golf cart before it had even fully come to a stop. She barely caught a glimpse of dark hair and broad shoulders as the driver turned back toward the front seat of his truck. "Sorry, we're not open for business to the public and I'm not giving any more interviews."

"You're what?" The deep baritone voice was as warm and rich as fine chocolate. "No, I'm not here for that."

Emma caught herself before she audibly gasped as he turned around. This man looked like a fitness model with his dark, spiky, slightly gelled hair, rippling physique and t-shirt showing off a sleeve tattoo on his right arm. Bumping the truck door shut with his hip, he walked up to the iron gate with a cardboard box cradled between his hands. "You're in charge?"

He didn't walk, he swaggered up to her gate. And when he smiled, she felt her entire stomach do a flip. *Who the hell* is *this guy?*

Her stomach righted itself and she clenched her jaw at the judgmental tone that reminded her that people weren't happy she'd taken over for her father. The torch had passed to her and several people were already voicing the serious doubts they had whether she was qualified or could handle it on her own. Apparently they didn't know about her veterinary degree or the fact that she'd worked as the head trainer at a large animal park in Southern California. Her experience didn't matter, or they didn't care. Not that working at the park had ever prepared her for the vast amount of work she faced here on a daily basis, alone for the most part. She couldn't deny that there were days she was sure people might be right about her capabilities being lacking. However, her father's death hadn't left her any other options.

"Yes."

"Thank goodness." He sighed in relief as he pressed the box in her direction. "This is for you. I was afraid I'd be stuck with him."

Emma felt relief wash over her as she heard quiet scratches coming from the box. He'd probably found some kind of bird and hadn't known where else to take it. This was something she could handle. Taking in a wounded bird was easy compared to dealing with the reporters who kept calling and refused to understand that "no comment" really meant exactly that. This she could handle in her sleep.

She punched the code into the keypad, waiting for the electric gate to slide open before holding out a hand. "I'm Emma Jordan, Conrad's daughter."

Mr. Fitness Model looked her up and down. "You?"

Emma arched a brow, waiting for him to explain. She didn't expect most people to recognize her. She'd kept herself secluded at the sanctuary as much as possible since her return. People weren't her forte, animals were. And it wasn't like she'd been to visit much over the past eight years. She was too busy finishing vet school and trying to land a job. Too busy to realize just how much was changing at the sanctuary over the last five years, after her father hired his two assistants, Jake and Brandon. Too busy to realize that he'd been second-guessing what they'd discussed for the future of Sierra Tracks and them working together for the past year.

"It's just that you . . . don't look anything like your dad. Well, other than the red hair."

"I'm assuming you were a friend." She didn't remember him coming around the ranch while she'd been here, and Emma wouldn't have forgotten this guy. It wasn't every day fantasies came to her door.

"Oh, sorry." He rubbed his hand on the side of his thigh before reaching for hers. "I'm Ben McQuaid. I'm actually on my way to the firehouse and stopped when I got a call. I figured it'd be better to bring this little guy to you on my way." She eyed the box as a curious mewl came from inside. "So? You want him here, or should I take him up to the barn?"

"I guess that depends on what 'he' is."

"Bobcat kitten. He was stuck in a tree up the road at the Quinn place. Hollister suspected he belonged to you."

She leaned forward, peeking into the box to see tawny fur and one round blue eye peering back at her.

The kitten gave a slight hiss but didn't cower as she expected him to. Her heart immediately melted slightly and she sighed. She shouldn't take any more animals in right now, especially since she wasn't sure she had the manpower now to take care of the sanctuary's previous rescues, but she knew if she refused, Animal Control would likely have to euthanize the poor thing since she knew they didn't have the resources to care for him.

"What made him think he was mine?" She glanced up at the man in front of her, trying not to notice the scent of crisp soap and laundry detergent that came from him and made her pulse skip slightly. She'd actually expected him to be drenched in cologne. In fact, it seemed rare to meet a guy these days who didn't bathe in the stuff, but she liked that he didn't.

"Well," he hemmed.

"The articles," Emma finished for him.

He shrugged slightly. "It's Hollister. He's loud and opinionated and doesn't like change. Is he? Yours, I mean."

Why did everyone assume any wild animal in the area was hers?

"Nope." She chewed at the corner of her lip, debating turning the kitten, and the sexy fireman, away purely out of principal. But turning him away would only hurt the poor kitten in the long run and wouldn't change anyone's minds. She couldn't do it. "Can you drive him up to the house?"

She watched as the guy turned and walked back to his truck. The view was just as good leaving as it was coming toward her. Sliding the box into the truck, Ben glanced over his shoulder toward her, catching Emma watching him. Unfortunately, it took a second longer for her to register that she was still checking out his ass.

A cocky grin lifted one corner of his mouth, speaking volumes. "It's okay. I can stand here as long as you like."

Heat rushed over her shoulders and up her neck but she wasn't about to let him think she was that impressed by a few muscles, or that rock-hard butt she'd like to try bouncing quarters off. Emma waved her hand at him. "Don't worry about it. Didn't see anything I liked anyway."

Take that, Mr. Muscles.

He chuckled quietly as he climbed into the truck and idled it past her slowly, waiting for her to climb back into her golf cart as the electric gate closed. "You sure? Because I think you've got a little drool on your chin."

Emma glared at him as the furious blush expanded to cover the rest of her neck, her chest and cheeks. Instead of answering him, she slammed her foot down on the gas pedal, pressing it to the floor, and wishing the golf cart would go faster than five miles per hour as she drove past the pompous ass in a pickup truck. She bit her tongue, consoling herself with the thought that any man who drove a truck that big and fancy must be compensating.

Chapter Two

BEN KNEW HE should head into the station now that he'd given her the kitten but he wasn't really in any hurry to clean equipment and they knew he was out on a call. The truth was, after reading the articles about her, he was intrigued to finally meet Emma Jordan.

She was so focused on the kitten that she acted like she barely even remembered that he was in the room. But Ben couldn't help but pay full attention to her. Emma Jordan was adorable, especially when he'd caught her checking out his ass and her cheeks turned bright red, making the smattering of faint freckles across the bridge of her nose stand out. She bent over the cat, holding him by the scruff as she looked into his ears and at his eyes before lifting the sides of the animal's mouth to look at his teeth. It gave him a perfect view of her heart-shaped bottom, cupped by a pair of cargo pants. He couldn't help taking a good look himself.

"You said you found him in a tree?"

Ben's gaze slammed into hers and she lifted a brow as she caught him checking out her backside. It was the first thing she'd said since she'd ushered him inside the makeshift exam room in the back of the house, so it surprised him. "Uh, yeah. He was about fifteen, maybe twenty feet up, stuck on a branch."

"Nope." She squeezed one paw gently, peering at his nails.

"What do you mean, 'nope'? Trust me, I'm the one who had to climb up there to get him down. I've probably still got bark on my butt to prove it." He almost asked if she wanted to check for him but she didn't seem like she was in a playful, teasing kind of mood and he didn't want to push his luck right now.

She might be adorable with her tiny stature but he had a feeling, if she was anything like her father, her temper matched her rich auburn hair—fiery. The long tresses drew his gaze again. She had it pulled back into a practical ponytail but that didn't stop it from catching the light coming through the window, making it shimmer. He almost reached out to touch it to see if it would burn his hand but she shot him a knowing smile, her sea-green eyes meeting his.

"And you have a little drool right there." She pointed at his chin and looked back at the kitten as if she'd hadn't just thrown his own words back at him.

Maybe he was wrong about her mood.

Ben laughed loudly, startling the kitten and she frowned at him, scooping the little guy into her arm and shuttling him to one of four empty kennels in the corner. "Keep an eye on him for just a second. I'll be right back."

Without waiting for his answer, she hurried out of the room, leaving him alone with the kitten again. Immediately, the little fur ball began yowling.

"Really? Again with the noise?" Wishing he knew what to do to soothe the animal, he tried to ignore it, wandering around the room instead, looking back at the miserable kitten helplessly.

It had been a few years since he'd come back to this room with her father after Ben rescued a pregnant opossum that had been hit by a car. She hadn't changed anything since her arrival after Conrad's death, which surprised him because most of the town was talking about how she wanted to change everything. Of course, Hidden Falls was a small town and you couldn't always trust the rumor mill.

But news traveled fast around town and he usually managed to keep a steady finger on the pulse of the place. Since people assumed police and firemen needed to know all the latest gossip, there wasn't much that went on that either he or his brother Andrew weren't the first to hear, whether they really wanted to or not. He'd heard plenty of talk about how she was taking over the operation of the sanctuary from Jake who everyone had assumed would run Sierra Tracks since he'd been Conrad's right hand. Not to mention the speculations about her qualifications. But looking the way she did, all those curves and luminescent blue-green eyes, he was shocked *that* didn't have tongues wagging and men falling all over themselves to get out here. She was beautiful, exotic-looking with her dark red hair and large, round eyes, but there was something in them that seemed to warn him to keep his distance. Which only made him curious about her.

He'd taken a gamble and just shown up, not even sure the place was open. He'd been worried he'd get stuck with the kitten when he found it locked and no one in sight.

"Here we go."

She came back in with a small bottle and plucked the kitten from the crate. Ben watched the cat begin sucking at the nipple eagerly, letting his gaze stray to the woman feeding the kitten.

She was so at ease with the cat yet seemed so uncomfortable with his presence. She cast him a quick glance, looking away just as quickly. She looked almost as skittish as the kitten and he found himself wanting to prove she didn't need to be wary of him.

Slow your roll, Romeo. You're here to drop off a kitten and that's it.

Ben recognized the logic in his thoughts. He'd sworn off women after his last relationship had ended so disastrously. He didn't need any women complications and should just get his ass to the station.

"So, since it looks like you've got this all under control . . ."

"Were there anymore?"

"More? Why would there be more?"

"Because this little guy shouldn't be away from his mother. He's too young so, more than likely, he was put in that tree. He physically doesn't have the strength to climb that high yet."

"Maybe there was a predator nearby so the mother carried the kitten up there," he suggested.

"Which means she left the rest? Where?" She shook her head. "Bobcats usually have two or three per litter so he has siblings somewhere, unless he belonged to someone as an illegal pet." She shook her head and looked down at the hungry kitten. "I'm telling you, someone put this little guy up into that tree."

Her dainty jaw clenched and her brow furrowed with concern. Ben would have to be blind not to see how much she cared about animals but that didn't mean there was someone out there, shoving cats in a tree for fun. Although, he knew better than most the stupid pranks teens pulled these days. It wouldn't be the first animal cruelty case he'd ever seen.

"Why would someone do that, especially if he was a pet? What purpose would that possibly serve?" Ben crossed his arms over his chest, waiting for her to elaborate.

"I don't know. But I do know he didn't get up there on his own. His claws would have been torn up. Because his nails are still soft, see?" She pressed the pad of the kitten's foot to show him. "But his aren't which means he didn't do any climbing."

"Maybe you're wrong about his age."

She cocked her head to one side. "I'm a vet. I think I can accurately age a kitten."

Ben's phone vibrated in his pocket and he tugged it out, glancing at the screen.

You coming in sometime today or what?

Angie, one of his crew and his ex. He really needed to head to the station but he hated to leave her in a lurch but, if Angie's text was any indicator, he was pushing the limit of his captain's patience. Duty called and that didn't include taking time off to flirt with Conrad Jordan's daughter, even if she did have some damn sexy curves.

Ben stopped his train of thought before it got any further down the track. Emma Jordan was a woman with her hands full. He didn't need any complications. Regardless of how attracted he might be, Ben was old enough to know that curves like Emma's indicated a need to slow down before things got dangerously out of control. He had enough danger on the job; he didn't need it in his personal life, even if those turquoise eyes did make him want to let her take the wheel.

"So, where are you heading now, Emma?" She turned to see Jake, her father's assistant for the past five years, leaning against the doorframe of the kitchen in the barn. "The birds need their first feeding of the day but now the cats are all behind since you're playing nursemaid."

She sighed as she stopped midway across the room. "I know. I'm moving as fast as I can. I had to get our newest resident settled."

"The fireman? Or something different?"

"Ha ha, funny."

She saw the disapproval in his face but that wasn't anything unusual for Jake. He didn't approve of much about her, never had and probably never would.

Jake was only a few years older than she was but he'd been a huge help at the sanctuary for her father for the past five years and especially once her father had been forced to slow down after his first stroke last year. Unwilling to give up the sanctuary, he'd leaned on Jake even more since Emma was finishing up vet school and starting her job at the animal park. Jake had been a rock for her father when she couldn't be there. Unfortunately, she and Jake had entirely different visions for what Sierra Tracks should be. He wanted it to be a strictly rehabilitation facility and, while she agreed that was her priority, Emma understood that they needed to keep the lights on and medication supplies up. Tours and educational programs paid the bills rehabilitation racked up.

However, she couldn't deny that, now that her father was gone, he was the only thing keeping this place running like clockwork. Emma wouldn't have even known the animals' schedules if not for him. But Jake knew she was dependent on him and seemed to be having a difficult time remembering she was managing this place, not him. He had no qualms treating her like some pissant annoyance he'd rather do without.

So far, she'd been able to keep him pacified with an abundance of compliments and praise, reminding him how she couldn't operate the facility without him, but his disrespect was becoming more blatant instead of less and she had about reached the limit of her tolerance.

"A bobcat kitten, looks about three or four weeks. I didn't exactly have much of a choice. He wouldn't survive if we didn't take him in. But," she pointed out, "he looks like a good candidate to be released again."

She didn't miss the dubious raise of Jake's brows or the way he pursed his lips. He didn't believe her.

"Don't give me that look. Once he's old enough we can put him into one of the indoor pens and then move him to the bigger pen outside in a few months."

"You mean, once he's a pet?"

"He's not going to be a pet."

He rolled his eyes. "Sure, he won't. You'll have him jumping through hoops or teaching him some tricks before you know it," he muttered.

What was it with the men around here today?

Emma sucked in a deep breath, trying to calm her temper before she blurted out something she'd just regret later. "Why don't you feed the birds and I'll do the cats. That way, I can try to get in touch with a few more donor prospects afterward."

"And leave me to do the shit work cleaning pens." She watched Jake sulk out of the kitchen toward the area her father had turned into an aviary, muttering under his breath the entire way.

Emma clenched her jaw, trying to keep her irritation with Jake at bay as she yanked a bag of raw chicken pieces and a bag of raw ground beef from the refrigerator. Dumping both into a bowl, she separated the mixture and weighed each bowl before adding the vitamins and minerals for each of the three cats on the property. She might not have spent the last three years rehabilitating wild animals but it didn't mean that she was incompetent. Not only had she grown up helping her father, but she'd been volunteering at zoos since high school. She was the one who'd gone through vet school, not Jake. She didn't need him getting judgmental because she'd spent the last year working as a veterinarian before taking a job as the head trainer at the animal equivalent of an amusement park. It wasn't like she'd worked there long, only two months, when her father's death had changed the direction of the future—both hers and that of the sanctuary—forcing her to quit and return to Sierra Tracks earlier than they'd planned.

Loading the passenger seat of the golf cart with the bowls, she headed for the cats as they shuffled slowly back and forth in their cages. Buster was vocal, as always, protesting the late feeding, even as she slapped the ball of meat onto the concrete, pushing it into his cage. He pounced on the food, dragging it into the cage and devouring it in only a few bites.

"You know, you aren't the only one waiting," she complained to the mountain lion, the tawny fur between his shoulder blades glistening like golden velvet. He glanced up at her with amber eyes as she slapped another piece of meat to the floor for him. He pulled it closer with a paw, his usual rumbling growl of pleasure sounding deep in his chest. "I didn't even get my second cup of coffee yet."

She slapped the third ball of ground beef to the ground but Buster simply stared at her expectantly.

"You can have the chicken after you eat this first."

He yowled loudly, as if he understood her, and she couldn't help but smile. In some ways, these big cats were exactly like house pets, if you overlooked the nearly three inch claws and the extra hundred and twenty pounds. Jake might think she forgot she was dealing with wild animals but she would never make that mistake. Her father had taught her to respect all wildlife from an early age. She'd been taught from the time she could walk how to read their body language, groomed to take over this sanctuary from her birth. It was simply part of who she was.

Buster finished eating the ground beef and she tossed the pieces of cut up chicken, bones and all, into the cage before moving on to their two adult bobcats, Millie and Bob.

Most of the animals in the sanctuary were there to be rehabilitated and rereleased into the wild so, as a rule, human contact with them was kept to a minimum whenever possible, especially if the animal was a candidate for reintroduction. It was hardest with animals who arrived as babies, like the kitten this morning, because he would need so much hands-on care in the coming weeks.

But there were others, like Millie and Bob, who arrived later in life with injuries, who could never survive in the wild and needed to be handled as safely as possible because of the human interaction they would be reliant on for care for the rest of their lives. Poor Bob had been the first of the pair to arrive, with a gunshot wound in his front leg that had become infected and required amputation. Millie, on the other hand, had been someone's idea of a pet, a kitten like the one this morning, that had been mistaken for a domestic cat, until her owner realized she was too big to be handled and tried to surrender her to a shelter.

Emma fed the pair the same way she had Buster before heading back to the house to prepare the meal for their black bear cub, Wally. As she passed by his cage, he bolted across the pen, leaping from his tire swing. Emma laughed out loud as he landed in his tub of water, unable to help her amusement at his clownish antics. Her laughter died when the water from the tub splashed up through the fencing and soaked her. Wally slid out of the barrel and bounded back across his pen.

Emma swiped her hand over her face, flinging the water aside. "Thanks a lot, brat. No jam on your bread today."

The bear cub leaned backward over the tractor tire in his cage, looking like he was laughing at her. Now she had to go change clothes and was going to be running even more behind. Days like today made her wonder why she'd ever wanted to run this place with her father. Treating cats and dogs was so much easier.

Chapter Three

EMMA HAD NO idea she was being watched and that was exactly how he wanted it. Cautiously, he slipped through the back door of the facility and into the area she was using as a nursery, housing the bobcat kitten he'd put up in that tree. It was sleeping soundly and he actually felt a measure of relief that the poor thing had survived without any harm. That was actually the last thing he wanted.

But, in reality, the kitten should have died. It would have in nature if he hadn't intervened, the way its siblings had after he'd hit their mother with his car while she was running across the road in the middle of the night. After nursing the kitten back to health, he'd realized he could use it as a way to put his plan for Sierra Tracks into action.

Emma Jordan had no idea what she was doing. She wasn't qualified, or equipped, to run this place. Just because she was a vet now didn't mean she knew what these animals needed.

She intended to reopen it to the public again, to reinstate the special events her father had once held, using the animals as *attractions*, putting them on display for guided tours and educational programs. Sierra Tracks was supposed to be a wildlife rescue, not a tourist trap. He wasn't about to let her turn her father's hard work into an amusement park.

BEN STARED AT the headline of the newspaper and wondered for the hundredth time how their small-town paper kept getting these stories.

Escaped Bobcat Terrorizes Quinn Ranch

It was beginning to look more like a tabloid, with its sensationalized headlines, than the *Hidden Falls Daily*. "Terrorize" was hardly the term he would use for what the tiny kitten had done, except maybe to his arm. He rubbed at the surface scratches absently. Hell, most of the people standing under the tree begged him to let them take the poor thing home. Where did any sort of terror fall into that scenario? And, other than Hollister's rambling accusations, what would make anyone think it had escaped?

His gaze slid over the piece in the paper. It was obviously skewed, every bit of the article attempting to convince locals that Sierra Tracks was a risk to the community and that, since Conrad Jordan's death, there was no one taking care of the animals other than a few overworked volunteers, going so far as to say the new manager was "ruining Conrad's legacy."

Ben leaned back in his chair, the sound of his father stomping dirt from his work boots on the back patio echoing in the stillness. Entering the kitchen, Travis McQuaid headed for the coffee pot, cursing quietly when he found it empty. Ben's brother Andrew slid his cup toward his dad.

"Here, take mine. I should get into the station early anyway."

Ben stood up. "I should probably head out too."

"Thanks." The patriarch of the McQuaid family chugged the lukewarm coffee in one gulp before looking around the kitchen, empty but for his two sons. "Where's your mother?"

"She ran into town. Said she wanted to get her grocery shopping finished early or something."

His father jerked his chin at the paper, still in Ben's hands. "Ridiculous, isn't it?"

"Which part?"

"Why on the earth would someone so unqualified come in to try to take over those animals? Either find a place that can take them in or sell the sanctuary to someone else. Conrad knew what he was doing, made sure those two boys and his volunteers knew what they were doing. That woman is going to get someone hurt."

Ben's eyes widened in surprise. It wasn't like his dad to believe gossip and this article was complete bullshit.

From what he'd seen when he'd dropped off the kitten yesterday, there wasn't an ounce of truth to any of this. Then again, he wasn't exactly an expert.

"Actually, that woman is Conrad's daughter," Ben pointed out.

Andrew shrugged. "People have always been critical of the place but it got worse when Conrad started not letting people in a few years back. I did the inspection on the sanctuary last month, when she first took over. I think she's planning on making some changes but she'd better hurry up before this bad press gets her shut down."

"She knows what she's doing." Andrew's brows shot up in interest at Ben's adamant proclamation. "I met her yesterday when I dropped off the kitten," he clarified as he shoved the paper away. "She seemed legit. Said she's a vet. I didn't question it since she knew exactly what to do with that kitten."

"A vet? She told me she used to be a trainer at some big animal park." Andrew frowned slightly and Ben wondered why Emma had lied about her experience.

Ben's father frowned into his mug. "Doesn't matter, either way. What I want to know is how that bobcat got out in the first place."

"She said he wasn't one of hers." Ben glanced at his brother. "And that he was too young to have been away from its mother, let alone climb a tree at all. She thinks someone put him there."

"Why?"

Ben shook his head. "No clue. But she's not happy

about these." He tapped the paper. His father rubbed at his chin thoughtfully and glanced down at the newspaper again. "Besides, you know as well as I do that the Daily isn't exactly printing hard news these days. The articles they printed about Grant were total crap. They don't give two shits about the truth or whose reputation they damage in the process anymore. I'm beginning to wonder if they aren't just saying anything to try to sell some papers. "

He stood up, trying to ignore the odd looks his brother and father were shooting his direction.

"Hmm, you're awfully worked up about this," Andrew teased. "You going to complain to the editor? Write a letter of protest?"

"Shut up." Ben shoved at his brother's shoulder as he walked past.

"It wouldn't hurt for someone to take another look at the place," their father suggested. "If everything is fine, then you could contact the paper to set the record straight and set some minds at ease in the town, Andrew. People are getting really worried about this."

"Hey!" Andrew exclaimed. "I know how to do my job, Dad."

Their father rolled his eyes and held up a hand when Andrew started to say more. "I know that, but it's not hard to make everything look like it's on the up and up when she knows you're coming to make an inspection. Maybe Ben here could swing by and take a look, see if he sees anything out of the ordinary. Just tell her you're checking up on the kitten."

Ben glowered at his father. "Like I have time for that. I have to get to work. Besides, it's not *my* job."

His father shrugged nonchalantly. "Whatever you say, son. It's not like keeping this town safe is your duty or anything."

Ben ignored his father's pathetic attempt at a guilt trip as he tugged his jacket from the back of the chair and reached for his keys on the counter before heading outside to his truck. As much as he might like to visit Emma Jordan, he got the distinct feeling that Fireball didn't appreciate unannounced visitors.

Then again, his dad did have a point. Looking out for the people in this town was his job and he didn't want any more close calls with bobcats. Maybe an un-announced visit wouldn't be a bad idea. If she'd been expecting the inspection, she'd have put her best foot forward. Things had seemed on the up and up yesterday but she'd also made sure he stuck close to her. Being suspicious by nature, now he was curious as to why.

Ben glanced at his watch. It wasn't like they were actually expecting him at the station for another few hours, he'd just said that to avoid his dad pinning him down for one of the never-ending chores around the ranch. "Hey, son?" His father poked his head out the screen door. "Don't you go letting her convince you she's the victim here. You keep your mind on what's best for this town as a whole, not just one woman, okay?"

"Got it." *What was that supposed to mean?*

Ben didn't even want to even think about how his father seemed to read his mind and know where he was planning on going. The last thing he needed right now was to find himself swayed by some sob story that might not be true. He didn't buy the article in the paper but he didn't know Emma Jordan either. This should be a simple solution. If there was no truth to the article, he'd be able to nip what he worried would turn into a witch hunt in the bud before people started taking sides. Hidden Falls didn't need that kind of trouble. Neither did he.

But Ben couldn't shake the feeling that Emma Jordan was going to be trouble with a capital *T*.

EMMA TWISTED HER hair back into a messy bun as the kitten swiped at the tendrils hanging around her face. She had no desire to have scratches on her cheeks so she tucked the strands behind her ear as she fed Kit, as she'd nicknamed him, the last of his bottle and settled him in front of the food she'd put in a bowl. It was going to take quite a while for him to be weaned, several more weeks of feeding him every four to five hours at least, but she needed to start him on solids right away so he didn't become too imprinted on her. She latched the door of the small playpen and removed the gloves she wore for feedings before slouching into one of the nearby chairs, letting him play and letting herself relax for just a few moments.

She was exhausted. Trying to keep the sanctuary running with only two employees and two part-time volunteers was killing her, especially now that she was up during the night to feed Kit. But she didn't have the money to hire someone else full-time. At least, not yet. If only she could get a few more donors . . . But to get donors, she needed to open the sanctuary to the public again. Reinstating the educational programs would earn her government grants but, in order to do that, she needed more full-time staff.

Her father's thick Scottish brogue practically echoed through the room. *If wishes were horses, then beggars would ride.*

She missed him. So much. After her parents' divorce, he'd been her one constant. While her mother was gallivanting around the globe, too busy for more than an occasional phone call to check in with her ten-year-old daughter, Emma's father had been teaching her animal psychology. When she'd begged him to homeschool her, insisting he could teach her everything she needed to know about animals, he'd given in because he'd known she planned to run the sanctuary with him eventually.

They'd been planning it for years, imagining it and discussing what it would look like. He'd encouraged her, even if her ideas had been wildly childish at the time.

They may have butted heads at every turn, often disagreeing on one another's methods when it came to working with animals, but he'd always been there to support her, regardless of who ended up being right. It had been his idea for her to work at the animal park, to gain more experience working with a wide variety of creatures. The plan had always been for her father to head up the rehabilitation efforts while she led the educational programs. But then he'd begun changing things over the past year, after his first stroke. At Jake's suggestion, in spite of her offer to return, her father ended the classroom visits and closed the facility to the weekend tours, which created a lapse in their government funding.

He'd begun leaning heavily on Jake and Brandon for assistance, only accepting animals for rehabilitation and fewer of those than ever before. In the process, he kept the people of Hidden Falls, and her, in the dark about what plans he had for Sierra Tracks. Although Emma had her suspicions that her father had wanted to make the brothers a permanent part of Sierra Tracks' future, he'd never made anything official, to her relief.

However, now she was here, trying to pick up the pieces alone, her home owned by the non-profit with her merely left in charge. She was the one left with the repercussions of decisions she'd never agreed with and wondering how to get the sanctuary back on track.

Tears burned at the back of her eyes and she took a deep breath, blinking them back. The truth was, she missed her father. Not to mention that being the town pariah was lonely.

Her two-way radio crackled, jerking her out of her thoughts of her father, and she heard Brandon, Jake's brother, call to her. "We have someone at the front gate. Want me to send them away?"

Again?

She'd been running the sanctuary for almost two months and, in spite of the recent influx of interview requests from the local paper, she knew the sanctuary hadn't seen this many visitors in the past year. Unless Kit's siblings had been found, two different visitors in the last twenty-four hours was pretty unlikely.

Unless they're shutting you down.

Emma refused to even acknowledge the nagging doubts and radioed Brandon back. "Is it a big gray truck?"

"Yeah, how'd you know?"

What in the hell is he doing back here? Her stomach fluttered quickly. Emma would rather believe it was out of concern for the other kittens, than anticipation at seeing the sexy fireman again.

"Go ahead and let him in. Tell him to just head to the house. Can you ask Sadie to come up here?" Kit shouldn't lose his playtime just because that pain in the butt fireman was back.

"Sure, boss. I'll send her your way."

Sadie, one of the sanctuary's long-time volunteers, hurried through the door a few minutes later. "What's up, boss?"

"Just need you to keep an eye on him while I deal with . . ." She wasn't even sure how to explain Ben's presence. "A visitor."

Sadie followed her to the door, catching a glimpse of Ben as he parked his truck and climbed out. "Huh. Wish I got visitors who looked like that. Take your time, boss," Sadie said with a wink.

Emma tried to still the way her stomach flipped and somersaulted but when he climbed down from his raised truck, she couldn't help but admire the fine figure he cut walking toward her. He had enough height that his massive muscles looked proportional instead of hulking. Yesterday he'd looked a little too pretty boy for her usual tastes but today, with his jaw unshaven and his hair slightly mussed, he was walking, breathing male perfection in maroon cotton and denim. He'd have been absolutely perfect, if she wasn't so worried he was here for an alternative reason.

"Two days in a row?" Emma crossed her arms in front of her. "To what do I owe the pleasure?"

"I'm here professionally this time, I'm afraid." He stopped in front of his truck.

Her pulse pounded in her veins, making her feel light-headed. She couldn't let this happen, but she had no idea how to stop it. Her only choice was to try to play it cool and stall for more time. A small voice of reason reminded her that he wasn't Fish and Game, Animal Control or the police department. She latched on to that one thread of hope.

"And what sort of business could the local fire department possibly have with me?"

Ben pulled a folded newspaper from his back pocket and held it up. She couldn't make out anything but one word: *Bobcat.*

She'd already read the article this morning, had already tried to convince herself that there was no reason for the paper's unwarranted attack to sting. She'd already begun planning ways to rebut the accusations made against her. But it was going to take time, and money, and she had neither.

It didn't take a genius to figure out that this wasn't going to be a benevolent visit. "Did you bring a warrant with you? Because no one is coming any further into the facility without one."

"Yesterday I was generous."

"Yet, here you are again." She didn't look away, wouldn't give him the satisfaction of seeing her fear, but she could feel the muscles in her back and legs quaking nervously, praying he didn't see it.

"Do I need to call my brother down at the police station and get one?" He mimicked her stance, crossing his arms over his massive chest. But when he did it, it made his biceps bulge and the sleeve of his shirt ride up his arm enough to reveal what appeared to be a wolf's head as part of the sleeve tattoo circling his right arm.

Heaven help me, she prayed as her heart bounced to her stomach and back up again before speeding up to triple time.

"Tell me, did this town harass my father this much? It might account for his stroke."

"I can't say it did." His tipped his head to one side. "You know, maybe shutting yourself and the sanctuary off from the rest of the town hasn't been the best idea. Perhaps if you let people see what you're doing here, they'd be backing you instead of believing this." He waved the paper slightly.

"You're saying that if I open my doors, they'll welcome me with open arms."

"Maybe."

"Bullshit."

She moved down the stairs to stand in front of him, trying to give him the impression that she wasn't intimidated by him. However, his sheer size was even more impressive this close and her idea backfired as her gaze slid up to meet his. "For your information, I wasn't the one to close the doors to the public. That was my father's doing. And I plan on reopening them as soon as I can, but it's going to take some time."

His dark gaze slid over her slowly, as if he was trying to read her thoughts, feeling more like a caress than an appraisal. It intrigued her, actually making her heart skip a beat. Her reaction to him annoyed her. She wanted to be unaffected by him, to not feel this slow heat sliding through her veins, to not have the urge to grab his shirt and jerk him forward for what she was sure would be a kiss to make her forget any before. A slow grin tugged at the corner of his mouth, a dimple creasing his left cheek.

Damn cocky man knows exactly what effect he has on women.

Emma wasn't about to be just another of the harem she was sure fawned over him. She didn't care how good looking he was or how his muscles might ripple when he walked. Okay, she *appreciated* it, but that wasn't the same thing as caring. She would keep her wits about her when this particular handsome man smiled at her, if only because she was sure most didn't, and she was smart enough to hide any attraction she might have to him beneath her annoyance at him wielding his authority over her this way.

She narrowed her eyes, studying him. She wanted to tell him to leave, to order him off the property and insist he not come back without a warrant. She had no idea what he really wanted and she already had enough trouble with the town and its rumors. However, she got the feeling that, if causing her more trouble had been his intent, Ben would have called in the police already. She tipped her head back, trying to get a better look at him and felt her makeshift bun loosen, coming unwound. Just like her resistance.

"Fine. I'm not sure why you're here, but I have nothing to hide." She jerked at the end of her hair, letting her auburn tresses fall around her shoulders, shielding her like a curtain, and headed for the golf cart. "Well? What are you waiting for? Hop in. I don't have all day to waste."

Ben slid in beside her, his arm brushing against hers, the heat from his skin practically burning her. He exuded raw sexuality, making the close confines of the golf cart seem even smaller, and she edged farther from him on the small seat. Twisting the key, her gaze fell on the folded newspaper Ben set in his lap, the words of the headline coming back to taunt her.

Damn! When was this town ever going to cut her some slack?

Chapter Four

BEN DIDN'T MISS the glare Emma shot at him as they made their way through the barn and toward the animal cages. He guessed he really couldn't blame her. He'd shown up unannounced, yet again, but this time he'd basically threatened her to take him on a tour of the animal sanctuary, whether he'd actually come out and vocalized it or not.

And, he'd lied, at least about being here on a professional call, which really stuck in his craw. He prided himself on being a gentleman and lying didn't really fit in the image he had of himself. But he hadn't known what else to say, especially when he really wasn't sure why he'd come. He could have just as easily called Animal Control. Or convinced Andrew to do this. His brother was the cop; he should be doing any inspection that was needed. Yet, here he was, seated beside her as the golf cart bumped along the gravel path.

She put on the brakes and the golf cart slid to a stop in the circular labyrinth of cages. The scent of clean straw wasn't enough to mask the musky odor of the variety of animals. He wrinkled his nose slightly. It wasn't a bad smell, but it was strong and took some acclimation. He caught the glance she shot his way, as if gauging his reaction before a smirk spread over her lips slowly, as if he'd reacted exactly the way she'd expected, although he couldn't imagine what he'd done.

"Emma, I'm not trying to cause any more trouble for you."

Emma turned toward him slowly, suspicion darkening her turquoise eyes as she glowered. "Sure you're not. You strut onto my ranch, like a damn peacock, and demand I show you around without any cause. I'm not stupid. I know this town would rather have my father here. I know everyone doubts my abilities, my experience. People are just waiting for me to screw up. I already know . . ." She threw her hands into the air.

"You know what?"

Emma took a deep breath, regaining her composure, her anger shuttered behind her closed eyes. "Never mind."

She opened her eyes, her demeanor making a one-eighty turn, appearing under control and professional again, waving a hand his direction. "So? Where would you like to start? The big cats are to the left, the birds are ahead in the aviary and the rest are over there, on your right."

There was far more to her outburst but her quick shift made it clear that it hadn't been intentional and she was finished with the conversation. He was smart enough to see what the people of Hidden Falls thought mattered to her, as much as she tried to hide it. She was trying to prove herself, and wanted to succeed.

Ben wasn't sure why he was still going on with this charade but if he turned away from it now, he'd have no reason to stay and he wasn't ready to leave yet. He'd be damned if he didn't feel that tug in his chest, that stirring of emotion he got when he wanted to do something to help. The same one that usually got him in over his head. He cleared his throat slightly, trying to clear away the heaviness building in his chest as he could see Emma fighting to hold on to her pride.

"Why don't we start with the cats and work our way around?"

"Fine."

Her clipped answer as she slid from the cart made it clear that while she might act cool, she didn't want or appreciate his presence. She headed toward the padlocked gate that led to the cats' cages and the wild smell of them hit him full force. Holding his breath, trying his best to ignore it, he hurried to catch up to her, unable to let her comment go.

Her accidental admission had surprised him and he wondered who had said something to give her the impression that she wasn't wanted here. Hidden Falls was a small town and, while people liked to speak their mind, often under the guise of concern for town well-being, he'd never known anyone to be openly malicious. "What makes you think people expect you to fail?"

She stopped abruptly and turned, causing him to run into her, knocking her off-balance. Ben reached out for her arms, to catch her. Instead, one hand splayed over her breast. Her gaze crashed into his and he jerked his hand back as if he'd reached into a fire. Heat traveled up his spine and burned over his shoulders. He would bet his face was as red as his shirt, but it didn't stop the rest of his body from responding instantly to her soft curves.

"I'm sorry. I didn't mean to . . ." he stammered. "I mean, it wasn't . . ." Ben jerked his offending hand through his hair. "Shit."

So much for looking cool and collected.

Emma eased away from him and tugged the bottom of her polo shirt down, pursing her lips prudishly, but choosing to ignore the fact that he'd just managed to get to second base without knowing he was even up to bat.

"Because that isn't the first article about this place and none of them have been glowing recommendations. This past month has been trying, to say the least. I'm fully expecting to see a 'get lost' sign on the front gate any day now."

"Why would someone do that?"

"Who knows?" She shrugged her slim shoulders, suddenly looking tired and defeated, as if she bore the weight of the world on them. "All I know is that I'm doing the best I can. I never expected to be running this place alone but I'm damn sure not going to let someone scare me away from my father's legacy."

Scare her away?

From what he'd already seen of Emma, she didn't

seem like the kind of woman to scare easily so something pretty significant must have already happened to make her this certain someone wanted her gone. Her father had run the rescue facility for the last twenty years and, while there were several ranchers who weren't thrilled to have it nearby, they tolerated it because of the tourists stopping en route to Lake Tahoe and the money it brought in during the summer months. They'd managed to somehow coexist in Hidden Falls without trouble. People had even started to come around when Conrad started his summer camp program for kids to experience some of the animals up close.

But something changed and he shut it down. Ben had assumed it was lack of funding, but maybe there was more to it than that.

If Emma's assessment was correct, and the article in the paper seemed to indicate that she was, she needed to regain the confidence of the town, both in her abilities to manage the sanctuary as well as in the benefit of the place. The real question was whether or not she could do it before she lost all support from the community.

"Maybe you should do something so people could get to know you, see your qualifications in action," he offered. "Once people realize—"

She rolled her eyes, cutting him off. "They'd act the same way Jake does. Like I'm nothing more than a glorified dog trainer. No one cares that I'm a vet because I just got my license. And they don't care that I was a trainer because I'd only worked at the park for two months when Dad . . ."

So, she hadn't lied about her qualifications. It was actually pretty impressive.

Emma sucked in a breath and he could see her trying to tamp down her frustration. "Look, I know you think you're helping but what I really need is some time to get my sea legs under me and figure out the best direction for this place. Whether that's getting more donors, opening it back up to the public or something else. But I will not be forced to shut it down because of some unfounded rumors."

He wasn't sure what else to suggest. As long as she was unwilling to open herself up to getting to know people in town, of letting them know her intentions, she and her abilities were going to continue being questioned. Like her father, she'd chosen a solitary path and, as of right now, made it clear she didn't want help. Ben fell silent as he followed her toward the pens that housed the big cats.

She pointed at two bobcats sprawled out in a patch of sunlight. The smaller of the two gave him a bored glance before opening its mouth wide in a yawn, baring sharp incisors, and turning away. He found it hard to believe that the kitten he'd rescued yesterday would end up like this pair, nearly double the size of a house cat and far more dangerous.

"This is Millie and that guy over there is Bob."

"You named a bobcat Bob? Isn't that a little too cliché?" She gave him a slight smile and a shrug before moving closer to the cage.

"My father named them. Bob came in after a hunter shot him. A rancher found him bleeding and barely breathing. Dad called me and I was able to talk him through patching him up but eventually he had to have the leg removed due to infection. He'll never be released back into the wild. Millie, on the other hand, was some rich lady's exotic house pet until she got a little too rough with those claws. They were about to dump her in the woods when Animal Control got the call and Dad took her in. She'd have never survived in the wild since she's too used to people."

"So, what do you do with them now?" She remained so intently focused on the animals, if she hadn't shrugged, he'd have wondered if she even heard his question.

"They've been rehabilitated, so they stay here. These two were a big part of the educational program Dad had going. Millie even went to some of the local schools with him for a while." Her voice took on a wistful note and he studied her.

"You want to start that up again?"

She sighed heavily. "I'd like to, but I can't right now. I don't even have enough staff to do even half of what needs to get done on a daily basis." She turned her gaze on him, piercing him with the deep longing he could read there. She was passionate about this place; there was no mistaking it.

His heart thudded heavily in his chest, heat slowly ebbing through his veins, circling his lungs and making it hard to breathe for a moment. He felt the desire to help her again, to offer whatever he could, even if it was just someone to lean on.

"I'm hoping I can send Kit back into the wild since he's not injured or domesticated," she said, breaking the tension that had suddenly enveloped them. "But if not, he'll probably move in with them. I hate to do that though because neither of these two would make good surrogates. They know nothing about survival."

She turned toward him and pointed across the compound area to a much larger enclosure filled with trees, ledges and rocky terrain, looking more like the mountainous hills surrounding Hidden Falls. "But Davis over there could, if he'll tolerate a kitten. I'll have to evaluate him, but I'm optimistic. He came in with a broken leg, but I was able to set it and he should be ready for release in a couple of months."

A low rumble of sound came from behind Ben, to his left. The hair on the back of his neck raised, although he couldn't quite place the sound. Emma must have noticed his sudden discomfort because she chuckled quietly and moved past him to where the sound continued. As they walked closer, he could make out a loud exhale and what sounded almost like a purr. Emma edged closer to the cage where a massive mountain lion rose and began pacing.

"This is Buster."

What should have been fear in her voice sounded more like a proud mother showing off her child's accomplishment. But this was no baby. This was an enormous beast that could tear her to shreds if she got too close.

"He was sent here from Nevada. Some guy thought he'd be a fun house pet so he had poor Buster declawed."

As if showing Ben that Emma spoke the truth, the big cat stood on his hind legs and pressed his massive paws against the chain link of his cage.

"Some moron wanted *that* for a pet?"

The idea seemed ludicrous to him, but there were a lot of things people did that made him scratch his head in awe of the human capability for stupidity. He took a step closer to the cage and the cat immediately crouched, curling his lip up and letting out a hiss that froze him in his tracks. He might not have claws but there were plenty of sharp teeth that could inflict some savage damage, and the only thing separating the cat from Emma was a flimsy chain fence.

"Don't worry, Buster," she cooed at the tawny beast like he was a house cat, "he has no idea what a good boy you are. Take it easy."

The cat stood up and rubbed his head against the fence where Emma stood, the low rumbling exhale sounding again. She seemed to have absolutely no fear of him and laughed at his antics as she moved away from the cage.

"Looks like Buster doesn't like you much," she pointed out.

"Yeah? I don't think I'm too fond of him either."

She pursed her lips. "Then I guess it's a good thing

I'm the one taking care of him and you're not around often."

"We'll see."

He wasn't sure why he said it. It had just slipped out. Maybe it had something to do with the way Emma seemed to make his brain stop functioning. She narrowed her eyes at him and he realized that he liked seeing the spark that lit in them when he pushed her buttons, like when he'd caught her staring at his ass yesterday.

Conrad Jordan had never been one to mince words and Ben wouldn't have expected anything less from his daughter, but she even surpassed her old man. This woman gave new meaning to the term "independent."

She arched a disdainful brow, her gaze skimming over him. "Why, Mr. McQuaid, are you offering to sign up as a volunteer here?"

Her eyes shimmered with humor, as if she expected him to turn down her offer. She was testing him, pushing back to see if he would continue to tease her. He could read the dare in her eyes and knew he needed to back off. He wasn't even sure why he'd given in to the urge to come at all. He should have just ignored the part of his brain that had seen a woman getting a bad rap and just headed in to the station. Clearly, she was no damsel in need of his rescue.

Ben squared his shoulders, looking her full in the face. Emma tipped her chin up toward him, making the sunlight dance over the freckles littered along the bridge of her nose as a confident smile spread. Desire settled deep in his gut, curling up as if preparing to reside there for some time.

But Ben didn't have any inclination for romance, and certainly not with someone like her. He had a knack for picking the wrong women and, after the last fiasco, he'd decided to make some changes. From now on his women, and his life, would be predictable. There was nothing about Emma that he could rely on. At the same time, he felt his common sense—or maybe it was his sanity—take a back seat as his mouth opened and he heard the words that tumbled out.

Ah, hell!

Chapter Five

"SURE, WHY NOT?"

Emma saw the slow grin that accompanied Ben's acquiescence and felt her stomach drop to her toes. She'd seen him wrinkle his nose in disgust as they'd driven into the compound. Granted, it was a smell that took some getting used to but Ben couldn't even hide his distaste. Why would he agree to this?

Asking him to volunteer had been a joke. She was sick of him pushing her buttons, having the authoritative upper hand, so she'd decided to push back. However, she'd never, in a million years, thought he'd say yes.

Emma took a step backward. "You don't know the first thing about these animals." She really wasn't sure what he might know, but it seemed like as good an excuse as any.

"So? You said you needed more people to get the

daily chores done. Teach me." He took a step closer, between her and the cage. She saw Buster drop back onto his haunches, his shoulders twitching as he opened his mouth, rolling his lip back, sucking in the newcomer's scent. Before Ben even realized what was happening, she reached for the front of his shirt and jerked him forward, away from the pen. The lion reared against the side of the cage, roaring in frustration when he couldn't reach his prize. Adrenaline coursed through her veins as she realized how close he'd just come to getting hurt. Even without claws, in spite of the chain link fencing between them, Buster could do some serious damage.

Ben's arms had instinctively wound around her waist when she reached for him and he lifted her off the ground, moving them both farther away from the cage. Her fingers were pinned between their bodies, curled in the soft cotton t-shirt.

"Are you okay?" he asked, looking down into her face, his dark eyes filled with urgency.

"Put me down," she ordered. Landing gently on her toes, she shoved against his chest, trying to gain some breathing room between their bodies. "Me? I'm fine. You were the one with a death wish. What would make you think you could get that close to him? Don't you realize what he could have done?"

"I wasn't much closer than you were to that *thing*," he argued.

"He knows *me*! I wasn't the one he was hissing at five minutes ago."

His lips split in a wide grin and he laughed. The damn pain in the ass was *laughing*?

"What in the hell do you think is funny about this? Don't you realize what could have happened?"

"You're kinda cute when you're mad."

She shoved against his chest. "And you're an idiot who could have gotten me shut down with your stupidity."

Ben frowned, as if the thought hadn't crossed his mind. Emma threw her hands into the air before pinching her thumb and first finger together. "I'm this close from being declared a danger to this town's welfare and you nearly hand them my head on a plate."

She turned on her heel, stalked back to the golf cart and snatched the newspaper from the seat where he'd discarded it. "You see this?" She snapped the paper so he could see the headline. "This isn't the first time I've been blamed for something I had nothing to do with. It's been happening at least once a week since I got back here. My animals and I are getting blamed every time livestock goes missing, something turns up amiss or some kid scrapes his knee. Hidden Falls is on a witch hunt and they've decided I'm riding the broom."

"People supported your dad, even if they didn't particularly love what he was doing here. I'm sure if they just saw your side, they'd rally around you." A frown furrowed his brow.

"Thanks, because a reminder of how much the people around here trusted my dad more than me is exactly what I need to hear right now." Emma shook her head slightly. "Look, I don't know why you're here, but

I seriously doubt that I'm due for another inspection just because someone found a bobcat in their tree. We live in the foothills. There are bobcats, and cougars and coyotes. I can't be held responsible for every wild animal that turns up around Hidden Falls."

"*Another* inspection?" He arched a brow and his lips pinched into a thin line.

"You're the second inspector in less than two months."

"A cop, right?"

"Yes, why?" she asked suspiciously.

"Yeah . . . um, that was my brother."

Emma opened her mouth, prepared to say more, but closed it quickly. She should have realized that Muscles was related to the officer who'd come by after she'd first arrived. Now that he'd said something, she realized they both had the same dark eyes, the same squared jaw, the same down-home, aw-shucks good-ole-boy attitude. But the police officer had been far sterner and had inspected the place by-the-books. Not to mention that he hadn't had Ben's lopsided, charming smile, nor did it feel like her entire body was catching fire when he looked at her, like his mere presence was about to spark dry tinder into a raging inferno.

Ben shoved his hands into his pockets and didn't meet her gaze, suddenly uncomfortable and looking guilty.

"Wait? Did he send you out here?" She looked around, almost expecting the cop to pop out from between the cages. "Is this some sort of set-up? You deliberately get hurt so he can swoop in and shut me down? Then you two can be the town heroes and get rid of the sanctuary?"

"Whoa, lady. You've got this all wrong. I just came by—"

She threw her hands into the air and spun on her heel, turning her back on him while she yelled. "You nearly get killed, then blame me for it."

Ben held his hands up and laughed as she spun back toward him. "Take a breath."

If he didn't stop laughing at her, she was going to lose what little rein she had left over her temper. When she didn't even crack a smile, his humor seemed to dissipate and he fell quiet.

"Look, I'm sorry. This wasn't some sort of set-up, just real-life stupidity on my part. Why don't we start over?" He held out his hand. "I'm Ben McQuaid, local firefighter, rescuer of kittens, and I guess I just came by today because I get the feeling this article if full of crap and I wanted to see it for myself."

"So, you're not really here professionally?" she asked, using his words against him.

He shook his head. "No, and I'm sorry I let you believe I was but I'd like to help you out if I can."

She folded her arms over her chest and stared at the hand he still held out to her. "Why?"

Ben shrugged, rolling his eyes. "Hell if I know. It's not like you're overly friendly," he teased, moving his hand a bit closer toward her, urging her to take it.

A grin tugged at the corner of his mouth and she

fought to maintain her stern expression. As much as she might want to stay angry, to release the frustration that had been building in her over the past month, Ben wasn't her enemy and treating him like he was wouldn't help anyone.

The corners of his eyes crinkled as he cocked his head to one side and shot her a lopsided smile that was far too charming to be in any woman's best interest. Her lips twitched in response and she pinched them together, trying to keep from falling prey to his panty-dropping smile and that sexy dimple creasing his cheek.

"You do realize, it's okay to have some fun. It won't hurt. I promise."

Little did he know that having fun was what had ruined her one serious relationship when her antics had gotten her boyfriend kicked in the face by a kangaroo. He'd ended up with a broken nose and she'd ended up with a broken heart when he demanded she quit her internship or lose him. It had taught her a good lesson early—never get too deeply involved with anyone who can't understand the risk.

Emma eyed Ben, pursing her lips, trying to keep from liking this guy, even as a shiver of heat slid down her belly and centered between her thighs.

Good looking and charming. Mr. Muscles is getting more appealing by the minute.

"Okay," he said, pulling his hand back when she didn't take it. "Do you think we could finish the tour?"

"Only if we head to the aviary. At least there I don't have to worry about you getting killed."

He chuckled quietly, his laughter falling around her like the first rains of spring, renewing her parched spirit. For the first time since arriving in town, she felt welcomed, like she might actually have someone who would go out on a limb for her. She might not be willing to ask for help, but a friend she could trust would be nice.

"I promise to stay away from cages if it means keeping you from having another near heart attack."

He slid a gentlemanly hand to her low back and Emma felt the sizzle of heat shoot up her spine, down her legs and warm every crevice between. Her pulse immediately throbbed, her breath catching. If she didn't get this under control, he was going to make her heart stop completely.

He seemed to read her thoughts, his gaze resting on her mouth as she fought the urge to lick her lips. "I'd have to resuscitate you the old fashioned way since I left the defibrillator in the truck."

Holy hell! Suddenly having a heart attack sounded like heaven.

BEN WAS ONE hundred percent out of his comfort zone.

He held his arm out, the way Emma had shown him, and eyed the massive talons of the red-tailed hawk digging into the leather glove—gauntlet, he corrected—as he held the tether between his fingers. The bird was far heavier than he imagined it would be, but he wasn't about to complain about the way the muscles in his arm had begun to burn with fatigue. He was sure Emma would have loved teasing him about it after he'd said a three-pound bird was nothing compared to the seventy-five pounds of turnout equipment he wore on the job. Of course, he hadn't planned on holding the bird for more than a second. After five minutes, his bicep had begun to quiver and ache.

The bird gave a shrill shriek and Ben cringed. "What'd I do?"

Emma grinned, holding back a quiet laugh. "Nothing."

She slid her gloved hand in front of the hawk and whistled. The bird immediately jumped onto her wrist and ducked her head into Emma's fist, retrieving a piece of raw meat.

"She was just letting you know she didn't trust you not to drop her." He watched as Emma turned the bird loose into her cage and locked the door behind her. "Poor Winger was up here one minute and, the next, your arm was down here." She dropped her arm dramatically, her eyes twinkling with laughter. "What's the matter? Was the tiny bird heavier than you thought?"

"I wasn't about to drop her," he insisted, fighting the need to reach up and massage his fatigued muscle.

She slid the gauntlet off her hand and slapped it against his arm. "Go ahead, admit it. You were starting to burn."

It was the first time he'd seen her playful, flirtatious even, and he liked it. Her eyes seemed to ignite from within, reminding him of the endless blue skies over Lake Tahoe. Her smile changed her entire demeanor.

She was suddenly open, inviting, and it make her look almost carefree. With her auburn hair pulled back over her shoulder in a quickly plaited braid, she was only missing wings and he'd have been convinced she was some woodland fairy nymph sent over from Scotland to torment him. Watching her bend over a large trunk of equipment to drop the gauntlets inside, he felt his body throb in response as he checked out the rounded curves. Suddenly he had no doubt she was here to torment him.

She stood up, turning quickly and catching him gawking at her. "What did you want to see next?"

You, with your hair loose around your shoulders like fire and my hands moving over that sun-kissed skin of yours.

A pretty pink colored her cheeks and he couldn't help but recognize the irony. He should be the one blushing, and probably would be if she had any inclination of the thoughts he'd just been having about her. He wasn't entirely sure where the fantasies had even come from, but that didn't stop them from coming, hard and fast.

Emma in his arms. Emma with her creamy skin bared to him. Emma beneath him as he rose over her.

Stop!

Ben halted his thoughts before they could go any further. He'd learned the hard way to avoid free-spirited women. As much fun as they could be, they also usually ended up being far more trouble than was advisable for any man, especially him. He'd been down that road, several times, and it always ended the same way—with him out on his ass and a long night bailing his fiancée out of jail before retrieving his belongings from the pawn shop.

He'd finally come to a place where he was content with his life, including his bachelorhood, even if his mother, sister and his brother's new fiancée, Bethany, were trying to convince him of something different. Okay, so maybe *content* wasn't the right word but Ben had convinced himself he was satisfied for the time being. And, when he decided it was time, he'd look for a woman more like Ellie—stable, easygoing and, maybe even a little boring by Emma's standards.

Perspective, that's what he needed. Maybe putting some distance between him and Emma would get his overactive libido in check. His palm still burned with the memory of her breast filling it.

Great, now it was going to take an ice bath to cool him down.

He took a step backward. He couldn't stay here any longer or he was bound to do something he'd regret. "I should probably head into the station."

He felt slightly guilty at the disappointment that flashed in her eyes, making him want to retract his words and spend the rest of the day doing whatever it might take to get that smile back on her lips. "My buddy, Will, is already planning to stick me with cooking duty since he covered for me this morning."

She nodded and tried to stifle the confusion furrowing her brow. "Okay, I'll give you a ride back to the house."

Ben wracked his brain for a reason to turn down

the offer. There was no way he could sit in the cart, that close to her, and pray she couldn't see the evidence her nearness was having on his body.

"It's okay. I'm sure you've got plenty to do and I've already messed up your morning."

He could read the suspicion shadowing her eyes and, for a moment, considered explaining himself. Before he could say anything, the look was gone, replaced by the confident self-assurance he'd seen in her yesterday with the kitten.

"Then I guess I'll see you here Saturday morning." His confusion must have shown in his face. "Your offer to volunteer still stands, right?"

Her satisfied smirk made him cringe, cursing whatever moment of insanity had urged him to agree. Images of torturous chores filled his mind and her smile promised Saturday was going to be something he wouldn't forget for a long time.

Chapter Six

BEN SCRAPED THE last of the shit up and twisted the spray nozzle to finish cleaning out the cage. Two red foxes ran playfully around their outdoor enclosure while Emma sat on a boulder watching them, jotting down a few notes and casually glancing his way. This wasn't exactly what he'd envisioned when he'd volunteered.

"As soon as you finish and I get them back inside, we can break for lunch."

"We?"

A guilty smile lifted her perfect lips. "I think lunch is the least I could do." She gave a sharp whistle and red fur seemed to immediately move to her feet like copper-colored tornadoes swirling around her legs. Emma laughed at their antics. "Okay, you two, I know you're having fun but it's time to head back inside."

Ben finished spraying down the cage as Emma clipped a leash to the harness on each of the animals and walked them back to their enclosure amidst their squeaking. Ben slipped out of the cage as Emma brought the pair inside, careful to keep his distance of the chattering devils.

"Okay, Trixie, you and Todd go play in there." She slipped the harness off the smaller female as the male twisted around her feet, tangling himself in the leash.

As she released the male, Ben watched, amazed at how relaxed her demeanor was around them. "Don't you ever worry?"

She looked back at him curiously. "About what?"

"I don't know. That you might get bitten? That they might turn on you?" She locked the door before they walked past several other cages, each containing a different type of animal. A black bear tried to reach through the chain link of his enclosure, almost giving the appearance of waving at Emma. "That's a bear. He could kill you pretty easily."

She gave him a patronizing shrug. "He could. But so could a lot of other things."

"Like?"

"Like running headfirst into a fire."

"Touché," Ben acknowledged as he hurried ahead of her to open the door when they reached the side of her house.

He followed her into a spacious kitchen. He'd been in here a few times with her father and the room had been remarkably sparse, simple but masculine. He looked around, surprised at how much had changed. She'd redecorated, adding bright yellow curtains, scattering daisy decor throughout the room. The counters were still the same dark granite with mahogany cabinets, but the entire room had gone from dark and dominant to cheery and welcoming. She went in, not noticing the falter in his step as he closed the door behind her.

"Why *do* you run into burning buildings? You're just as likely to get injured as I am with the animals."

"It's not like I run into every building. When we do it's usually because someone needs help."

Emma turned and faced him, growing serious. "Well, then, we have something in common. These animals need mine, more than any human ever has."

Ben leaned back against the counter and crossed his arms, studying her as she moved around the kitchen. The woman was hard to figure out. One minute she was playful, completely relaxed and at ease with a fox or a mountain lion, and the next, she was a warrior, fiery and passionate, only to do a one-eighty and make a joke. She was like a butterfly, unable to settle on any one emotion too long, but he found himself wanting to try to keep up.

Not this time, Ben. You want predictable, remember?

He steeled his resolve. He'd had more than his fair share of bad relationships. There was Angie. He'd walked in on her, straddling the guy who lived two doors down from their apartment as she screamed his name. But even that couldn't top his latest romantic fiasco, Laura. That time, he'd found out with a call from Andrew, from the police station, where he was holding Ben's fiancée for selling stolen goods. Those "goods" being all of the memorabilia his brother Grant had given him spanning his NFL career, most of their furniture and the car that she'd stolen from his house while he was on call at the firehouse.

Nope, he wasn't dating unless he found a woman who was straightforward. No games, no pretenses, and nothing he'd need to figure out—or find out about later.

However, he couldn't deny that Emma Jordan had gotten under his skin, making him want to know more.

From the first moment he'd met her, dropping off the kitten, she'd intrigued him. Sure, she was pretty, but that hadn't been why he'd come back the second time or why he'd agreed to volunteer. She was difficult to figure out but there was a genuineness about her that she didn't bother to hide. Whether she was unabashedly staring at his butt or defending her misfit tribe of animals, this woman was an intense force to be reckoned with and she kept him guessing what might happen next.

"I mean, you'd have done the same, right?"

Ben was jolted back to the present where, if her question was any indication, she'd been holding a one-sided conversation he hadn't been paying attention to. Emma stood in front of him, her arms crossed, expecting an answer but he could only watch those perfect, luscious lips of hers and wonder if they tasted as sweet as they looked.

If she hadn't been staring at him, he'd have laughed at the idea. He was pretty sure that if he tried to kiss her, she wouldn't hesitate to claw his eyes out. Just like one of her bobcats. In spite of the common sense that typically reminded him of how ridiculous fantasies were, his fingers itched to see if her hair was as warm to the touch as it looked. He wanted to see if her skin tasted like the sweet vanilla scent he'd caught as she walked past, reaching for a loaf of bread. In the end, he was too big a chicken, settling for self-preservation over desire.

"Um, I need to get in that cupboard."

She pointed to the cabinet door behind his head and Ben stepped aside as she stretched on her toes to reach for the glassware inside.

"Here." He moved behind her, easily grabbing two glasses from the shelf.

"I've got it," she protested, pressing her shoulder into him and turning.

The movement brought her body flush against his, igniting a desire he could no longer pretend didn't exist inside him. Lust slammed into him, his entire body responding almost violently. Blood pounded hotly in his veins while every nerve ending seemed to come alive, oversensitive and heightened to the nth degree. Setting the glasses down on the counter before he dropped them, he found he couldn't quite let them go. His fingers gripped their slick sides tighter in an effort to keep from reaching for her.

Ben knew he should just take a step backward and stop this exquisite torture but, with her body pinned between his and the counter at her back, he couldn't quite force his feet to move. When her hands landed on his biceps, electric jolts of longing rippled through his veins, making him quake with yearning.

Emma opened her mouth, ready to speak, but her eyes darkened and he could see he wasn't the only one affected. He was just about to step backward when her hands slid up around his neck. Standing on her toes, Emma connected her mouth with his and Ben's world immediately rocked on its axis.

WHAT THE HELL are you doing?

The logical side of Emma's brain was practically screaming at her, but she didn't care. When she'd turned and felt Ben McQuaid pressed against her from shoulder to knee, her bones had turned to gelatin, leaving her a quivering, hungry, mess of yearning. The man was solid muscle, and it had been pure torture watching him clean pens all morning, every movement causing the flesh to ripple and flex deliciously. She might have given him a filthy job, but it hadn't compared to how dirty her thoughts had been as she eyed every chiseled inch of him, like living stone-carved perfection.

To be completely honest, she'd been fantasizing about him from the first time she'd seen him getting out of the truck with the box in his hands, but the more time she spent with him, the more she realized it wasn't just a physical attraction. The man was as inept with the animals as he was charming, but he had a way of making her feel heard, of getting her to open up and feel safe, even in her vulnerabilities. She'd already confessed more to him than she had to anyone, even her father, especially about her doubts in her own capabilities.

Her fingers brushed over the nape of his neck, his short hair bristling across her palms deliciously as his lips moved over hers and she opened beneath his seeking touch, sending spirals of heat to curl low in her belly, making her entire body tremble. She rose on her toes to better access his mouth and nearly moaned as her breasts brushed against the wall of his chest. He caught her sigh in his kiss and Emma swept her tongue into his mouth. Ben leaned into her, his presence surrounding her completely.

Without thinking, just knowing she wanted—*needed*—to be closer, Emma barely separated from him long enough to hop up on the kitchen counter, putting her face at the same level as his, even if her butt was only halfway on the counter.

"There," she whispered on a sigh, fusing their mouths again, wrapping her calves around his hips, her heels locking around that tempting ass of his.

Emma dragged him as close as she could, her thighs clasping his body, and felt the heat explode in her core where they were only separated by the thin barrier of their clothing. Her heart beat faster than she'd ever imagined possible. Faster than the first time she'd worked with a timber wolf, harder than the time a bull elephant had charged her at the park. Ben McQuaid affected her in a way that no burst of adrenaline ever had.

His hands slid from the counter to grip the side of her hips. It wasn't enough. She wanted to feel them move over her, under her shirt, against her bare skin.

She wanted him to touch her, to be able to touch him, and to let this unexplainable maelstrom of desire engulf them both. Emma arched her back, pressing against the wall of his chest. Her body ached for more, demanding release, and she could feel the heat of his body where she burned the hottest.

His fingers clenched slightly, digging into the denim at her hips but, other than that small movement, he seemed relaxed, almost as if he was merely tolerating her kiss. Realization struck her hard, like a kick she'd received once from a donkey but twice as painful, because this time the sting was coupled with embarrassment. It flooded through her making the back of her neck prickle, burning her cheeks, nearly as hot as the lust still circling through her lower body. Emma drew back but avoided looking at him, not wanting to see passive indifference in his gaze while she was still reeling with the intensity of her reaction to him.

"Is that how you thank all of your volunteers for cleaning cages?" Ben slid his finger under her chin and lifted her face, forcing her to look at him and see that cocky smirk. "Or am I just one of the lucky ones?"

His gaze was dark with a lazy amusement. There was nothing to indicate he shared the same urgent hunger she felt.

Ben's gaze slid over her face, lingering for a moment on her mouth before he inhaled deeply, cocking his head to one side, as if she was a puzzle he was trying to solve. "You're almost as wild as those animals of yours."

Emma's stomach did a flip before it sank to her toes.

In fact, the way he said it sounded more like an insult than an innocent observation.

Wild, impulsive, brash, daring . . . she'd had them all linked to her in one way or another during her lifetime. She didn't usually mind since, in her line of work, she needed to be all of them at times. But she wasn't stupid, and she usually didn't rush headlong into a situation without considering the consequences, not like this. Not anymore. It was that balance that kept her and her staff safe.

But somehow, Ben made her undeniably aware, and for the first time she understood the meaning of "animal attraction." Even now, with her pride stinging, she still had the urge to rip his shirt off and lick the well-defined abs still pressed against her. But, obviously, the feeling wasn't mutual and she wasn't about to make a complete idiot out of herself. Once a day was the limit for her own stupidity.

Emma had two choices: either continue to blush furiously and let him know the depths of her embarrassment, or brush it off as no big deal, pretending he didn't affect her in the slightest. It was a no-brainer, although she could still feel her cheeks burning.

Sliding off the counter, letting her body brush slowly against the front of him, Emma deliberately tried to get some reaction from him while ignoring the electric shock waves the contact set off in her own body, turning too many parts liquid.

She lifted his arm from the counter and reached for the glasses, brushing past him and giving him a quick shrug. "Eh, it's out of my system."

Chapter Seven

THE AIR BETWEEN them practically crackled with electricity as Emma walked away from him to fix their lunch. Ben kept his back to her, gripping his fingers around the bull-nosed edge of the counter and sucking in a slow breath as silently as possible, trying to regain some semblance of control over his inflamed body. His heart rate wasn't yet slowing and everything south of his waist was throbbing. He'd fought with every bit of self-control to hide his reactions from her, not wanting to look like a randy teenager on prom night, but it was going to take more than a little will power to keep from wanting to ravish that mouth of hers again.

Out of her system? Damn, if she could do this with just a kiss . . .

He couldn't even allow himself a moment to think about what else Emma might be capable of because regardless of how much he might want her—and *damn*, did he want her right now—Ben couldn't allow himself to get swept up in a moment. He'd done that before and learned the hard way not to let it ever happen again.

Especially if he was "out of her system."

Her comment actually smarted a bit. He was tempted to kiss her again, to prove her wrong. Just the thought was enough to make his knees feel weak, like he'd just finished carrying his turnout gear up thirty flights of stairs. Emma already had a way of making him ache and yearn for more than he could have. She was a temptation that was just too dangerous to give in to.

"You want mayo?" she asked, casually, making him wonder if the sexual current he felt sparking between them wasn't completely one-sided.

Ben inhaled deeply through his nose again, pushing himself away from the counter and tugging his cell phone from the pocket of his jeans, pretending to get a text. "You know, I should probably take that to-go. Looks like they need me at the station." He wiggled his phone, grateful she couldn't see the screen well enough to figure out he was lying.

Emma arched a brow and leaned a hip against the side of the counter. "I thought you told me this morning you had the day off."

"I do, but I'm always on call, so . . ."

"Hmm." She nodded slightly but he could tell she didn't believe him.

It was better for them both if he left now, before he did something stupid. Like pinning her against the counter again and lifting her legs back around his waist. *Out of her system, really?*

Emma slapped the rest of the sandwich together and held it out to him. "There you go. Drive careful." Ben took it with a mumble of thanks and headed for the door. "You think they're going to need you tomorrow too?"

He paused with his hand on the doorknob and looked back over his shoulder at her. The sunlight streaming through the window caught her deep auburn hair, turning it flame red. Ben knew this was one fire he couldn't let himself get caught up in, couldn't run into fearlessly, even if he wanted to—and he *really* wanted to—but he had the distinct impression getting too involved with Emma would only end up with him getting burned. Even so, he couldn't quite bring himself to turn down her request.

"I'll . . . uh . . . let you know."

She rolled her eyes at him, with a bitter laugh, and went back to her own sandwich. "Never mind, hero. I've managed to keep this place standing without you so far. I can do it on my own for as long as I need to."

EMMA WASN'T SURE which was more humiliating—the fact that Ben hadn't been nearly as affected by their steamy kiss as she had or that he'd bailed on volunteering just to get away from her afterward. She sighed as she quickly made herself a sandwich and took her lunch outside, onto the front porch, just catching a glimpse of his truck driving through the electric gates at the end of the driveway.

"Good riddance," she muttered before taking a bite.

She had enough trouble on her plate with judgmental locals. She didn't need to be worrying about a sexy fireman wandering around her place with his rock-hard abs and a butt she could bounce quarters off, getting himself in trouble.

Her body instantly responded to the memory of her legs hooked around that butt, heat flaring from within at the mere thought. She twisted the cap off a bottle of water before swallowing some, letting it quench the heat building inside her, praying it would douse the attraction she felt.

"Hey, Emma, we're out of jam for Wally," Jake announced as he came out of the barn and made his way toward her. "You want to head into town for some or you want me to do it?"

"I just bought some. It should be in the cupboard."

Jake wiped the sweat from his forehead with his forearm. "Yeah, it would be, if your new boy toy hadn't dropped the jar and broken it when I was showing him how to get their breakfast ready."

She sighed at the disapproval in his voice. He didn't need to say the words for her to hear his judgment loud and clear: *you're not your dad. You can't do this.*

"Then use honey. Wally will appreciate the change."

"Ran out three days ago, remember? And I'd say

not to worry about it but Wally's so accustomed to it now that he'll tear that cage apart if he doesn't have his snack." His gaze was accusatory, pointedly reminding her that she'd been the one to insist on giving the treat, against Jake's warning otherwise.

Emma tossed the sandwich back onto the plate and stood up. "Of course," she complained. "Okay, I'm going, I'm going. In the meantime, let's keep everyone housed and we'll get them exercised when I get back, when there are more eyes on them."

"Not a rookie, boss." Jake rolled his eyes as he turned back to the barn. Sarcasm dripped from his tone but Emma chose not to respond.

She had every right to say something, after all, technically, he was her employee, but it was easier to keep quiet. It wouldn't be prudent to piss off either of her last two employees. He and his brother, along with Sadie and Monique, her two part-time volunteers, were the only ones who hadn't up and left when her father died, leaving her in charge of the sanctuary filled with too many animals and not enough hands to do the never-ending chores. But, so far, Jake wasn't coming around the way the others had.

What in the world had her dad been thinking, assuming she could take charge of this place without him and no source of income for it? She couldn't even manage to keep honey or jam on hand for a bear, how was she going to run this entire facility single-handed?

He watched Emma as she headed out of the facility. Now was his opportunity, while she was gone and everyone else was busy. Sadie and Monique were working in the nursery and his brother was too busy to even notice that he wasn't where he'd said he'd be.

It didn't take long to drive his sedan to the entry. Retrieving the cans of spray paint from his trunk, he tagged the front of the entrance, watching the heavy red paint drip down the wall. It wasn't fancy. It barely even made sense, but it was nothing more than a diversion. Emma would be so busy cleaning up the mess that she wouldn't even realize what was happening inside the compound. By the time she did, it would be too late.

Emma was too incompetent to be running Sierra Tracks the way it should be run. He was going to make sure that everyone else finally realized it too.

Ben headed into the station, but he hadn't bothered to stay long. It was quiet and they didn't need him. Why would they? It was technically his day off and, while this was their peak fire season, the past few weeks had been unusually quiet. Under normal circumstances, he would have welcomed the peace but the way his body was still thrumming with adrenaline after that kiss with a particular redhead who knew exactly how to light him up, he needed a release. Instead, he'd had to make due with taking his frustrations out on the weight machines, leaving the crew on duty carefully skirting his ire after one of the new probies had made the mistake of asking who shit in his cornflakes.

It wasn't likely to be repeated anytime soon. Not after his ridiculous overreaction, shoving the poor kid against the wall hard enough to rattle the hanging plaques. Thank goodness Angie had been there to convince him that the rookie was nothing more than a dumb kid. So far, thankfully, they'd all been willing to let the matter drop but the probie eyed him warily now and he was going to have to do something to make it up to him.

It wasn't like he could confess the real reason he'd lost his shit. There was no way he was telling anyone else in the station that he'd been shaken up by his reaction to a woman who kissed like sweet sin personified. As much as he liked the crew, Ben wasn't about to take that razzing. They'd never let him live it down. Especially Angie. They might be friends now, but she was nothing less than brutal when it came to giving him dating advice. Quick sound bites like *Love 'em and leave 'em, Ben.* Or his personal favorite, *sometimes you just need to get your rocks off.*

It was easier to sneak out and head home than wait to hear her lesson for today.

Ben slowed as he turned down the long stretch of road in front of the sanctuary. He'd never admit it out loud, but there was no doubt he was trying to catch a glimpse of Emma, even if it was pretty unlikely that he'd actually be able to see her from this distance. It didn't stop him from leaning forward as he neared the edge of the property line, watching for the flash of red from her hair in the sunlight. Just as he came to the driveway, Ben slammed on the brakes.

Emma stood on her toes at the front gate with her back to the road, trying to scrub what looked like blood from the top of the enclosure wall.

Pulling the truck onto the shoulder, he parked behind her golf cart, and jumped out. "What the hell happened?"

She looked back over her shoulder at him. "What does it look like, genius? Someone thought they'd come by and spray paint my wall."

"But who? Why? When?" It hadn't been there when he drove out earlier. Ben could see what was left of the paint spelling out "Free the slaves" with the last "s" smeared thanks to her clean-up efforts.

Emma dipped the plastic scrub brush into the bucket of soapy water. "Some nut? Protester? Activist? I don't know. I headed into town to get a few things and came back to this. Again."

"You mean this has happened before?"

She sighed heavily, her head dropping forward, as if it pained her to admit the truth. "I told you people around here don't like me being in charge. Did you think I was joking?" She dropped the brush into the water and rolled her shoulders back, trying to loosen the kinks, before shaking her head at the writing on the wall. "When are people going to get it through their heads that I'm not running a circus or a zoo? I don't keep these animals for entertainment. I only keep the ones that can't go back into the wild."

"But your dad used to have visiting hours, like a zoo," Ben pointed out, earning himself a dirty look.

"Yeah, well, vet care is expensive when all that comes through your doors are injured and needy animals. Vaccines and surgeries still cost money and there needs to be some sort of steady income to make up for the constant unpredictability of donations."

Ben threw his hands up in supplication with his palms facing her. "No judgment, just playing devil's advocate." He stepped closer, sliding a finger through the paint that was still tacky to the touch.

"Yeah? Well, go advocate somewhere else."

"Brake fluid."

"What?" She didn't bother to hide her annoyance.

"Try using brake fluid instead of soap and water. Do you have some? It should break up the paint and make it easier to clean."

"Yeah, in the shop at the house. I have enough equipment that seems to constantly need repair, so we keep plenty on hand."

Ben didn't miss the exasperation in her voice. She was beat—both physically and mentally. Overworked and stretched far too thin. Yet, in spite of it, her conviction propelled her on. He wasn't sure she would succeed but he made the decision that he wasn't going to let her go down fighting alone.

He wandered around the entry to the sanctuary, looking for some sort of clue as to who might be causing her trouble. Several tire marks marred the ground at the exit. She eyed him suspiciously as he stared down at the dirt. Ben squatted on the balls of his feet and ran his fingers over what appeared to be a narrow tire track. Emma drove a truck.

"Did anyone else come out while you were gone?"

"Not that I know of. The gates stay shut and Jake didn't mention it. Everyone is still here."

Ben made his way back to the painted wall, turning her to give him her full attention. "You're sure?"

"I guess."

Ben pulled his phone from his back pocket and began dialing Andrew. "Radio Jake to have him bring you the brake fluid. But stop cleaning for now."

"Why? What are you doing? I don't have time for this, Ben."

"I'm calling my brother. He needs to come out and see this."

"The police? I don't think we need to involve them." She pulled the two-way radio from her pocket and asked Jake to bring the brake fluid to the front gate. She tucked the device into the back pocket of her jeans and reached for the brush, nudging past him, dripping water along the way. "I mean, it sucks but—"

"Emma, this is vandalism. You need to report it, especially if this isn't the first time." When the call went to voicemail, he sent his brother a quick text.

"Wow! Thank you, Captain Obvious." She sighed heavily, making him wonder if she got this annoyed with everyone or if he just brought out the best in her.

"I know that, but there's no sense in involving the police in something that is so low on their list of concerns that it won't do any good."

"My brother's a good cop. He'll follow up on it and make sure he gets to the bottom of this."

"Not if he's too busy dealing with other shit."

Why was she being so difficult? He stood and made his way back to her, opening his mouth to argue. She didn't even give him the opportunity.

"It's just paint, McQuaid. It'll wash off. No sense giving someone the satisfaction of all the drama calling the police would cause."

"This could get a lot more troublesome than just spray paint on a wall."

Emma glanced past him to where he could see a car pulling up to the gate. Jake jumped out and ran toward them, looking panic-stricken.

"Emma, Buster's missing," he yelled.

"What?" She threw the brush back into the water and jerked the bucket onto the back of the golf cart. "How long?"

"I don't know," he said, heaving for a breath. "Monique and Sadie have been in the nursery all morning, Brandon was with the raccoons and I was cleaning the deer pens. No one else has been near the cats since you fed them this morning. I was bringing this to you like you asked and when I went by his cage, it's wide open and he's not in it."

Ben could see the panic rising in her at the thought of even a declawed mountain lion loose on the premises.

He could also read between the lines. Emma had been the last one at the cage.

"Shit," she whispered under her breath. "Get in, Jake. We've got to get to the barn and get tranquilizers before he gets into any trouble."

Or kills someone.

She didn't need to say the words for Ben to hear them in his head.

"Get in the truck," Ben ordered. "That way you two won't be in the open. Radio everyone else to stay inside."

Chapter Eight

THIS CANNOT BE happening.

Emma's gaze slid over the tree line, searching for any area Buster might be hiding as they drove back to the barn with Ben, praying to catch a glimpse of him, even as she prayed she'd find him back in his cage. She'd radioed Sadie and Monique, warning them to stay together inside but to keep watch for Buster. So far, there had been silence from everyone. She wasn't sure if that was good or bad. While it meant everyone was safe, it also meant no one had seen Buster. He could have been loose when she left for the store, somehow gotten outside of the sanctuary enclosure without her noticing. He could be anywhere at this point.

Stop! You're going to find him and everything will be fine.

It had to be.

Ben parked the truck in front of the barn. "We'll find him, Emma," he said, as if reading her mind.

Jake leapt from the cab and ran inside, reappearing after only a few minutes with two tranquilizer guns, several packs of darts and two brown bottles of sedative. He passed one set to Emma.

Ben's gaze darted between them. "Hey, what about me?"

"Do you know how to use one?"

"A gun? Yes."

"A dart gun is very different. You have to aim differently and account for how much sedative is given." She shook her head. "If you shoot him in the wrong spot, it'll kill him."

"And if he gets a hold of me?"

"Hang on." Jake ran back into the barn, returning with what looked like an automatic weapon and a container of large plastic BBs. "Here. Be careful with this."

"A pepper ball gun?"

Emma was surprised he knew what it was. "Yes. It'll be enough to deter Buster and turn him the other direction if he comes after you. It's the same thing Monique and Sadie have. Jake and Brandon have been trained—"

"Yeah, I get it." He reached for the phone in his pocket.

"Who are you calling?"

"My brother. I texted him about the vandalism, remember? I need to warn him. The last thing we need is for one of the department to drive in and run into a mountain lion on the loose."

She reached for his wrist before he could dial. "The

last thing *I* need is the police overreacting about this. Especially if I can get it under control quickly."

"Emma, he's probably already on his way."

"Thanks to you," she accused, opening the door, using it to cover one side of her while she prepped the darts. "Get into the house. Jake and I will comb the area looking for him." She turned toward Jake. "You have your radio?"

"I am not letting you go out alone looking for a mountain lion."

Emma's brows shot up at the audacity he had, ordering her around. "*You* can't stop me. And I'm not going alone. Jake's going with me."

"Emma, he's right." She should have guessed that no matter what decision she made, Jake would find a reason to quibble. "It's going to be getting dark soon. It would be stupid to go traipsing over the property at dusk and think Buster won't be stalking you. We can set a trap out here, in the open for him, and I'll set up another in his cage. He's pretty lazy so we'll make it easy pickings for him. I'll keep watch on his cage and the other animals from the barn. You can keep an eye out for Buster from the house." He looked at Ben. "Call your brother and tell them to stay away. Give him some sort of B.S. reason. A cop will want to call in Animal Control and those guys will just make a mess of things. We can deal with them after we find the cat." He frowned at Emma, his disapproval evident. "At least that way, it won't look quite as bad."

"Buster isn't the only mountain lion out here, Jake."

Emma argued. "If he runs into another one, he has no way to defend himself."

"He has his teeth and we both know he's not going to go far." Jake shook his head. "This is what happens when people make wild animals into house pets."

Emma wasn't sure whether Jake meant Buster's original owners or her but she didn't miss the deliberate look he shot her way. He had accused her of doing the same numerous times with several of the animals at the sanctuary.

"I'm not going to leave you in the barn alone."

"The four of us can crash in the office. Mo and I have before."

A sly grin split his face but Emma wasn't about to give him the satisfaction of inquiring about his questionable relationship with her volunteers. They were grown women and it wasn't her business to warn them off dating a jerk like Jake. Emma rolled her eyes, disgusted by him.

"There's enough to worry about without your overactive sex drive, Romeo." Ben glared at Jake. "One animal on the loose is all we can handle right now."

He snorted. "Can't make any promises."

"Don't make me have to shoot you in the ass with one of your own darts," Ben warned.

Jake laughed arrogantly. "Says the guy holding a BB gun. Just make your call, hero, and stay with her at the house."

"I don't need protection." She glared at Jake, then at Ben. "From either of you."

"Sure you don't." Jake grabbed the radio clipped to his side pocket and called for Sadie, informing her and Monique to get to the barn before he called for his brother. He hurried to the barn doorway and pointed at Ben, ignoring Emma altogether. "Help her get that trap set before the sun goes down. That cat may not have claws but he's still wild enough to figure out how to use those teeth. I may not agree with her methods, but I don't really want to see Emma dead."

Emma's heart thudded in her chest at his words, driving home the very real possibility of someone getting hurt.

Aw, Jake, here I thought you didn't care.

BEN HUNG UP the phone after lying out of his ass to persuade his brother that he'd call him later with the details of the vandalism and that Emma didn't want to report it. Luckily, Andrew had assumed Ben was trying to keep him away in order to put the moves on the "hot vet" and Ben wasn't going to argue just to save face. He'd confess the truth later, when his brother wouldn't be tempted to single-handedly face down a mountain lion just to show off. He walked back into the kitchen.

"Get everything taken care of?" Emma glanced his way as she slid a package of ground beef from the refrigerator, tossing it into a mixing bowl. Going back, she retrieved several pieces of raw chicken and she cut the thigh from the drumsticks before dropping them into the bowl as well.

"Are you just going to put some anesthetic into that?" She didn't even look his way. "No."

"Wouldn't it be easier just to drug Buster with food than to try to wait for him to show up and then *attempt* to shoot him?"

She paused, turning toward him, irritation practically oozing from every pore. "First, I wouldn't know how much anesthetic he was actually getting if he didn't eat all of the meat. Second, if, for some reason, he's able to eat the meat without getting trapped, he could escape with only a partial dose. This way, if we trap him, I have the dart stick. If not, I can dart him with the gun from a distance and it will take effect almost immediately. It's safer."

"It sounds like you're more worried about Buster than everyone else."

"A half-drugged mountain lion isn't safe for anyone. I don't want to put anyone at risk. That's how we do things here, with the safety of *everyone* in mind."

"I highly doubt that."

"Excuse me?" She narrowed her eyes, flames of fury lighting them. Any mild irritation she might have felt toward him earlier disappeared in the smoking aftermath of her rage. She threw the raw chicken leg into the bowl with a *splat* and advanced on him, looking almost as dangerous as the lion that was the cause of this mess. Her eyes glimmered with indignation. "What would you know about how this place runs?"

She might be dangerous, but Ben wasn't about to run. Not when he was right. He'd done what she asked, against his better judgment and called his brother, but there was still a wild animal on the loose and that put the entire town at risk until he was captured. She either needed to catch this cat right away or he was calling in reinforcements. Emma needed to face the truth of this potentially dangerous situation, even if it was brutal.

"I knew your dad and I may not have been out to the sanctuary that often, but it's a small town. People talk, Emma, and I don't once recall hearing about animals on the loose. I'm sure this isn't the way you *normally* run the sanctuary but—"

"Don't lecture me."

"I'm only giving you until morning and then I'm calling Andrew in. There are lives at stake here. I'm not saying you can't do this but, Emma, you need more help."

"I *can* do this and I *don't* need more help. I locked that cage." She turned her back on him, but not before he'd seen the uncertainty flood her eyes.

"Emma?"

"Before I went into town, I checked the cat enclosures. I always do." She shook her head and pursed her lips, frowning. "I know that cage was locked."

Ben narrowed his eyes and tried to comprehend what she wasn't actually saying, what she seemed too afraid to say aloud. *Free the slaves.* After the graffiti he'd seen at the front entrance, it wasn't far-fetched. But why would someone have done something this extreme?

"You think someone let him out."

"I don't know. Maybe."

Her gaze sought his, pleading. He couldn't tell if she was more worried that he might agree, or that he wouldn't and this might be her own fault. She threw up her hands and finished with the raw meat before washing them at the sink and brushing her hair back from her face.

"I don't know. I can't believe that anyone would misunderstand what I'm doing here so much that they would risk lives."

There was more to her suspicions than she was telling him. He could see it in the way she was avoiding his gaze. He watched her profile, willing her to look at him but she deliberately focused on everything else.

This was too dangerous a situation for Ben to let this drop. "Emma, this isn't the first time, is it?"

He saw the muscle in her jaw clench, as if she were biting back the admission. "It is, but I think someone's been tampering with the cages," she confessed. "The chain link on Wally's cage was cut last week but I found it before he was able to really do anything but scrape himself on it. Then I found the door unlatched on Mama Hoot's aviary." She faced him. "These animals can't survive in the wild. I would never risk them getting out, they'd die. But I think someone is trying to let them out. I think someone wants to sabotage me by making it look like I'm unfit to run the sanctuary."

"Who?" Ben's mind ticked through anyone he could think of who might not agree with her vision, or that of the sanctuary. But people in Hidden Falls loved her father, even if they hadn't always agreed with his ideals for wildlife preservation. There was really only one reason for someone to target a sanctuary. "You think it's some animal rights group?"

She shrugged and for the first time, Ben saw fear in her aqua eyes. "I really have no clue, but it's escalating. If someone let Buster out on purpose, it wasn't just to scare me or make me look bad. Buster is probably the most dangerous animal here, even if he was once a pet."

Ben took a deep breath and glanced up at the ceiling, praying this feeling of dread would go away. He didn't want to get mixed up in her civil war, didn't want to feel responsible for her. He didn't want to be a hero.

Except that he was lying to himself and he knew it. He absolutely wanted all of those things and more.

"Mountain lions are like a wildfire. Most of the time, you don't see the danger coming until suddenly it's right up on you."

Fighting back the urge to draw her into his embrace, to promise he'd protect her, Ben gave her the most confident, reassuring smile he could muster.

"Then it's a good thing you have a damn good fireman on hand."

Chapter Nine

EMMA STARED OUT the kitchen window, watching the trap she'd set nearly four hours ago. She hadn't meant to tell Ben about her suspicions. Talking about sabotage and someone being out to get her only made her sound like a paranoid freak.

But Ben hadn't laughed off her fears.

In fact, he hadn't even questioned it, which only made her more concerned because it meant he thought she might be right. Which surprised her because Ben seemed like a Boy Scout, the kind of guy inclined to believe the best of everyone, the kind who followed every rule and regulation, the kind who looked at the big picture. She actually liked that about him and, under normal circumstances, it was something they had in common. Although she could be impulsive, charging headfirst into matters but she did it within the confines of regulations. However, when it came to keeping her sanctuary open, she'd break every rule in the book if she had to in order to make it happen.

That started with luring Buster back in his cage safely. It was going to be a long night, staring out into the stillness of the night, waiting for Buster to, hopefully, decide to return to the easy meal they'd laid out for him. She prayed he'd return; he had to. Then maybe she'd take Ben's advice, do something to reach out to the community and let them see she was able to run this place just as well as her father had. If she could keep her animals safe.

"Hey, Emma?"

Ben's voice was husky as he came down the hall, into the kitchen, rubbing a towel over his dark hair, making it stand in spikes.

But it wasn't his voice or his hair that made her throat close. It was the man, standing in her doorway barefoot, wearing nothing but a pair of jeans, unbuttoned at the waist, with droplets of water from his shower still clinging to his skin. One broke free and slid down his chest, over his well-defined abs and past the opening of his jeans.

Oh, to be that bead of water.

His dark gaze slammed into hers and Emma felt a fire ignite within her. She actually squeezed her thighs together in an effort to hold back her body's response to the Adonis standing before her. Ben McQuaid wasn't just a fine specimen, he was a statue of perfection, carved by the hand of a god. The man was rippling muscles, long and lean, chiseled and carved flesh, and Emma wanted to trace the lines that crisscrossed and overlapped like marble artwork. The sleeve tattoo that covered most of his right arm, from the forearm to his shoulder, made the clean-cut fireman look dangerous.

Maybe he wasn't as safe as she'd first assumed.

His mouth tipped in a lopsided grin, as if he knew exactly what she was thinking.

Please, don't let him realize what I'm thinking.

"Where'd you want me to put this towel?"

"The . . . uh . . ." she stammered, unable to get her brain functioning again. "Um . . . in the . . ." *Shit, what was that room called?*

"Laundry room?" he filled in for her, his lips quirking to one side and deepening that damn dimple.

"Yes." She jumped up from the table, needing something other than his rock-hard body to focus on. "I think I still have some of my dad's t-shirts if you need a clean shirt to sleep in." She plucked the towel from his fingers and felt her entire body throb when his hand reached out, grasping her wrist.

"Don't worry about it. I always have a bag in the back of my truck, in case I stay over at the station."

His voice was more gravely than she'd realized. His eyes practically glowed with golden flecks in the depth of his dark gaze as it skimmed over her, caressing her face and lingering on her lips.

Please, don't look at me like that. I can't be responsible for anything I might do.

Ben's thumb brushed along the inside of her elbow making goose bumps break out over her arms. She could smell her own soap mixed with the male scent of his skin—so tantalizing. Emma fought back a shiver of need, wishing she could just lean into him.

Hell, who was she kidding? What she really wanted to do was to drag him into her room and have her way with him. Her breath caught in her chest at the fantasy.

"You think it's safe for me to go grab it?"

"Safe?" she repeated, dumbly, wishing her brain would get with the program.

"Because of Buster," he reminded her, lifting his brows. He was probably questioning her sanity at this point. "Do you think I could go out and grab my bag?"

"Oh . . . oh! Yeah, because of Buster." She took a step back, away from his spellbinding touch, needing to put some space between him and her so that her brain could function properly again. "I'll get it."

She hurried past him, holding her breath and trying desperately to get through the doorway without touching the bared skin of his chest. She didn't need anything else that might scatter her thoughts, or her senses, and touching him would definitely do it. Emma rushed through the front door, uncertain whether she was more anxious to get away from Ben or to get some clothes on him so she could stop thinking about how much she wanted to see exactly how warm and wet his body would feel beneath her fingers.

"Wait a second," he called, running after her, his feet padding quietly on the hardwood floor.

"It's fine," she yelled back. "You don't have shoes on."

"No, you need this."

Emma ignored him, jogging down the steps and threw open the passenger door of his truck, leaning inside, grateful for the respite to cool the very hot fantasies about a certain half-naked fireman and what sort of fire she'd like him to put out for her. She glanced around the front seats, but saw no bag.

Where would I put a duffel bag?

Emma climbed into the truck, looking into the backseat. Sure enough, tucked partially out of sight under the backseat was a black duffel bag. She tugged on the handle, sliding the zipper back to reveal what appeared to be several changes of clothing. Emma fought back a grin. He was a Boy Scout, for sure.

"Got it!" she yelled, holding the bag up as she backed out of the truck.

"Don't move." Ben's voice was low but authoritative.

She looked back toward the porch, where he waited. "What? I'm just—"

Then she heard it, that low rumble she'd recognize anywhere. Buster's warning growl. She looked past the back of the truck, on the other side of the driveway, where she'd set the trap up under the trees.

Buster was crouched low, as if he'd been trying to get at the meat she'd left out without getting caught in the trap but without claws, he couldn't quite manage to grasp the meat. His golden eyes glowed in the near dusk as he focused in on her, the shadows making his tawny fur look darker than usual, more like a panther. She would have had a perfect shot to dart him in the hindquarters without risking any injury to him, if she hadn't been in such a hurry that she'd forgotten to bring the dart gun.

Emma cursed her impatience. In her hurry to get away from Ben, she'd left the dart gun sitting beside the door on the porch. She hadn't expected the cat to come for the trap so quickly. She hadn't been thinking clearly and she'd broken her cardinal rule—safety first.

Hearing footsteps, she glanced back to see Ben approaching, gun held to his shoulder. "Don't. It has to be in a certain spot."

"I've got this."

As if comprehending his intent, Buster bared his teeth at Ben, hissing and hunching lower, raising his hindquarters in the air. His shoulder blades twitched as he readied to disappear in the dusk. Or worse, pounce.

"Stop," she ordered quietly. "He's going to run."

"Good."

"Not good. I need to catch him, remember?" Her voice had taken on a higher pitch and she knew she had to get it under control before the cat picked up on her anxiousness. He'd been a pet once, he seemed to like her. Maybe she could edge her way back to the house safely. She took a step backward, moving toward Ben.

"Hand me the dart gun."

Buster's eyes flicked toward Ben, still approaching slowly, and his fangs flashed dangerously as he screamed, piercing the stillness with his rage.

"Stop," she warned, wishing she'd been able to get a few steps closer to Ben. "He's feeling threatened."

"Yeah, well, so am I."

Emma took another step backward, shuffling her feet carefully over the worn dirt surface. Instead of relaxing his stance and returning to his meal, Buster raised up, stalking toward her slowly. It wasn't the reaction she'd expected, nor was it usual for him. He might be wild, but he also knew she wasn't a threat.

Unless that was the problem. She needed to change tactics.

"Hey, hey!" she yelled at the cat, putting her arms up high and waving in an attempt to regain the upper hand with him and force him to see her as a predator instead of prey.

"Emma?"

She heard the concern in Ben's voice. She couldn't blame him. Buster didn't seem inclined to back down now that he'd started toward her. She eased back, moving behind the truck door, ready to use it to help block Buster's attack if needed.

"You're going to have to do it. But aim slightly higher than normal and for his back legs. Only shoot once."

"He's getting closer to you. I can't see his back legs."

"Don't hit his lungs. You'll kill him."

"Yeah, that's my concern," he muttered.

She heard the quick whine of the dart gun and Buster jumped into the air slightly, his scream loud in the stillness. Animals inside the compound began to sound off and Buster immediately ran toward the back of the truck, attempting to hide from this new threat he hadn't expected. Emma reached for the truck door to shut it so she could edge to where she hoped the cat would fall to rest, when she heard the whine of the dart gun and barely jumped back against the truck in time for the dart to graze the edge of the door before falling to one side.

"What the hell are you doing?" She spun on Ben. "I said once."

"I didn't pull the trigger."

"Obviously you did." She picked up the dart, holding it in front of his face. "You almost shot me!"

"You said you needed to catch him and he was getting away."

She hurried to the back of the truck but Buster was nowhere in sight. Emma sighed. "Correction. He *got* away. Now I've got a half-drugged mountain lion running around. He's a target for any other predators in the area."

"What other predators? He's the top of the freaking food chain."

She scowled at him as he lowered the gun, before looking out at the tree line where Buster must have gone. "Not if he's encroaching on another mountain lion's territory."

Emma grabbed the gun from his hand, slipping on the safety, as she walked past him. Brandon came out from one side of the barn. "Where were you? You were supposed to be in the barn."

"I heard the commotion and grabbed a couple darts in case you needed me. Did I miss the fun?"

"Something like that."

"Please tell me you got him."

She didn't have the energy to bother reliving the experience with him, or the rest of the crew. She had no doubt Jake would only find a way to make it her fault and take the opportunity, yet again, to remind her of how she didn't come close to measuring up to her father and lacked his expertise.

She looked into Brandon's face, so filled with trust and dismay that he hadn't been able to help. But, he shouldn't have to. She should have remembered the gun, should have been more careful, shouldn't have ever let Buster get away.

Maybe Jake and Ben were right. Animals didn't escape on her father's watch, not ever. Maybe the best thing for everyone would be for her to just shut the doors and let it all go to hell.

BEN FIGURED IT was in his best interest to give Emma some space for the rest of the evening. She'd been pissed enough that they'd missed the chance at catching Buster, but compounded by the fact that he'd nearly shot her with her own dart gun made being scarce seem like the only viable option for him at this point.

But he wasn't sure that's what happened. Not that he could tell her that. He'd barely slid his finger to the trigger of the dart gun when the dart hit the edge of his truck door. And the angle had been off. If he'd shot it, Emma would have been directly in his line of fire. It scared him to think what could have happened, and who might have been responsible.

He glanced out the bedroom window again, eyeing the still empty trap. He was definitely in over his head. He didn't know the first thing about capturing a wild animal, let alone how to help this woman who'd decided she didn't need any assistance. Even though it was perfectly clear she did. There was someone out for her, some sort of attacker, and now they'd made it personal, trying to shoot her with a dart.

Ben twirled the dart in his hand. He'd picked it up when she wasn't looking and she'd been too distracted looking for Buster to notice. The needle was long and a large gauge, big enough that it would have hurt, but he had no idea what the sedative would have done to her. Luckily, it had spilled onto the ground and they hadn't had to find out. But even if it hadn't killed her, it would have taken her out of commission, long enough to spread the word and get the facility shut down if that was the intent.

Her words earlier came back to haunt him, chasing his own. *I'm damn sure not going to let someone scare me away* . . . Someone was doing more than trying to scare Emma.

Ben should walk away while he still could. His brain warned him that he was getting in too deep, caring too much, that he was doing the same thing all over again, falling back on old habits. Logic told him to head for his truck, jam the pedal to the floor and get the hell outta there, as far and as fast as possible.

Except he knew he wasn't leaving until that cat was caught. And there was no way he was leaving Emma here alone—well, alone with her volunteers—because Ben didn't trust Jake any more than he did that cat. The man rubbed him the wrong way, and seemed useless in a crisis. If he'd been watching, like he was supposed to, he'd have been out there to shoot that cat. Emma needed him, even if she wouldn't admit it, and he wasn't one to walk away from someone in need.

Of course, that wasn't taking into account his own needs, and Emma had those needs twisting through him like he was caught in a tornado, blowing every which way, and unable to right himself. The more he tried to convince himself that he shouldn't want her, the more his body seemed to reject the logic of walking away. But, when his lust put her in danger . . . Ben ran a hand through his hair, cursing his own stupidity.

He should have headed out to get his clothes himself, or brought them inside in the first place instead of leaving them in the truck, but his brain seemed to forget to function around her.

Either way, there was a cougar on the loose and, while Emma might think she had the situation under control, it didn't take an animal expert to know that mountain lion had been ready to attack her. He knew it and, from the way her hands had been shaking when she took the gun from him, so had she.

A knock on the door jerked him from his reverie and he jumped up from the bed in her guest room. "Yeah?"

Emma opened it, tentatively. It was the first time he'd seen her act anything but self-assured and he wondered why. She took a deep breath and crossed her arms but remained in the doorway, as if she was trying to build up courage to speak.

"I just want to apologize for yelling at you the way I did. It wasn't your fault. I should have known better than to go out to the truck without the gun. I put you in a dangerous position."

"Emma, I should have been more careful, or grabbed my clothes out of the truck before I came in, but I wasn't thinking straight."

Emma shook her head. "No, this was my fault and it wasn't right for me to push the blame on you."

Ben narrowed his eyes. "You know, you don't have to carry *everything* on your shoulders all the time."

Her eyes flickered brightly for a moment before shuttering and growing cold. "What? I don't."

"No?" Her hair was still damp from her shower, making wet circles on the shoulders of her t-shirt. He moved close and lifted a thick strand that was stuck to her cheek, tucking it behind her ear. "Because it sure sounds like you are."

She turned her head, refusing to look at him, but he noticed she didn't duck her head. That would show weakness and his Emma only showed strength, even if it was going to get her killed.

And when did she become your *Emma?*

"You don't know me, or what I'm dealing with here."

It was as if she'd read his mind. Her gaze clashed with his, reminding him of a storm he'd been caught in while deep sea fishing in Hawaii, when he'd gone for the Pro Bowl with his brother Grant. Crystal clear, glittering turquoise, but tempestuous. He could read a deep longing in its depth but it wasn't due to attraction, it was a need for approval.

He knew it well. He'd seen it enough times from his twin brothers, working with their father. Had seen it in the faces of each of his other four siblings when they explained to their parents that they didn't want to work the cattle, that other pursuits were calling them from their father's dream of a family-run ranch.

He saw the same desire in Emma's eyes, that same fear that no matter what she did, it wouldn't be enough to measure up. But, unlike him or his siblings, Emma was seeking validation from a ghost, and a town that had qualms about giving it. He wanted to pull her into his embrace, to show her the support she so desperately needed, but he could see by her rigid stance, she wouldn't accept that offer from him.

"You're right," Ben admitted. "I don't know exactly what you have to deal with, but that doesn't mean I can't see the weight you're trying to carry on your own."

There was a flicker in her eyes, a vulnerability he knew she would never admit to, tethered to regret. He could only assume it was about her father more than concerns about the town. He might not be able to bear the burden for her, but he could remind her that she wasn't alone.

"This place is going to be fine, Emma. I'll help you make sure of that. You don't have to run it the way anyone else says you should. You know what you're doing and the sanctuary is yours now. For what it's worth," Ben began, then brushed his thumb over her chin, "I think you're doing a pretty damn good job." He gave her a half-shrug and a grin, hoping to lighten the heaviness that seemed to surround them. "Escaped mountain lions aside."

His joke managed to do exactly what he'd intended and a faint smile tugged the corner of her lips to one side as she shook her head.

"And I promise not to shoot at you from here on out. So, are we friends again?" he asked.

She lifted her gaze again, but this time, her eyes didn't hold the vulnerability that had been there a moment ago. They glimmered like jewels and Ben thought he might lose himself in the hungry desire he saw there.

"Is that what we are?"

He knew he should keep his distance. There was something that burned hot between them and he shouldn't fan the flame, especially when he suspected it would only lead to one of them getting hurt in the end. But knowing what to do and convincing himself to do it when he was around her were two entirely different things.

"I'll be whatever you want me to be, Emma." The words slipped past his lips before he could stop them.

Ben's thumb brushed over the line of her jaw, his fingers moving behind her damp hair to cup her neck and draw her close. Emma's breath was warm against his face and, rather than close her eyes and wait for his kiss, her long lashes brushed against the arch of her brows, meeting his gaze with intensity, just before she stood on her toes to take what he so willingly gave.

Like their first kiss, it was an explosion of seduction as soon as their mouths met. There was no hesitancy, no testing the waters. Emma knew exactly what she wanted, exactly what he needed, and he was content to let her take the lead. Her tongue slid over his lower lip before plunging into his mouth, dancing with his in sensations of slick sweetness and velvety heat, searing him. She branded him, making him forget why he'd decided this was a bad idea.

Her body fit against his, curving into him as his hand slid down her spine to rest at her lower back. He groaned when she tipped her hips into him, pressing against his arousal, already throbbing for release, as his body ignited with the yearning raging through him. He had to regain his control. She needed a friend, a champion, not a man to take advantage of her in a moment of weakness. He wasn't that kind of guy, and he wasn't about to give in to primal lust, no matter how tempting it was.

Ben's arms tightened around her slightly, lifting her closer even as he withdrew from their kiss. Emma's arms wound around his neck for balance, her breasts pressing against his chest, and he fought to force himself to end this moment of pure pleasure. It didn't matter how many times he reminded himself he'd been raised to be a gentleman; he couldn't make himself end it. Not yet. Just one more kiss because it would have to be their last.

His lips found the hollow near her ear and Emma let out a small whimper of yearning. That small sound killed any control he thought he had. He'd been crazy to think he could keep from wanting her.

His hand slid under the hem of her shirt, gliding over her ribs to cup her breast, his thumb brushing over the taut peak beneath the thin fabric. Her fingers dug into the flesh of his back, her short nails biting into his skin slightly. Her response to his touch made the blood pound through his veins. He sucked at her neck, tasting her, his tongue swirling over her pulse, feeling it race in time with his own.

She leaned back slightly, her hips pressed against his arousal, making him swell with hunger and growl with the exquisite torment. Emma jerked her t-shirt over her head and pushed against his chest, guiding him backward until the bed in the center of the room hit his calves. Her hands slid around his waist to his back, down to cup his ass.

He wanted her. Every cell in his body was aching with hunger for her. It was primal, ravenous and he knew it would devour them both. He had to stop himself but he was having difficulty convincing his body. With him wearing nothing but sweatpants and only her thin flannel pajama pants between them, he couldn't hide the ridge of his erection pressing against her.

"Emma," he protested, gulping for air, trying to regain the restraint he'd become so proficient at over the past year. Emma's lips parted in her siren's smile as she pushed him backward and he fell onto the mattress.

She caught her thumbs in the material at her hips, sliding the pajama bottoms over the curve of her hips and letting them fall to the floor with a whisper. She stood there, wearing nothing but a thin cotton bra with white cotton underwear, and the magnificent simplicity of this woman struck him like lightning, sharp and powerful. The strength of his reaction to her left him feeling exposed.

He'd been this vulnerable before. It had led to him losing everything. He didn't want to go through that again.

Chapter Ten

"WE SHOULDN'T."

Ben's words felt like he'd just thrown a bucket of ice water on her. He'd been the one giving her the come-hither signals. She could feel his arousal, still rising to the occasion. What the hell was his problem?

She planted her hands at her hips as he stared up at her from the mattress. "Do you have a girlfriend?"

"No."

"A boyfriend?" She doubted it even as she said it, but it wasn't impossible.

"No!"

She slid one knee onto the edge of the mattress, her fingers itching to trace the ridges over his abs, to follow the lines of muscle. She wanted to taste him, to feel his skin against hers. "A medical condition?"

Ben blinked slowly, clenching his jaw as he let out a tortured sigh, and she could see he was fighting for restraint. "I'm not going to take advantage of you, Emma."

She couldn't help the incredulous laughter that burst from her. Just the idea that he thought he was taking advantage of her was ludicrous. Ben frowned, not seeing the humor in the situation, and she pursed her lips, trying to be serious for him.

"I'm sorry, I didn't mean to laugh but do I look like some virginal teenager? This isn't the 1800s. We're two grown, consenting adults. It's just sex. Assuming we have the same thing in mind." She met his dark gaze, letting her mouth curve into a wicked smile then glanced below his waist where his erection strained against the soft cotton of his sweat pants. "And it appears we do. So, what's the big deal?"

Ben rose on his elbows and scooted back on the bed, moving into a seated position. "Just because I *want* to do something doesn't mean I should." Even as he said the words, Ben's eyes smoldered with desire, his gaze sliding over her like a caress.

She bit back a laugh, pinching her lips together. "That's very pious of you." She moved closer, sliding one leg over both of his, straddling his hips, his arousal pressing against where she burned for him. Emma let her hands trail over his bare chest. "What happened to being whatever I want you to be?" He sighed and opened his mouth to speak. "Maybe you shouldn't make promises you don't intend to keep, Mr. McQuaid."

She knew she was being bold, but she was a woman who followed her instincts and every fiber of her being wanted Ben. He'd reached deep inside her on an emotional level, something she hadn't let anyone do in a very long time. When he'd reminded her that this was her place now, something in her clung to his words. He was the first person since her arrival here in town to recognize the value her experience brought. And, in spite of the stray dart, he'd proven he could handle himself in a crisis. He didn't blame her for the danger or the risk. For the first time, she wanted to let the instinct that ruled her in her work spill over into her personal life. She wanted to embrace that passion she felt when she was with him and quit worrying about what tomorrow might bring. She wanted to just let go and be able to trust her intuition again.

And then there was the raw, primal hunger.

She wanted to make love to Ben. Longing swelled through her with every touch, every kiss wreaking devastation on her usual sense of sexual ambivalence. She'd been attracted to men before, had a healthy sex life even if lovers had been somewhat infrequent. Most of the time, attraction fizzled quickly. Those not in her world couldn't understand the risk and tried to convince her to walk away. Men she met in her line of work wanted to control, and she would be subservient to no one.

But Ben made her want to give in, to surrender the control she usually wore like a badge of honor. This wasn't simply attraction. The best way she could describe it was pure, unadulterated, emotional and physical lust.

She lay her palms on his flat stomach and felt his muscles clench in response, his erection twitched beneath her and she bit back a groan, feeling the tension already building within her. She might regret this later but, now, she wanted to feel him buried inside her.

Ben slid his hands up her thighs to settle at her hips, his thumbs brushing over the lace trimming the top of her underwear. "Emma."

His voice was a murmured plea, a tormented rumble of sound beneath her palms. She rolled her hips against his in answer, the thin material between them creating a glorious, torturous friction. He growled and, moving with surprising dexterity, flipped her onto her back, hovering over her.

"You're sure this is what you want?" His question brushed over her lips as he tasted her again. She savored it, letting the frisson of heat move through her.

In answer, Emma wrapped her legs around his hips as he nestled himself between her thighs. "Quit thinking so much. You want me, I want you. Let's just accept it and enjoy it until it runs its course, okay?"

She heard the words fall from her lips but she questioned the truth in them. One time with Ben wouldn't be enough. She doubted if an entire night would even come close. If the inferno surging through her blood was any indication, this was a fire that might never be quenched.

She wasn't into romance and flowers, she wouldn't let herself be tied down to anyone, not as long as she worked with animals as dangerous and unpredictable as hers were, but she needed him tonight. In spite of nearly shooting her, she felt safe with him. Ben offered her the freedom to be weak and strong at the same time, to be vulnerable yet still maintain control. She didn't want to miss the opportunity to grasp this moment with both hands, before it was gone. And it would be, probably quickly and when she least expected it. Her mother's abandonment, father's sudden death had taught her that.

Ben lowered himself over her and she let her hands trail down the length of his back, feeling the muscles bunch and release beneath her fingertips. His mouth pressed hot kisses over her shoulders, his teeth nipping at the sensitive skin. Emma arched into him. Deftly, he unclasped her bra and slid it down her arms, tracing the curves of her breasts in languorous circles with his tongue, moving closer to the peaks as she strained for his touch. He brushed his thumb over one and her back arched, pressing her into his hand. His laugh was a low rumble against her flesh, making her shiver with wanton need.

"You are so beautiful." His lips covered her breast, sucking her into the heat of his mouth, his tongue flicking against her nipple, making her see stars behind her eyelids. While his mouth decimated what was left of her senses, his hands fondled her, caressing her stomach and cupping her rear, bared by her thong.

He paused and chuckled quietly. "Well, that wasn't what I expected."

She smiled up at him, enjoying the teasing note in his voice and the mischief in his eyes more than she'd thought possible. "I'm all about the surprise ending."

"Is that right?"

Ben shot her the most devilish grin she'd ever seen and felt herself grow wet anticipating what it promised. Maybe he wasn't quite the Boy Scout she'd believed him to be.

Moving to one side, he rolled her onto her stomach, brushing her hair aside and kissing a trail over her shoulders. His fingers hooked into the side of the underwear as his mouth moved down her back, his lips tracing every curve. Emma trembled beneath his touch, squirming as his teeth grazed over the cheek of her butt while his hands caressed the back of her thighs, to her ankles, before replacing them with his lips. After exploring every inch of her backside, Ben rolled her over, his shoulders between her ankles.

"You're driving me crazy," she whispered, looking down at him.

"I've only just gotten started," he promised, pressing kisses to the inside of her thigh, nipping the flesh, before laving the sweet pain away with a sweep of his tongue. "I want to make you go wild, Emma."

His words teased her and desire rushed through her. Ben lay a hand over her abdomen, kissing her hipbone, letting his hand move over her until his thumb brushed her folds, parting her, stroking her. She let her head fall back against the pillow, giving in to the passion washing over her, crying out when his tongue replaced his hand. Her body bucked in response but he held her, tormented her, and her fingers wound into his hair, pleading with him to stop even as she begged him not to.

Ben stroked her, lifting her higher, until she finally gave in, succumbing to the euphoric release that left her shattered, unable to control her limbs as she sank into the bedding beneath her. Ben trailed his hands over her abdomen, moving to lay beside her, skimming his fingers over her still quivering body. He brushed over the taut peaks of her breast and she moaned softly, wishing she could move but unable to convince her body to cooperate.

Ben chuckled softly beside her. "You okay?"

Emma cracked open one eye. "I'm not sure yet. I'm still numb."

"That's a good thing, right?"

"Yes." She couldn't help but laugh at his self-assured smirk. She forced herself up, leaning over him as he dropped back against the pillows, her hair falling around them in a damp curtain.

"You did say something about a surprise ending."

A smile as impish as his curved her lips as she thought about what she planned to do to him tonight. "This isn't the ending. It's only the beginning."

Swinging her legs off the side of the bed, she walked out of the bedroom, giving her hips a little extra sway.

"Where are you going?"

"Just wait there," she yelled as she headed into the hall to her bathroom. "And you'd better have those pants off by the time I get back."

BEN WATCHED EMMA walk out of the room, unable to tear his eyes from staring after her, taking in the sway of her hips, the curve of her spine, and the satisfied smile he'd put on her face. He'd been with his fair share of women but he'd never had a woman respond to him the way Emma did, nor had he ever wanted to please one more. Somehow, she'd managed reach into him and grab a hold of him. Fulfilling her needs became his only desire, to feel her squirm in his embrace as he brought her to the edge, to see those eyes light from within as she found her release. He needed to get a grip before he found himself too attached to let go.

Who was he kidding? He'd gotten attached that first afternoon, watching her with the bobcat kitten and he'd only tightened his grip each day since.

Emma's footsteps padded quietly down the hallway, back to his room. She came inside and set a condom on the nightstand, dropping another on the mattress by his shoulder.

He arched his brow and shot her a grin. "I hope I'm up to your expectations."

"You've already set the bar pretty high." She laughed as she slid back onto the bed and he lifted himself on an elbow, her breasts tantalizingly close to his face. "Or do you not think you're up to the task?"

He reached for her wrist, pulling her down on top of him. His cock jerked to attention, the blood rushing from his head to his groin. Ben brushed her mussed hair back from her face. "I have no doubts about my stamina."

Her hand slid down, sneaking beneath the waistband of his sweats to cradle him. "You were supposed to be out of these."

"It isn't very nice to tease."

"I never promised to be nice."

Ben couldn't think as her fingers moved over the length of him, stroking him until he thought he'd lose his mind. She pressed kisses over his abs, moving lower, before she pulled his sweats off and dropped them on the floor. He grabbed the foil package and tore it open.

"That was my job."

"Next time." Ben sheathed himself and positioned her over him, his fingers gripping her hips tightly. Need crested in him, rising high until he was sure it would drown him. "Now, Emma. I need to feel you around me now."

Unable to think any longer, he groaned as she slid down his length. Ben could only feel—the heated satin of her skin under his fingertips, the way her body clutched at him tightly, and the yearning blazing through him, sending him closer to the precipice. She sighed in relieved pleasure as he buried himself in her again, deeper, and she let her head fall backward.

Emma gripped his ribs as she lifted herself, riding him, teasing him into a frenzy. Ben lost himself in the feel of her surrounding him, the heady scent of her intoxicating him. Her curves in his hands. The way her body rocked with him, taking as much as she was giving. Gasping, Emma's fingers dug into his ribs as she gave in to her passion, driving him toward his own.

Nothing in his entire life had ever felt this good. Burying his hand into her hair, he pulled her down toward him, plundering her mouth as she rode him through her climax, letting it consume them both. Emma cried out, her entire body quaking, her response overwhelming him. Ben couldn't hold back any longer, shuddering with the force of his own release, he tumbled into the abyss with her.

Emma collapsed against his chest into a heap of soft curves and fiery tresses, with him still buried within her. She gasped, panting, her breath hot against his skin.

"Wow," she whispered.

"You could say that again." Nothing in his life had ever felt as euphoric as making love to Emma. No other woman had ever compared, not even his ex-fiancée and he'd been ready to commit his life to her.

Whoa, Ace, let's keep this in perspective. This was nothing but sex. She already made that very clear.

He caught a lock of her hair with his finger, brushing it from her cheek so that he could look down at her. "Have you ever . . ."

She shook her head slightly, her eyes wide. "Never." She looked up at him, resting her chin on her hand, her gaze languid and completely relaxed. "That was even more benefit than I bargained for with this friendship."

Her comment took him by surprise. Is that what they were?

He'd never been in a friends-with-benefits situation. He was more of an all-or-nothing kind of guy. But since his ex-fiancée had up and stolen half his shit last year, it had been a lot of *nothing*. He'd never been one to sleep around, or have one-night stands. That was more Andrew and Linc's scene. It didn't matter that his brothers harassed him for being the most likely to tie the knot, he just hadn't ever seen the point in sleeping with women he barely knew. But, in spite of her comment, Ben wasn't sure that's what this was.

He had no doubt that what he'd just experienced wasn't common, not with one-night stands, not with friends. Shit, he'd been with his ex for three years, and Angie for almost a year before that, nothing had ever come close to what he'd felt with Emma. He wasn't sure what *this* was, but he was sure it didn't happen every day.

He felt himself grow hard, still buried within her, and her eyes darkened, desire flaring up again. "Already?"

Ben was just as surprised as she was, but he couldn't deny that he wanted her again. And again after that. In fact, he couldn't honestly imagine *not* wanting her.

She shifted, rolling her hips, her body clutching his. The hunger he'd thought was sated, ignited again, flaring brightly in his chest. "Looks like we'll be needing that second one after all."

Chapter Eleven

EMMA WOKE SLOWLY, stretching her arms toward the head of her bed and her toes toward the end when they hit the foot board. She instinctively jerked her knees back up to her chest. Her bed didn't have a foot board.

She blinked, looking around the room as the dim sunlight filtered through the blinds and the thin sheer curtains. Sounds carried from down the hall through the closed door and she quickly sat up, reaching for her head as she tried to regain her senses. The sheet slipped, revealing her naked breasts and memories from the night before came crashing in.

Images of Ben in his own naked splendor. Above her, below her. How many times had they made love last night? She couldn't even remember.

She looked over the side of the bed for her pajamas and her gaze fell on the half-empty box of condoms. She barely recalled returning to her room for them. Holy hell, that man had even sat up with her during a midnight feeding with Kit before they returned to bed to start over again. A furious blush burned her cheeks as she covered her face with her hands, remembering how she'd begged him to touch her.

What had she been thinking? How was she ever going to face him?

"Where's Emma?" She heard Jake's demanding voice just before the back door slammed closed.

"Excuse me?" Ben sounded pissed.

Oh shit! The sound of the pair in her kitchen was enough to jerk her from her remorseful stupor. *Please let Ben at least have clothes on.*

Emma leapt out of the bed and yanked her pajamas on, running her fingers through her hair before giving up and twisting it into a messy knot at the top of her head. She ran down the hall to find Jake standing in the back doorway with his arms crossed, frowning at Ben who stood at the stove, scrambling eggs. Brandon was pouring several cups of coffee. As she entered, Jake glanced her way, arching his lip in a sneer.

"Morning, Emma," Brandon greeted cheerfully.

Ben glanced her direction, giving her a quick wink, and she couldn't help the blush that spread over the back of her neck, knowing it was creeping into her cheeks and making it obvious to all three of the men, confirmed far more than she wanted for Jake.

"So, Buster wasn't the only animal on the loose last night, huh? And you were worried about me?" Jake shook his head at Ben, clearly disgusted by the thought of them together.

She was a grown woman and didn't owe him any explanations.

"Coffee's ready." Ben motioned toward the mug he'd left beside the pot. "Brandon was getting some for the two girls. Jackass . . . I mean, Jake, here didn't want any."

Brandon frowned at Ben, not happy with him teasing Jake. Jake, on the other hand, glared maliciously at Ben, looking ready to explode, but somehow kept his mouth closed for a change. Emma bit back her smile, grateful that Ben had shut him up without causing a scene. As Ben glanced her direction, she saw the guilty grin spreading over that sinful mouth of his. As if she needed another reason to want him even more.

"Thanks." She accepted the mug Brandon held out to her. "I should hurry up and get another trap set up for Buster. I doubt he'll come this way during the day but—"

"He's already back in his cage," Brandon informed her.

"Which is actually why we came by," Jake said. "I saw him prowling the cages about six this morning, probably looking for food. We managed to get a couple darts off while he was trying to figure out where breakfast was." Jake must have noticed the shock on her face. "What? I figured you'd want to check on him while he's out but the clock's ticking. It's almost six thirty. He's been out about twenty minutes already." He turned, heading back outside. "Oh, and you might want to check out that new headline."

Emma turned toward the counter where someone had tossed a folded newspaper. Opening it, she could see a picture of her front gate, still dotted with the graffiti, with a headline below that read:

Danger on the Prowl

"Damn it," she muttered. She barely scanned the article before shoving it back on the counter. "You said you gave your brother some bullshit excuse."

"I did."

"Well, someone found out what happened and only six of us knew the truth. The others wouldn't do anything to jeopardize this place or they'd be out of work."

"So, of course, that means I'd turn on you?"

"Well, Sadie and Monica were with Brandon and me in the barn all night. I know none of us made any calls," Jake pointed out. "You were the one talking about calling your brother. It's a lot more likely one of you two tipped off that reporter than one of us."

Ben clicked off the stove and dropped the spatula in the pan. Turning, he faced Emma, ignoring Jake and Brandon's presence altogether. "Seriously?" He narrowed his eyes and she could easily read his expression.

You'd think that after what happened last night?

She tried to keep her gaze on his face but it was nearly impossible when he stood there, looking like a statue of a Greek god. Her entire body warmed as she remembered exactly how it had felt to be lying with her body curled against the wall of his chest. She couldn't quite ignore the sizzle of heat that spiraled in her belly. Emma found herself focusing on his mouth, the lips that had worked magic on her last night, helping her escape her fears. She couldn't do this. Turning away from him, she headed for the back door.

"You really think I'd do that?"

She didn't answer for a moment, pausing before turning back toward him slowly. "I don't know," she admitted.

Anger flashed in his eyes. Hurt followed immediately. "Fine."

Ben stalked out of the kitchen and she found herself wanting to forget about Buster and follow him, to apologize and beg his forgiveness, but Jake and Brandon were watching, waiting for her to go to Buster's cage. Emma sighed, letting Ben go.

It was for the best. She was bound to say and do the wrong thing at every turn. Her mother liked to remind her that she had quite the track record for being her own worst enemy. It was better for Ben to leave now, before she overcomplicated his life too. In truth, her career was too unpredictable for any sort of relationship. Her priority needed to be getting the sanctuary back on the right track, before she needed to worry about a relationship with anyone. She knew it but she'd allowed herself to get caught up in her lust last night. Besides, most men didn't want to date a woman who wrestled with tigers. While it might make intimacy interesting, having a girlfriend who could be mauled was definitely not high on the qualities men wanted in an ongoing, serious relationship.

Jake cleared his throat and rolled his eyes before shoving the back door open again. "How about if I just meet you at Buster's cage. That is, if any of this even matters to you anymore."

She met Brandon's gaze but he simply gave her a helpless shrug. "You know how Jake is."

Yeah, she knew. "Son of a bitch," she mumbled under her breath, dumping the coffee down the drain and heading out to Buster's cage in her pajamas.

If this was the start to her day, it could only go up from here. At least she prayed it would, because it couldn't exactly get much worse.

WHAT THE HELL was her problem?

He ran a frustrated hand over his head as he watched her inspect the mountain lion. This should prove to everyone how unfit she was to run the facility. Her father had even had his qualms. He knew because Conrad had told him and his brother that he was considering changing his will to name someone else co-director so that Emma didn't shoulder the entire burden, but then he'd gone and had a stroke before he'd had the opportunity. Now he was forced to take matters into their own hands.

How many animals did he have to plant, or let loose, before she realized that she wasn't prepared to handle this? Instead of concentrating on finding Buster, or even trying to figure out who was behind the graffiti, she was busy boning this fireman. It had taken her almost an entire day before she'd noticed he'd cut Wally's cage. And she'd barely even looked for Buster.

It was pissing him off.

She should have known she wasn't ready to take over when she'd first arrived. It should have been completely clear when he'd unlocked the aviary door and she hadn't spotted it until the next morning. He was starting to run out of ways to convince her to call it quits so someone else could take over. Unfortunately, it looked like he was going to have to take this to the next level, to up the stakes of the game. He liked Emma, and didn't want to hurt anyone, but he had to get rid of her.

Somehow.

BEN HAD KNOWN better.

He'd *known*.

He berated himself as he stuffed his clothing into the duffel bag. He'd fucking known better than to give in. Sex just for sex's sake was impossible for him. He was trying hard not to let her accusation wound him. She didn't know him, not really. Any more than he really knew her. He hadn't earned her trust.

However, that wasn't the way it felt when he was with her. He'd thought they had some sort of connection, a mutual understanding of one another, something that defied explanation. Obviously, it was one-sided. Staring at the mussed sheets, he couldn't stop the memories from last night that crashed over him, like waves of glory, as he relived each and every kiss.

Friends with benefits.

Friends didn't make unfounded accusations.

The back door slammed shut and Ben paused, waiting to see if it was Emma coming to apologize. The silence of the house spoke volumes.

Jerking his t-shirt down over his head, Ben grabbed his toothbrush from the bathroom sink where he'd left it and shoved it into his bag as well. He didn't deserve this crap. He'd gone out of his way to help her, not to mention the fact that he'd been willing to put himself between her and a cougar.

His cell phone vibrated on the nightstand, next to the box of condoms. His body jerked to attention at the mere reminder of their night together and, just as quickly, he forced the visions from his head. There was a reason he didn't do one-night stands, friends-with-benefits—whatever bullshit name she wanted to give it. Because he couldn't separate his emotions from the act.

Reaching for the phone, he saw his brother's face on the screen.

Shit.

Andrew was the last person he wanted to talk to right now. He must have seen this morning's paper. It didn't take a genius for Ben to know that this call wouldn't end well. It was better to get it over with now. Ignoring him would only make Andrew fume and build steam, like a volcano.

Ben swiped his finger over the screen to answer it. "Hey, I was just about to call you."

"Sure you were, you lying son of a bitch."

"You kiss your mother with—"

"You lied to me about the mountain lion when I talked to you yesterday. That's something the police should have been called in on, don't you think?"

"I didn't lie and no, it's something Animal Control would be called in for."

"Okay, smartass, they work with the police department. And you deliberately withheld the fact that there was a puma on the loose. What the fuck, Ben? That's something you should have told me about."

"I was helping Emma—"

"Emma? She's *Emma* now?" Ben could hear the disdain in his brother's voice. "Well, you be sure to tell *Emma* that I'm on my way out to investigate this matter."

"They've already caught him and put him back in his cage. He never even left the property." He might not have seen the animal yet but he didn't have any reason to doubt Jake, even if he was a jackass. "There's no need to forgo your morning ritual at the coffee shop. Just finish your doughnuts and relax."

"Ha ha, you're hilarious." Andrew didn't sound as if he saw any humor in the situation. "This isn't a laughing matter. That woman put a lot of people in danger by not calling us in, or Fish and Game, at the least. It's a fucking mountain lion, Ben."

"And it's caught."

"That's not the point." His brother took a deep breath. "Look, I'm on my way out there now. Warn her, don't warn her. I don't care. I'm getting some answers with or without your help."

Andrew disconnected the call, leaving Ben trying to figure out the best course of action. Andrew was a good guy but, like Ben, he tended to be a stickler for the rules, doing everything by the book, every time. Which was how he'd ended up the one arresting Laura. It was how they'd all been raised—to do the right thing, even when it was the hard thing to do. To be the good guy, the hero, to be honorable. But what was he supposed to do when what he and his brother thought was right put them on opposite sides?

Even though Emma's accusation had wounded him, he didn't want to see her subjected to Andrew's iron-handed sense of justice without some sort of an intermediary. Especially when Andrew was already this pissed off. Andrew wouldn't be interested in appearances, or the fact that someone *might* be setting Emma up. He wanted facts. And, right now, the facts were that the town needed protection, or thought it did, from Emma's incompetence.

Ben carried his bag out to the truck and slid it under the backseat before heading to the cages housing the big cats, arriving at the edge of the enclosure in time to hear Jake's outspoken criticism.

"They're going to shut you down, Emma. Maybe it's better if they do it now." The hair rose on the back of his neck and he forced himself not to clench his fists.

"I'll handle this."

"The way you have been so far? This place used to be a premiere facility. Your father had an impeccable reputation for rehabbing these animals, not *accidentally* letting them run out."

She glared at him over the sedated cat from inside the cage but, even from this distance, Ben could see the self-recriminations eating at her.

"I didn't do that."

"Then who did? You were the last one to work with the cats. Maybe you need to get your head back into the game and quit flirting with firemen."

This time, Ben couldn't help but clench his fists at his sides. It was the only thing keeping him from punching Jake in the mouth.

"Are you sure you're worried about the sanctuary or your own reputation, Jake?" She jerked her stethoscope from around her neck and placed one end on the cat's chest.

"Don't even," he warned. "You know this place means as much to me as it does to you, or your dad. Which is why we should have partnered up to run it, like your dad wanted."

Emma didn't even look up at him. "You convinced him to cancel all the educational and kids' programs, so what would we do together, Jake? I'm not about to let you bully me into doing things your way. I'm in charge now."

"Education wasn't your dad's vision for this place and you know it. It was always what *you* wanted. He wanted to rehab the animals for release. That was his dream."

So there was far more to the contention between Emma and Jake than just him being a jerk. At least, from his side of it.

"The government funding that comes from those programs helped keep the doors open. You know, as well as I do that we need—" She fell silent when her gaze touched on Ben.

He hadn't meant to eavesdrop but he wasn't exactly sorry he had. If nothing else, it gave him a better understanding of the added pressure Emma was under. She was facing it from within her staff as well.

"How's he doing?"

"Fine." She quickly inspected his massive paws for signs of trauma, plucking what looked like a pine needle from where it had lodged in the pad of one. "He should come to in about fifteen or twenty minutes and be no worse for his little adventure last night. I'll just have to keep an eye on him."

She exited the cage, locking the gate and then jerking on the door, testing the lock again.

"My brother's on his way over."

She paused with her fingers in the chain link and he waited for her response, hating that he was the one adding even more trouble on her already full plate. She took a deep breath but he didn't miss the way her shoulders slumped in defeat.

"Okay. I should probably go open the gate for him." She glanced over her shoulder at Jake. "Can you feed the cats? Don't forget Kit too, okay?" She brushed past

Ben, careful to avoid touching him as she headed back toward the main gate.

Ben reached for her hand. "I thought I'd hang out here until Andrew arrives."

Emma slid her hand away from his and squared her shoulders, standing erect and proud. She didn't even bother to look back at him as she steeled herself for what was likely to come. "Thanks, but I can handle this."

Her tone was frigid as she spoke the same words he'd just heard her say to Jake. Regardless of what Ben thought they might have shared last night, this was no longer the woman who'd set his passions on fire. She'd been replaced by a woman on a mission, one who no longer trusted him.

Chapter Twelve

EMMA STEPPED OUT of the shower and wrapped a towel around herself, using another to wring the water from her hair, wishing she could stall another few hours. She had no idea what she was going to say when Ben's brother arrived. What *could* she say?

Somehow Buster had gotten out. Whether it was due to someone tampering with the cage or her own forgetfulness, ultimately she was responsible for everything that happened at this sanctuary. Unfortunately, since she'd taken over for her father, there had been far more failures than successes and now it looked like it would be culminating with a cop coming to shut her down. Especially since she had no proof that anyone else had been involved.

Emma dragged a comb through her long tresses and flipped on the blow dryer, wishing she could just hide out for the rest of the morning.

"Hey?"

She jumped at Ben's voice and his sudden appearance in the doorway, yelping as she dropped the blow dryer into the sink.

"Shit!" She fumbled to turn it off which managed to loosen the towel knotted at her breasts, causing it to slip and pool at her feet, leaving her completely naked. "Get out!"

Ben arched a brow, a hungry smile spreading over his face as his dark gaze slid down her body, warming her from her head to her toes. Or maybe it was the blush covering her that warmed her skin. She quickly turned her back on him and bent to retrieve her towel.

"Nice view in either direction."

Wrapping herself in the terrycloth and tucking the end between her breasts, she scowled at him over her shoulder. "What happened to the gentleman from last night?"

The grin fell from his lips as Ben leaned against the doorframe. "He bailed after getting falsely accused of calling a reporter."

Emma had already planned to apologize for blaming him. While it was possible he'd made the call, it was just as likely that Ben had simply mentioned it to his brother and the police called the paper. For all she knew, it could have been anyone at the sanctuary last night. Just because Jake, Brandon and the girls were together all night in the barn didn't mean someone hadn't snuck off to make a phone call. She couldn't rule it out. Honestly, she couldn't even really blame them. All of their lives had been in jeopardy. If she was in their shoes, she might have called for backup too.

Either way, she'd had no proof it was Ben and he'd been nothing but helpful, even at the risk of his own skin. She wasn't normally one to jump to conclusions, but Ben had her doing a lot of things she didn't normally do. Even so, accusing him had crossed a line.

"About that . . . I'm sorry. It wasn't right and it certainly wasn't warranted." Ben's brows lifted high on his forehead as she stated the obvious. She waved a hand toward her bedroom before trying to close the door on him. "Um, you think you could wait out there until I get some clothes on?"

His cocky, lopsided grin returned and his dark eyes glittered devilishly, making her heart skip irritatingly. She needed to figure out a way to get her body to stop reacting like he was the first boy to kiss her, even if he was the first one in a long time that made her want something more. Just how much more, she wasn't sure.

Emma reached for the blow dryer in the sink, flipping it back on and leaning to one side, pretending not to care that he stood in the doorway watching her, but holding her towel in place with one hand all the same.

"Nothing I haven't already seen in glorious detail."

Her eyes widened at his blatant comment, her cheeks warming as she stared at his reflection in her mirror. She'd blushed more around this man than anyone in her entire life.

"Get out." She flipped her wrist, aiming the blow dryer at his face as she let go of the towel long enough to shove her other hand against his chest. She jerked at it when the top of the towel loosened and nearly fell again. "This is still *my* house."

Ben took a step back and she took the opportunity to slam the door shut, twisting the lock. Emma heard his deep laughter just as she realized she'd left her jeans and t-shirt lying on the foot of her bed.

Son of a bitch.

He rapped lightly on the door. "You're probably going to need these."

Mentally counting to ten, trying unsuccessfully to contain her frustration, she opened the door, quickly yanking the clothes from his hands before slamming it shut again.

"You sure you don't need some help? I'm not as good at getting them on as I am off, but I could try," he teased.

Oh God, please let him be teasing.

Recalling the heat she'd felt as his gaze slid over her a moment ago, she wasn't so sure. Nor was she sure she really *wanted* him to be joking. Working her jeans over her still wet legs, Emma danced around the bathroom, slipping on the tile floor and catching herself against the door with a loud *thud*.

"Are you okay?" She heard him test the knob, prepared to enter, and was grateful she locked it.

"I'm fine."

She hooked the clasp of her bra and tugged the shirt down over her head. Forgoing any makeup, she tugged her still-damp hair back into a ponytail and opened the door, walking past him into the bedroom. Dragging her hands through the drawer, she found a pair of matching socks and sat on the bed, glancing up at him.

"Look, maybe we should get a few things cleared up."

He snorted slightly. "You think? We have so much to choose from, Emma. The news article, the situation you've got going on here . . ." His eyes smoldered as he met her gaze. "Or do you mean about us and last night?"

She looked away, avoiding his penetrating gaze by focusing far more on tying her sneaker than was necessary. Why was she finding it so hard to distance herself from him emotionally?

She'd known from the start Ben was most definitely a different sort of guy than she usually hooked up with. Most men would be thrilled at the prospect of sex with no strings. It made life easy, without complications. But he made her feel like she was missing out on so much more. He made her question whether she could really be happy with something noncommittal from him.

After the way he'd made her feel last night, she wasn't sure she could go back. He'd branded her, taken her to a different realm, and she didn't want to give it up. That alone made her wonder if last night wasn't a mistake they shouldn't repeat. But the mere idea of not touching him again, of not *being* touched by him, made her chest ache. She looked up at him as he stared down at her, waiting for her response. But she could see the disappointment in his eyes, as if he already knew what she would say. It was just one more regret heaped on the pile of disappointments she was already dealing with.

"I'm not sure that subject really needs discussion.

We should probably just chalk that up as a one-time deal." She finished tying her shoes and stood up. "I was talking about my dealing with your brother—alone. You need to let me handle this. I don't need help."

His expression remained stoic.

"I mean it. This is my sanctuary. You said so yourself." She rose from the edge of the bed, pacing the room slightly. "And, while I appreciate your help yesterday—I really do—I'm not some damsel in distress or some kitten in a tree for you to rescue, okay?"

"Okay." He took a step back, giving her some space to make her way through the door but she couldn't help feeling like a chasm had been carved between them. All she really wanted was to cross it, to curl against his chest and let him fight with her, to let him rescue her from the trouble she was facing. She wanted to let him be her hero, her savior.

Emma mentally shook herself. She was a grown-ass woman. She didn't need anyone else to fight her battles, even if it meant losing the war. Her pride wouldn't allow it. She'd worked too hard to fall into some simpering female stereotype just because it was easy.

Easy had never been a part of her vocabulary and she didn't see the point in adding it now.

IN SPITE OF her adamant insistence, Ben wasn't about to let Emma deal with Andrew alone. She might think that because she could handle a bear, she could handle Andrew, but Emma had no idea what sort of temperamental beast he could be when riled. And he was riled thanks to Ben's omission about Buster last night.

Ben couldn't really fault Andrew. The cops had probably already received hundreds of complaints coming in from "concerned" townspeople about the most recent article. However intense he might be, Andrew was also fair. Once he realized that there was a good chance Emma was, in fact, the victim in this situation, he'd settle down and get to the truth.

Ben watched as his brother slid the patrol car to a stop, parking it in front of Emma's house. It was going to be hard for Ben to keep his distance, yet remain close enough that, should Emma change her mind, he could jump in. Not that she'd ever cave and ask for help.

As if reading his thoughts, Emma glanced at him over her shoulder. She started down the porch steps to greet Andrew and mouthed a quick "stay here" to him.

He followed her, ignoring her frown of disapproval. "I'm not one of your animals to give commands to."

"Then that means I should be able to get rid of you, right?" she grumbled as he moved to flank her. "I told you I don't need help."

"I heard you," he replied from the side of his mouth. "I'm only here to say hello to my brother."

In spite of her protests about his presence, Ben reached for her hand, twining his fingers between hers, giving her hand a supportive squeeze as they made their way to where his brother waited.

"It's going to be fine, Emma," he whispered.

It was a testament to how nervous she really was

about this meeting when she didn't pull her hand from his. As they reached the patrol car, Andrew slid his sunglasses from his face slowly, his gaze falling on their hands for a moment before a shit-eating grin spread over his face. Ben inwardly cringed at what that could mean.

"Emma, I think you've met my brother Andrew right?"

"Officer McQuaid," Andrew corrected, shooting him a warning look. "And, yes, we've met." He looked at Emma, apologetically. "I hate for us to meet this way but I'm here on official business again, investigating the complaint in this morning's paper. Have you seen it?"

At Andrew's businesslike manner Emma slid her hand from Ben's and nodded. "I assure you that it was a one-time circumstance that has never happened before, nor will it happen again. I am thoroughly investigating how it happened myself."

"I'd like to have a look around the premises?"

Emma paused, as if uncertain which option would be in her best interest. She could refuse; however, it would only bring more suspicion on her and the sanctuary, as if she were deliberately hiding something. Although Ben knew Andrew was fair-minded, he didn't want him making up his mind before he knew all of the circumstances. Then again, saying yes would open her up to anything Andrew chose to investigate.

Ben didn't wait for Emma to decide, answering for her. "Did you bring a warrant?"

Emma shot daggers his way, making it clear he should keep his mouth shut and let her handle this.

Andrew turned toward him, obviously annoyed. "I didn't realize we were at that point. I'm only here to gather some information from Miss Jordan. I didn't realize she'd hired you as her representative."

Emma stepped between them and Ben didn't miss the glance they exchanged.

Don't worry about him. This is between us.

My brother is a pain in my ass.

"Why don't we head over to the main office where I keep all of my paperwork. We can gather anything you might need from there, then I'd be happy to take you around the facility again, Officer McQuaid, starting with Buster's cage."

"Excellent."

Emma motioned for Andrew to follow her across the driveway toward the barn. Ben immediately fell into line behind them. They might not want him around but he could be just as stubborn as Emma.

Andrew glanced back at him. "I don't think we really need the escort, Ben. Don't they need you at the station, to clean equipment, or hold down a couch or something?"

"Nope, but you might want to hurry up so you aren't late for one of those full cavity searches you enjoy so much."

"Nozzle jockey," Andrew muttered.

"It smells like bacon. Emma, did you make bacon?"

Emma held open the door for them both, rolling her eyes at the pair and giving Ben a look that begged him to stop. He was also well aware that his jibes were only serving to ratchet up his brother's ire but this way it would be directed at him, making Andrew less likely to press Emma for information or blame her for what might be nothing more than an unfortunate accident, one that had already been safely resolved and didn't need his interference after the fact.

The smell of antiseptic hung heavy in the air as Emma escorted them past a veterinary exam room and through a pair of double doors.

"Why don't you two have a seat?"

She motioned toward a pair of chairs across from a cheap office desk, covered by open files, a basket overflowing with bills and a closed laptop. Ben dropped into the chair near the window, not surprised when his brother refused, pulling a notepad from his shirt pocket.

"What I really need are some answers from you, Miss Jordan, starting with whether you're registered with Fish and Game as a rescue facility."

"My father has had this facility set up with them for years."

"Yes, but were *you* approved. Once your father died, that licensure goes into a pending state until you, personally, have been approved to take over. I probably should have made sure the last time I was here."

"The paperwork has already been submitted through proper channels and we are waiting for the documentation, but yes, I am an approved wildlife rehabilitation expert. Would you like to see my veterinary credentials as well?" Emma moved to a safe at the back wall.

"I can get copies if it's deemed necessary."

Ben shot his brother a curious glance. That was information he would need for his report. Why was Mr. By-the-Books letting her off that easily?

"Tell me about this mountain lion. How long has he been at your facility?"

"My father rescued Buster from an illegal pet situation five years ago. They'd had him declawed but, as you can imagine, there are other ways he can cause damage. The story we were told was that the owner was showing him off at a party and Buster was playing a little too rough. He gnawed on someone's arm a little too hard and Animal Control was called in. They were going to euthanize him, but Dad stepped in and brought him here."

"A cougar as a pet?" Andrew sounded as appalled as the thought had originally made Ben. "A cat is bad enough."

She shrugged. "What can I say? There are a lot of people who think exotic animals make good cool pets only to find out the hard way how wrong they are. It's not the animal's fault."

"So, he's dangerous?"

Emma cocked her head to one side. "If you're asking if he's ever hurt someone, the answer is no. Even that one time, he didn't break the skin. But he *is* a mountain lion, so I can't say I'd ever trust him *not* to hurt someone given the chance." She cast Ben a wary glance before turning back to Andrew. She obviously wasn't going to mention how he'd gone after her yesterday. "He doesn't seem to like your brother much."

"So, a cougar with good taste." He pretended to jot the information down on his pad, giving Emma a conspiratorial grin. "Has he ever gotten out before?"

"Not that I'm aware of and I believe my father would have mentioned it to me if he had."

"And what are your procedures for making sure it doesn't happen?"

"You've seen our cages before, but each one has a heavy latch and a padlock. The only time it's opened is when Buster is taken out for exercise or when someone cleans up after him. He hadn't been taken out on the day he got loose. I had to run to town unexpectedly for some supplies and we'd rearranged the cats' exercise schedule. After I returned, I was cleaning graffiti from the front gate when Jake came to tell me he'd escaped."

"I saw that when I came in." He turned to look at Ben. "That's what you originally texted me about, right?"

Ben nodded. "Apparently, this isn't the first time and there was only one set of fresh tire tracks other than hers leading to the gate."

"Hmm." Andrew rubbed at his chin with a thumb, thoughtfully. "Does anyone else have keys to the cages?"

"Everyone. And a spare set over there." Emma pointed at a set of keys hanging just inside the doorway.

"So, anyone could have had access to the cages while you were gone?" Andrew sounded surprised.

Flashing a glance at Ben, she narrowed her eyes at Andrew. "I have four people working here, helping me to maintain more than is humanly possible so for one person, in answer to your question, yes, anyone who works here could have access to a set of keys. But they rarely use them unless I've asked them to."

Andrew nodded. "I'm going to need to talk to all of your staff. Volunteers as well."

"Then there's your first one." She jerked her chin toward Ben. "Although, he doesn't have keys and only managed to last a day."

Andrew spun on him, a smug grin on his face. "You? Volunteered here?"

"Yeah, so?"

Andrew snorted. "That's right, I forgot how much you Dalmatian molesters love animals."

"Like I haven't seen you blue canaries eyeing your K-9 units."

"Children, please," Emma interrupted. "If you two are through bickering like four-year-olds, I have a sanctuary to run, cages to clean and animals to take care of. Not to mention, that I still need to finish cleaning the graffiti off the front gate. Officer McQuaid, do you have any more questions for me, or should I start sending my staff in? Unless you'd rather start with that tour."

Ben almost laughed out loud at the shocked tilt of Andrew's chin. He'd rarely seen his brother speechless and never while on duty. It was definitely a welcome sight, especially when it was a pip-squeak redhead with a feisty attitude who finally managed to do it.

Damn, she was hot. Too bad they'd already decided last night was a one-time thing.

Chapter Thirteen

"I DON'T KNOW, Officer." He played innocent, pretending that he didn't know anyone who wanted to see the sanctuary closed down. Of course, that was almost too predictable an answer, so he decided to elaborate a bit. "I mean, there are always people who don't understand what we're doing, or maybe don't agree. But I don't know of anyone that would go so far as to turn Buster loose."

"What about the graffiti on the gate?"

He frowned. "What about it?"

"What do you know about it? Is this the first time?"

In truth this was the fourth time but he wasn't sure what, if anything, Emma had already told this cop. *Damn it!* His story had to match up or, at the very least, seem plausible.

"No, but I haven't kept count and Emma doesn't like to talk about it so I really couldn't give you a specific number."

The cop narrowed his eyes, his gaze as penetrating as any television detective. The only thing missing was the interrogation room and crappy lighting. "Between you and me, what do you really think of Emma?"

"What do you mean?" He was careful to keep his expression blank, passive, maintaining a poker face that could break the house.

"I mean, you have to know what people are saying, thanks in part to these articles. But, unlike most people, you're around her all day. You know her and you've worked with her father for years. What do you think? Are the articles right?"

He leaned forward, clasping his hands between his knees. "Well, officer, here's the thing. I'm not stupid and I like my job. I'd like to keep it as long as possible."

The cop shrugged and waved one hand his way. "I'm not here to tattle on you, or turn your boss against you. I'm just trying to protect this town and get to the bottom of whether Emma Jordan is detrimental to it. Whether it's due to negligence or . . ."

This was his shot, a clean kill. Just tell this cop she was dangerous, that she didn't take care of the animals, that she was completely incompetent and he could watch Sierra Track close its doors. Except he didn't want to see Sierra Tracks closed. He simply wanted it under new management—with him and his brother in charge. The only way to do that was to run Emma out while not letting anyone know who was responsible. He needed the town to turn on her personally, not the facility. To do that, he had to walk a thin line of loyalty.

"Emma's not perfect and she's trying. Sometimes she succeeds and sometimes she doesn't. You want to know what's going on here, do your job and investigate. I *do* know Emma, but I don't know or trust you."

"I could arrest you for obstruction."

"But you won't, because you need my help. You need someone to give you the behind the scenes info. So, what's in this for me?"

EMMA FINISHED CUTTING up the rats she needed to feed their newest addition in the aviary, a great horned owlet that came in a couple weeks ago. Dropping the pieces into a Baggie, she soaked it in a bowl of hot water to warm it for mealtime. After washing and drying her hands, she tossed the towel aside and leaned back against the counter, rubbing at the ache forming behind her temples.

Ben's brother had already talked with everyone else and was finishing up with Monica, but she had no idea what to expect from him afterward. She prayed he wouldn't really make her take him on a tour of the facility just to turn around and close her down. Or maybe he'd just call the state immediately to come take possession of her animals? She wondered if she could convince him to give her a few days to find rescues to take them in.

"Miss Jordan?" She heard Office McQuaid's voice just before he knocked lightly at the door, as if uncertain whether she was inside.

"Come in," she called, standing up again as he came inside. She watched the doorway, expecting Ben to follow him, and not wanting to acknowledge the disappointment when she saw he wasn't there. It looked like he'd finally listened to her and left.

There was a hint of humor in the cop's eyes as he glanced behind him. "Expecting someone else?"

Smart ass. She wasn't about to give him the satisfaction of admitting she was. "Are you ready for that inspection?"

"I wanted to talk to you first. After talking to your staff, I think we have a bit of a problem." He slid the door shut with a quiet snick.

Here we go. Emma squared her shoulders, taking a deep breath, trying to prepare herself for the bad news that was coming. Somehow she'd managed to single-handedly destroy her father's legacy, and in record time.

"I think it's pretty fair to assume someone is targeting your facility."

Emma's heart plummeted hearing her worst fears confirmed. She'd seen more than her share of animal rights' activists while working at the animal park but never here, not when Sierra Tracks simply cared for animals who couldn't do it for themselves. Most of her animals were eventually released back into the wild. Why would someone mark her facility when there were so many other, more questionable, facilities nearby?

"I can't prove that cougar was released on purpose but after hearing your staff confirm your procedures and meeting you, not to mention seeing that front gate,

I'm pretty certain this wasn't an accident. I'd suggest you reserve keys to the cages for only those who absolutely need them."

"I already do." If she took the keys to the cages back, she'd spend her entire day running around just locking and unlocking doors.

He shrugged. "Of course, it's up to you. But, as an added precaution, if I were you, I'd also change the locks and the code on the gate."

"Do you realize what sort of expense you're talking about?" She mentally calculated how many locks she had on the cages and other facility gates as well as what it would cost to replace them. It was going to cut deeply into her already dwindling budget.

"Whatever it is, it's going to be cheaper than if that lion escapes again," he pointed out. "I can explain it escaping once, especially in light of the vandalism you've experienced, but if it happens again, the people of Hidden Falls are going to demand answers." He shot her a careful look. "Not to mention, your resignation."

He was giving her another chance. He wasn't going to shut her down.

"Which brings me to my next issue. I think whoever let that cougar out is also tipping off the newspaper. You haven't seen any suspicious cars at the gates, or parked off the road outside your fences? Anyone lurking around who has no reason to be here?"

She cocked her head to one side. "You mean, other than your brother?"

Office McQuaid laughed and, in spite of the serious

cop persona, it sounded natural coming from him. "Yeah, what's that all about?"

She crossed her arms. She still held her suspicions that he'd sent Ben to spy on her the morning after dropping off the kitten. She wasn't about to discuss her relationship with Ben, even if it was nothing more than a lapse in her better judgment and unlikely to be repeated.

"Okay," he acquiesced with a grin. "I guess I should apologize since I'm the one who sent him here in the first place. I had no idea he'd turn into your guard dog when I sent him out to pick up that kitten."

"It was a bobcat," she corrected. "And are you really going to stand there and pretend that's the only time? That you didn't send him over here yesterday too."

"Actually, that wasn't my suggestion."

She tipped her head to one side and rolled her eyes.

"Nope, can't pin that on me. He took that all upon himself," he assured her.

If he didn't send Ben, then why had he really come over?

He twisted his lips to one side, not about to be deterred from his own questions. "I have to admit, I'm surprised, because you're not really his type."

"No?"

"It's funny," he continued. "I've never known my brother to have such a compassionate heart for animals. Now that I think about it, I don't think I've *ever* seen him interested in their welfare at all before."

Her heart skipped for a moment, allowing her to

believe she might actually mean something to Ben. She squashed the feeling just as quickly, reminding herself that she couldn't let emotions become involved. For the first time, Emma regretted the solitary, lonely path she'd chosen.

Growing impatient with the roundabout questions, she decided to put an end to this discussion about her relationship, or lack of, with Ben. He might think he was being clever, but she could see right through Ben's brother. "You're right, that is odd. Perhaps you should address your questions with Ben. I hope you'll excuse me but I have an owlet whose lunch is late."

She reached for the bag of meat and a package of sterile forceps from the drawer.

"You know, I find it strange that my big brother would jump to your defense so quickly."

She was tired of this man beating around the bush. If he wanted to ask her a question, then he better get to the point. She spun on him with a loud sigh of exasperation. "And what is that supposed to mean, Officer McQuaid?"

"Andrew," he corrected, "and it doesn't mean anything." He gave her a smug grin. "Just do me a favor. Don't make me arrest you too. I don't want to have to be the one to put his girlfriend in handcuffs."

"This is a professional call, remember Officer McQuaid?" Emma frowned. "I'm not his girlfriend."

"Hmm." Andrew bobbed his head, changing the subject before she could say more. "I left my card in your office with my cell number on the back. Call me if anything else happens, and that includes any more vandalism or escaped animals. If you see anything out of the ordinary, don't hesitate to call me. Otherwise I'll check in with you in a few days."

Turning on his heel, he headed for the door. "I'm not his girlfriend," she repeated, more confidently this time.

"Not yet." Andrew laughed as he raised a hand, letting the door close behind him.

"You SAID WHAT?" Ben clenched his fists at his sides. He couldn't believe his brother would hang him out to dry this way with a woman. "You had no right mentioning what happened with Laura."

Andrew leaned against the side of his patrol car, looking far too sanctimonious, making Ben want to wipe the smirk from his face.

"What are you getting so worked up for? It's not like everyone doesn't already know about Laura." Andrew rolled his eyes and pushed himself off the car. "And she missed the reference anyway. She was too preoccupied with me calling her your girlfriend." Andrew let out a sigh. "You want to know what I think?"

"Not really."

His brother went on, ignoring him. "I think you really did want to put the moves on the *hot* vet last night."

"In case you're forgetting, there was a mountain lion on the loose and four people in the barn watching the other animals. I wasn't about to leave her alone to watch the house and the trap. Besides, you've met her.

She would have headed out here alone to catch that damn cat."

"Oh, I see," Andrew began with a laugh. "So, this was about you being a hero?"

"No. This was about me protecting your ass so you didn't drive up and get ambushed."

"Ah. So, you were being *my* hero?"

Ben tried to still the irritation welling up, threatening to be unleashed. It was better to save it for the football game coming up. Chances are, that was why his brother was trying to get in his head anyway. The cops had lost the last three years running and it wasn't sitting well that they'd been bested by firemen in the last four competitions: the Thanksgiving food drive and Christmas toy drive last year, and the baseball and basketball tournaments earlier this year.

"Look, I don't care what you think," Ben interrupted. "Emma needs our help. Somebody let that cougar out and people could have been hurt. This isn't just about vandalism anymore."

Andrew grew serious, a frown creasing his brow. When it came to discussing their actual duties to Hidden Falls, he was all business.

"I know. I don't like the fact that the news of this cougar has gone public because of that article. Our phone at the station has been ringing off the hook all morning. People are upset, and rightly so but, although I don't think Emma is to blame, I'm worried the town'll be out for blood. I think I'll head over to the paper and see if I can find out who wrote the article. It's pretty unlikely they're going to give up their anonymous source but I have to try. You heading to the fire station or are you *volunteering* here today?" He made air quotes with his fingers.

Ben looked toward the barn, ignoring his brother's insinuations. "I'm heading home to shower first."

"Sure you are. And she's not in there, she's in with the birds. Said something about an owl." Andrew chuckled as he rolled his eyes and pushed himself off the side of the car, pointing at his brother. "You need to be careful, Ben. You don't need to be everyone's hero, you know."

"I'm not trying to be a hero."

"I call bullshit. It's what you do. You find a woman who needs help and you try to rescue her. You did it with Angie after she broke up with her boyfriend and had no place to stay. That ended up with her cheating on you. Then you did it with Laura and she emptied your apartment. You would have done it with Bethany, but she was too smart to fall for a water fairy."

"Don't even go there." Ben was grateful he'd never dated the woman who was now very happily engaged to their older brother, Grant.

Andrew laughed as he slid into the patrol car. "I'm just telling you to watch yourself." He jerked a thumb at the barns. "This one doesn't seem to want or need your help. Know when to walk away, bro."

"Thanks for the advice, Dr. Phil. Don't you have some evidence to tamper with?"

Andrew glared at him. "Yeah, that's not funny. Especially after we just suspended one of the guys for stealing marijuana from a crime scene."

"Only cops."

"What the hell are you talking about? You guys just let it burn and inhale the smoke. I saw that fireman on television. Don't act all high and mighty with me."

Ben shook his head, waving as his brother made his way down the driveway and back toward the highway. He wandered back into the center of the facility, hoping to find Emma in the aviary. They needed to talk—about last night, about her accusations, and the truth about the trouble the sanctuary was facing.

"You know, it's all well and good that you want to help her." Ben turned and saw Jake leaning outside one of the cages with a clipboard. "But Emma's bent on doing things her own way, even if it takes all of us down."

"Excuse me?"

"Don't get involved, man. Conrad was a stand-up guy, ran this place like a well-oiled machine. He knew exactly what to do to make it work and where to prune so it got better. He made sure we all shared his vision. But since Emma's taken over . . ." He shook his head sadly. "Let's just say, I'm keeping my options open and my ear to the ground for another position. I'm not sure how long this place will last with her in charge."

Ben was struck again with how much he didn't like this guy. Or trust him. There was such an open animosity in the way he looked at Emma. The way he talked about her that made Ben wonder what had happened between them. However, it wasn't his place to ask and neither of them seemed inclined to offer up a reason for what he believed was a mutual hostility.

"Emma seems to know what she's doing."

Jake scoffed as he jotted down a few notes. "Yeah, if this place was a zoo or one of those animal experience joints like Sea World. This is a rehab facility—but I haven't seen one animal leave this place in the last month since she's arrived. She's not rehabilitating animals, she's hoarding them."

"If it were me," Jake continued, not even bothering to look up from the cage of raccoons cleaning themselves, tucked into a shaded log in the corner of the cage, "I'd watch my back. Just because she's beautiful, doesn't mean she's not dangerous. Like these guys, she's just doing what comes naturally. But Emma is trouble, plain and simple. She doesn't have to go looking for it. It just seems to find her. Her dad knew it too, which is why he didn't want her running the place alone. Maybe that brother of yours should ask her about that."

EMMA HELD THE meat out to the baby owl until he snapped it from the forceps. He was getting stronger in the short time she'd had him and was ready to be released into the pen with Mama Hoot, the female her father had rescued after being hit by a car and left to die on the side of the road. The accident had caused her to lose an eye, but she'd made a fantastic surrogate for owlets and, because of her, her father had released four young owls back into the wild just last year. Soon, this one would be able to begin hunting for live prey.

"What's wrong with him?"

Emma jumped at the sound of Ben's voice. A lot of things were making her jumpy lately and she hated feeling that way. She was usually alert to her surroundings, aware of everything around her and constantly assessing various scenarios. It came from working with unpredictable wildlife. But lately, she was getting so lost in thought, or her stupid fantasies about a certain fireman, that she was forgetting to pay attention, and it was proving to be a hazard.

She looked at him through the netting surrounding her face. It kept the owl from recognizing her as a human but, for now, she was grateful that Ben couldn't really see her face through it either. It hid her conflicting thoughts about him. She was drawn to him, wanting to lose herself in him, something she'd never felt with anyone else. Her body practically hummed with anticipation when he was near. She wanted to ask him to stay again and knew if she didn't, she wouldn't be able to stop thinking about last night, or the way his hands had moved over her body. It was easy for her to let the physical attraction take over, to enjoy the pleasure of his touch, his kiss, and let him carry her away with it.

But it wasn't right to put him into the middle of her turmoil. She was on the cusp of being ruined professionally and she couldn't let him follow her over that cliff, especially when he felt a so much responsibility toward the town. It would destroy his credibility and, honestly, she liked him too much to be the one to cause that. He was a nice guy who didn't deserve the judgment siding with her would bring him.

"Emma?" His brows furrowed in concern and she realized she'd been staring at him.

"He was abandoned by his parents. At least, that's what we were told by the lady who found him. Unfortunately, there's a good chance he's already bonded to humans and can't be released. He should be trying to fly by now."

"How old is he?"

"About seven weeks." She glanced back at him, standing outside the room, and saw his frown. "I'm introducing him to his surrogate mother after he eats. Hopefully, she'll teach him how to be an owl."

"And if she doesn't?"

"Then I'll finish taming him down and add him to an educational program once I start it up again." She held another piece of meat up to him between the forceps and the bird took it gently this time, a sign he wasn't as interested in the food as she'd hoped he'd be.

"A pet."

Emma felt the muscles in her shoulders bunch with tension. She didn't turn toward him, regardless of how much she wanted to challenge the accusation she heard in his tone.

"No." She kept her voice level but inside, disappointment gnawed at her. She needed to cut him some slack. He didn't know anything about these animals, maybe he wasn't judging her. But she couldn't quite convince herself. "An unreleasable bird that can't survive in the wild because someone has imprinted with it before I could keep that from happening."

"Have you thought of getting another opinion?"

She clenched her jaw. He was questioning her judgment and her ability. She had enough people criticizing the way she was running the facility, but until now, she hadn't lumped Ben in with them. She'd thought he was different. He'd said all the things she'd wanted— *needed*—to hear, until now. Now he sounded like Jake, and whoever was writing those articles.

Ben didn't say anything else as she placed another piece of meat in the forceps. This time the owl turned his head away, refusing to eat more. Rather than causing any unnecessary stress on the animal before turning it in with the surrogate, Emma exited the space serving as a nursery, stripping off the protective gear, to prepare for his move.

"I am more than capable of making this decision."

"I know that." His voice was contemplative, thoughtful, but she also heard the doubt.

"Do you?" She spun on him, trying to control her temper. "Because it sounds like you don't. It sounds like you think setting this owl in a tree and letting nature roll the dice for his survival might be a better option. It sounds like you might agree with everyone else that I'm not qualified to run this place, regardless of my experience, training and degrees."

She brushed past him, shoving open the door, the sun blinding her as she stepped outside. Ben reached for her arm, turning her to face him.

She squinted up at him, trying to ignore the burning in her eyes, unwilling to entertain the thought that it might be from anything other than the sunlight. She certainly wasn't going to admit that it might be tears. There was no way she would cry over some guy she barely knew, even if she'd ignored her better judgment and trusted him. And she had.

After the way he'd stayed to help her with the graffiti, or to try to help her get Buster back. He'd soothed her worries last night, offering her support. Hell, he'd even stood up for her to his brother. But like everyone else, he'd turned on her.

"You're putting words in my mouth, Emma. I didn't say that. I simply asked a question."

"No, you didn't." She jerked her arm from him, jabbing her finger into his chest. "You were doing the same thing everyone else around this damn town has and making assumptions about how I run this place. You talked to Jake, didn't you?"

Emma could see the guilt in the way he shifted his gaze to the horizon, as if searching for answers there. She didn't need any other confirmation.

"Calling him a *pet* was a dead giveaway." She shook her head. "You should go. I've got enough people judging me. What I needed was a friend, not another critic."

Emma turned her back on him. She didn't care what he thought. She *couldn't*. Because if she did, she'd have to admit that his lack of confidence stung far more than any one-night fling should.

Chapter Fourteen

BEN PULLED INTO the driveway of his parents' ranch just as the twins, Jefferson and Jackson, rode up to the fence line. He slowed as they waved him over and rolled down the passenger window. "Dad has you two running fences again, huh?"

"Well, we can't all spend the night with pretty red-heads," Jackson teased.

Damn.

The fact that they knew he'd been at Emma's instead of the station meant Andrew had already been shooting off his mouth. Ben didn't even want to know how that conversation started. He rolled his eyes at the pair and turned back to the windshield.

"Are you two finished for the day? I was going to head to the station but I could saddle up and meet you somewhere if you need me."

"Don't worry about it." Jefferson looped one leg

around the saddle horn. "We're just about finished. But Dad's got plans for all of us this weekend, unless you're working. He's got some burr up his ass about another family work day."

"Gotta *love* 'family work days,'" Jackson complained. "The last one had me up on the barn roof patching shingles in hundred-degree weather."

"Would you rather do it in snow? Either way," Ben said with a shrug, "I'm on shift, so you guys are on your own."

"Of course you are. Would that be a shift at the station or at the animal sanctuary?" Jefferson exchanged a dubious look with Jackson. "You barely know what to do with cattle and horses. What do you even do there?"

"Oh, I'm pretty sure I can guess who—I mean *what*—he's doing." Jackson laughed at his own joke.

"Watch yourself, Jackson," Ben warned, his jaw clenching.

"Maybe she's taming his wild beast."

Jefferson snorted but Ben wasn't amused by his younger brothers. "Are you two through?"

"Maybe he's just watching her like a *hawk*," Jefferson supplied.

Jackson's laughter died. "That's wasn't even funny."

Jefferson glared at his twin and sat up straighter in the saddle. "Shut up."

"Why don't you both shut up?" Ben wasn't in the mood for their jokes, especially since he wasn't sure where he stood with Emma now. He'd managed to piss her off with his questions and, when she'd walked away, he left without saying goodbye. As much as he'd wanted to clear the air about what had happened last night between them, he had enough brains to know this wasn't a good time. However, he also knew that waiting wasn't going to earn him any brownie points either. He was basically stuck between a rock and hard place with nowhere to turn.

Dropping the truck into gear, he left his brothers at the fence and headed for the house, feeling only slightly guilty as dust from his tires encircled the pair on horseback.

What he needed was to talk to someone without a penis. There were two women in the house but only one he would consider taking dating advice from. He could only pray that luck was on his side and his sister, Maddie, was home from work.

"MADDIE!"

Ben knocked on his sister's bedroom door. He recognized the ridiculousness of the fact that most of them still lived with their parents. They all had lives and jobs outside of the ranch, with the exception of the twins, but they had all chosen to remain on the property—Maddie in the house and all six brothers in the bunkhouse across the driveway. Only Grant and Linc had moved away but even Grant had returned after his recent retirement from professional football. He and his fiancée, Bethany, along with her son James were already building a house near the east pasture. As unnatural as it seemed at times, Ben wasn't sure what he'd do without his close-knit family. Especially when he really needed his baby sister's advice.

"Come on, Maddie. Mom said you were in here."

She yanked open the door with a sigh. "What?"

The sight that greeted Ben made him feel like he'd been transported back in time at least ten years, when she was still in high school, preparing for a date. Maddie stood in the doorway, holding a handful of her light brown hair to one side, wearing nothing but a pair of jeans and a thin camisole top.

"Christ, Maddie! Put clothes on before you answer your door."

"What the hell do these look like to you?" she countered, swiping a free hand over the front of her shirt. "I *am* wearing clothes. Maybe if some idiot wasn't banging on my door, I could finish getting ready for my date so that I'm not late to dinner." She turned her back on him, leaving the door open for him to follow her inside.

Ben held a hand up to shield his eyes and entered. She waved a hand at the end of her unmade bed and headed into her small adjoined bathroom, laughing at him. "For crying out loud, Ben. It's not like I'm in my underwear. Now you know how I feel when you guys strip down to jump in the creek when we drive the cattle."

His sister had a point. They outnumbered her six to one, but their boxers weren't practically see-through the way the lace along the top of her camisole was.

"Could you just please put on some clothes?"

She rolled her eyes and reached for the button-down, plaid shirt hanging in the doorway. "There. Are you happy now?" She pointed the curling iron at him. "But you're picking off every loose hair that ends up on my back, *capisce?*"

Ben breathed a sigh of relief. It was worth it. He didn't care that she was almost twenty-five. He didn't like the fact that his baby sister, the only girl and the youngest of seven, was old enough to date at all. He and his brothers had all been in more fights than he wanted to count because some moron shot off his mouth or cat-called their sister. He certainly didn't want to think of her showing any skin, to anyone.

"Fine, but I need your help."

She poked her head around the doorway. "This wouldn't have anything to do with Emma Jordan, would it?"

"I'm seriously going to kick Andrew's ass when he gets home. That guy gossips more than most women I know."

"Hey! I take offense to that." Her voice was slightly muffled as she turned back to her reflection in the mirror. "Besides, Mom told me and she heard it from Jackson."

"Who heard it from Andrew," Ben finished.

"Then you tell me. What's the real story?"

He rose from the edge of the bed and shut the door to her room. The last thing he needed was someone else in the family overhearing this conversation. His brothers would never let him live it down.

"You know me."

Maddie slid a curl from the hot iron as he leaned against the bathroom doorway. "That serious, huh?"

Ben shrugged a shoulder. "I don't really know. I like her."

"And?" She headed back to the sink, turning around to look at him over her shoulder. "I'm not seeing the problem."

"Laura."

Maddie lay the curling iron back on the counter and crossed her arms. "What about her?"

"What do you mean, 'what about her?' I think the fact that she is a part of my past at all goes to prove that when it comes to dating, I'm not exactly the best judge of character." Ben felt suddenly tired and walked back to Maddie's bed, slumping on the mattress and letting his hands hang between his knees. He dropped his head forward, staring at the floor. "I can't do that again."

"First of all, *you* didn't do anything, Ben. Laura was messed up. You didn't ask her to steal Grant's shit or sell it, and you weren't the one who pressed charges. She had her chance to come clean and you were willing to forgive her, although none of us understood why."

"Because I loved her."

Maddie's eyes softened with sympathy. "I know you did. But she never loved you back, Ben. She was using you."

He nodded. "And I had no clue."

He looked up at his younger sister. He was supposed to be the one giving her advice. How had their relationship gotten so topsy-turvy? How had he ever screwed up so badly?

"And second, you don't tend to make the same mistakes more than once."

A bitter laugh broke through his lips. "Um, did you forget about Angie?"

"Angie was different. You guys were young and, let's face it, you tried to fit a round friendship peg into a square relationship hole. You and Angie were never going to last. I think you knew it too."

"There was Becca."

"You were sixteen, Ben," Maddie laughed. "No relationship works out at sixteen."

"I gave her a ring."

"And you were lucky she gave it back when she went away to college. You guys weren't ready and she was wrong for you. They all have been."

He shrugged, feeling defeated as they rehashed the mistakes of his past. She sat down beside him. "You're not really afraid that Emma is like Laura or Angie, are you?"

"No."

"You're afraid of falling for someone and then having the relationship fall apart again."

Ben shrugged. "I've spent the past three years in doomed relationships. We lived together, talked about the future and then they both walked away. I don't want to put myself out there, build a relationship, only to find out it's just lies again. I should just not date at all." He ran a hand over his face and shot his sister a self-deprecating smile. "I'm kind of a disaster."

"You are not. You're the one macho, alpha male in this family who actually believes in love." Maddie squatted on the balls of her feet in front of him and she lay her hands on his knees. "Ben, you don't have to fall in love with every woman. Dating is about the journey, not the destination. You don't have to be so serious all of the time. Just have fun. Get back on that horse and take her for a ride."

His gaze flicked up to meet hers as guilt slid through him.

Her mouth dropped open. "You didn't?" When he didn't answer, Maddie shoved against his shoulder and jumped up. "You did!"

"I'm not exactly proud of myself, Mads."

"You might not be, but I am. It's about time." She giggled as she headed back to the bathroom. "Welcome back to the club, Ben."

"Ew." He grimaced at the thought of his sister with a man. "That is not something you want burned into my mind, unless I'm kicking someone's ass tonight."

She pulled a strand of hair from the few still needing to be curled. "But, why her? After all this time. She's not exactly your type."

"Why not?" He wanted Maddie's opinion but there was a small part afraid she'd agree with Andrew.

"Well," she hemmed, cringing a little. "Emma seems pretty strong and self-sufficient. I mean, the woman deals with bears and eagles. That's kickass." He didn't miss the awe in her voice. "You tend to pick women who need help, or are going to moon over you being their hero. In spite of the recent articles, I get the feeling she can take care of herself."

"Maybe, maybe not," Ben acknowledged.

His sister brought up the same thing Andrew had. Did he really have a *type*? It might be true when it came to other women. Laura and Angie both needed him and told him so. He'd rescued them both and would have continued until they dumped him. But it wasn't like that with Emma. She didn't want his help and she made it clear he was a pain in her ass. But, he wanted to help her, not rescue her, but work *with* her to save the sanctuary because it was right. However, she wasn't ashamed to admit she needed him, at least for one reason. His body instantly reacted, throbbing with longing at the thought.

Ben inhaled deeply, letting it out carefully. "I don't know." She shot him a doubtful smirk. "I really don't. From the first time we kissed it was like an explosion went off." He shook his head. "Nothing at all like with Laura, or anyone else for that matter. This was almost violent, but in a good way."

"Aw, my big brother's finally got the hots for a girl again," she teased, wrapping a strand of hair around the curling iron.

Hot was definitely the right word for it. Blazing hot, enough to sear him, to brand him. Even now, he could remember the heat of her skin beneath his hands. He rubbed a thumb in his palm to keep from thinking about the way her breasts had filled them during their fierce lovemaking last night. Running the same hand through his hair, he couldn't help but recall the way Emma had tugged at it as he pressed his mouth to her.

"Whoa, wait a second." He met Maddie's gaze in her reflection. "I know that look. Ben, please tell me you're not getting serious about her already."

"What look?" He didn't even bother to deny her suspicions.

"That one," she said, wiggling her finger in the air at his face. "The same one Grant had when he asked me about Bethany and James. I told you to take a ride, not buy the whole horse."

"I'm not buying anything."

She sighed at him again and slid the curling iron to the counter, fluffing her curls before facing him again. "Then what's the issue? Why are you even in here?"

"I need advice."

"No, you're wanting permission. You don't need it. You're a grown man, with needs and wants and desires, and as long as she wants the same thing, I don't see the problem."

"The problem is that I don't know how to do casual."

She laughed. "Most men don't want the complication of a relationship, so why do you seem to?"

"I'm not like most men."

"Trust me, I know." She cast him an adoring smile. "And I love you for that, but you're making this far more complicated than it needs to be. Relax and just see where this goes. Maybe the whole thing will fizzle out after a couple dates."

Maybe Maddie was right. Emma had basically said the same thing. They didn't know each other well and they'd never been out on a date. They might find that without mountain lions, bobcats and dart guns, they had absolutely nothing in common.

Yeah, nothing but those sultry kisses and an untamable attraction that neither seemed to want to deny.

HE STARED INTO the kennel at the back of his rental house, watching the wolf huddle in the back corner, eyeing him warily, its lip curling slightly as it bared shimmering white teeth. No one else knew he was here and this hadn't been the way he'd wanted it to happen but it looked like Emma wasn't going to give him much of a choice.

Cana was the perfect animal to finish this for him. The black wolf-dog looked every bit the part of a violent wolf and when he was found with blood on him and nearby livestock dead, it wouldn't be difficult to put together two and two and have it equal the last straw, the one that convinced local ranchers to demand Emma no longer be in charge of Sierra Tracks. The people in this town knew how much Conrad had entrusted much of the responsibilities of the facility to them since his first stroke. It only made sense that they would be suggested as replacements for the non-profit. They could finally turn Sierra Tracks into the rehab facility it was supposed to become.

He squatted down as the wolf growled low in his throat. "I'm really sorry about this but you have to play an integral part of a much bigger plan."

Jaws snapped at him but he knew the wolf was timid

enough to stay back. "You should have been put down a long time ago, but Emma stopped that too, didn't she? She tried to make you a pet and instead, you're a wolf that doesn't know how to be a wolf."

"Holy crap!" Without warning, the beast lunged forward, throwing itself against the chain link of the kennel, trying to attack the man on the other side. Cana yelped as he bounced off the metal.

He jumped backward, losing his balance and falling to the ground. Picking himself up, he laughed nervously. "I didn't see that coming from you. That kind of unpredictability is exactly what I want you to do after she finds you, okay, boy?"

This was going to be easier than he'd expected it to be.

Chapter Fifteen

IT HAD BEEN a quiet three days, too quiet, and Emma couldn't help but feel antsy. The animals seemed on edge, testing her at every turn. Even Wally had taken a swipe at her, something he'd never done before. But she couldn't blame them. She had no doubt that they were picking up on her anxiety and reacting to it. She was the one on edge. She couldn't even blame it on the early fall heat wave.

She couldn't stop thinking about him, or their one night together. She wasn't even sure why. It wasn't like she'd never had sex before.

Who are you kidding? It was never *like that.*

Unfortunately, that was true.

Every time she and Ben were together, there was something that ignited between them, something hot and violently seductive. It was like the crackle of electricity sizzling in the air just before a lightning storm, raising the hair on her arms and making her jittery. And when they kissed, a bolt had touched down, striking her and leaving her weak. But Emma had no time for weakness right now and being distracted this way was going to get her killed if she wasn't careful.

Across the compound Buster paced in his cage. Ever since his escape, he'd been unhappy and let everyone know it. Between his loud yowls and the way he was jumping against the door, testing the new lock, she worried he was going to somehow escape again, or hurt someone trying. She sympathized with the poor boy. He'd gotten a taste of freedom but hadn't known what to do with it. The same way she had.

At her father's insistence, Emma headed to college, fully prepared to get a degree in business management. The plan was for her to return to run the business side of the sanctuary, which her father claimed was his weakness. She suspected he'd just wanted her away from the danger and risk. But only one semester in, she found she'd missed working with the animals. Against his wishes, Emma changed her major and spent the next eight years getting a degree in veterinary medicine. Within a few months of getting her licensing, he'd convinced her that she should take a job offer she received at an amusement park in order to gain more experience before returning to the sanctuary.

They'd agreed on two years. Two years before she would return to run Sierra Tracks with her father. And they'd had big plans—camps, events, programs. Her father had always wanted to combine his love for animals and rehabilitation with hers for teaching people to respect wildlife. She was going to work *with* him, side by side on a daily basis and someday, years into the future, decide how to deal with his retirement. The plan had never been to leave her to run the sanctuary alone, with nothing but a few very opinionated helpers.

But, while she was away, Brandon and Jake had joined her father. After her father had his first stroke, he'd begun making changes she'd never foreseen. Shutting down programs, turning away animals. He'd begun taking Jake's advice over hers, even going so far as mentioning that Jake might be a good replacement after he retired. She'd turn over Sierra Tracks to Wally and let the bear run it before she let Jake take over. He was obnoxious, opinionated and overly critical of anything that wasn't his own idea. If he had his way, Sierra Tracks would only rescue a few species and the rest of the animals deserved to be euthanized.

"He's going crazy in that cage now." Jake's voice grated on Emma's already frazzled nerves as he and Brandon approached from behind.

Speak of the devil, she thought. She might be better off running the sanctuary alone than trying to do it with Jake. At least then she wouldn't have someone bent on destroying every ounce of confidence she'd once held in her skills.

"I know," she admitted. "Why don't we give him—"

"Please tell me you're not going to drug him just so you don't have to give him up?"

"Jake," Brandon scolded him. "She's just trying to help Buster."

"With more drugs."

"No," she answered slowly, trying to quench her temper. "But I don't want him stressed out more than he needs to be at this point, either. Just until he settles back in again."

"You need to put him down."

"What?" She spun on Jake in disbelief. "Because he's pacing?"

"And voicing his discomfort. He's going to start getting violent if this keeps up."

"I'll make some calls and see if I can't find a rescue with a larger enclosure, one where he can move around more and climb." She glanced back at Buster, rubbing his face over the chain link fencing, searching for a way out of his predicament and she felt her heart clench.

"No, you won't." He shoved his worn cowboy hat back off his forehead. "Because you're still trying to turn these animals into something they aren't. If they can't be rehabilitated and rereleased, they need to be put down." He pointed a finger at the mountain lion. "Doing *that* to him is inhumane."

"I'm not euthanizing him because some idiot unlocked his cage. It's not Buster's fault."

"I think you need to at least consider what he's saying, Emma," Brandon said, his quiet voice surprising her. "Buster may not be at fault but Jake's right. This isn't fair to him. He's miserable now."

Jake crossed his arms, widening his stance, as if daring her to push this further. Brandon was usually the voice of reason between them when they disagreed, which was practically hourly. But, she couldn't euthanize Buster, not because someone used him to target her. She didn't want his death on her conscience.

"Let's see if he calms down after a few days."

Jake tipped his chin up. "And what happens when he turns on someone? You think I'm taking that blame? Or that risk?"

"I didn't ask you to—"

"If you keep him here, Emma, you are." Brandon took a step closer to his brother, making her wonder when this had come to taking sides. "What would your father have done?"

She'd had enough of people questioning her decisions for the sanctuary, enough of Jake's open animosity and disrespect for her position. Sierra Tracks was hers now and she needed to run it her way.

"You know what, you're right."

"I know I am." Jake's stance relaxed slightly and he tucked his hands into his pockets which seemed to pacify Brandon as well.

"And you shouldn't be worried about your safety while you're working."

"Exactly."

Brandon shot her a sideways glance, narrowing his eyes as if curious about her sudden acquiesce.

"You should probably grab your gear and leave."

"What?"

"What?" Brandon repeated. "You can't—"

"Oh, that's where you're wrong. I can, and I just did."

"But Conrad said—" Brandon sputtered, choking on his words.

Emma didn't give either of them the opportunity to say more. "I'm the one in charge now. I don't know what went on between you and my father, or why he was willing to listen to some of your ideas, especially when they contradicted what he told me for years he wanted for Sierra Tracks, but I'm not going to have anyone here who doesn't believe in the way I'm doing things. We've obviously come to that point."

"What?" Jake sputtered again. "Your dad hired me. He wanted me in charge."

His words were a knife to her heart, chipping away at her confidence. Emma took a deep breath, steeling herself. Maybe her father *had* wanted him in charge, or wanted them to work together, but that wasn't the way it turned out.

"I understand that the two of you worked well together but I can't say the same about us. So, thank you for what you've accomplished here over the past few years, but this is where we part ways. I'll have your final check ready for you in the morning."

Jake clamped his jaw shut with a snap. She could see the muscle twitching with his rage as he glowered at her. "You'll regret this. I promise you."

Spinning on his heel, Jake headed back to the main office, gravel kicking up behind his boots.

Not any more than I regret keeping you here so long.

"Emma, you can't do this." Brandon watched his brother walk away. "You're barely keeping the place afloat now."

"I understand your loyalty to your brother, Brandon. I really do. But the conflict between us was causing more problems than it was solving."

"Then you'll understand why I can't stay?"

She'd thought he might follow his brother. "I really hate to see you leave, Brandon. Where your brother and I butt heads, you and I tend to see eye to eye."

"Do we?" His eyes were suddenly cold, almost callous, as he pinched his mouth into a thin line and shook his head. "Because if we did, you wouldn't have fired Jake. Jake," he called, running after his older brother. "Wait up. I'm coming too."

Emma watched them leave. As worried as she was about finding someone to replace Jake, or running the facility without him, and as disappointed as she was to see Brandon leave, she couldn't deny that it felt like a weight had just been lifted from her shoulders. It was as if the negativity was exiting the premises with them.

"THAT BITCH HAS no idea who she's dealing with."

Ben instantly recognized Jake's voice from where he sat with Angie in the bar. He quickly glanced around, praying Emma wasn't here and saw him sitting in the back corner with his brother and a few other friends. But Emma was nowhere in sight.

He still hadn't gotten up the nerve to call her. He wasn't even sure what he wanted to say. And the more time that went by, the less certain he was that there was anything he could say to make it right. He'd hurt her, although he still wasn't entirely sure what he'd said or done, and he wanted to fix it.

In truth, the past two days had been hell. Every moment had been consumed with thoughts about her—was she okay, which animal was she working with, what could he do to help her—and being on duty had only made it harder because he struggled to maintain focus to keep his crew safe. He had to keep his mind on his duty and not on a woman who'd made it clear that she didn't want him around.

They'd put out three grass fires in the last forty-eight hours, thanks to people and their damn cigarettes. Between the fires and the tossing and turning he'd done, trying not to think about Emma, he was beat. But when Angie offered to buy him a beer after their shift, he didn't turn her down. Not only did he need to wind down but it gave him a reason not to call Emma.

Besides, Angie didn't drink often but when she did, it was never just one and always because of trouble with a guy. It was safer for him to keep an eye on her and drive her home rather than leave her to her own devices.

"Pipe down, Jake," his friends said, slapping his shoulder and sliding a beer his direction. "You didn't like working for her as it was." Ben caught a glimpse of Brandon trying to calm his brother as he waved the waitress over for another round.

"That doesn't mean I can afford to be unemployed. Damn bitch! That place is going to crash and burn without me." Jake slid off the side of his chair and landed on his ass.

Brandon pulled him back up. "Shut up. We'll be fine and I'll take care . . ."

Ben missed the rest of what Brandon said as Angie continued to bemoan her latest ex, a lowlife who wrecked her car while he was out on a date with another woman.

"I can't believe that cocksucker . . ." Angie slapped a hand on the top of the table. "Hey! Are you even listening to me?"

"Yeah," he lied, watching from the corner of his eye as Jake wobbled and fell against the side of the table. The man was completely smashed and he was tempted to go over to find out whether Emma had actually fired him and why.

She tipped her head to one side, her dark hair falling over one shoulder, brown eyes gleaming with humor. "Really?"

"Okay, halfway," Ben admitted with a lopsided grin.

"Why do I even bother talking to you? You haven't been on a date in at least a year and a half."

"Because I'm the only guy at the station that isn't trying to get into your pants."

She rolled her eyes before they took on a hopeful gleam. "You think Ryan might be interested?"

"Are you kidding, woman? That is why you end up sitting here with me. Because you keep picking assholes. Why don't you pick a guy who's interested in more than just a one-night stand?"

"Because I'd end up with a guy like you, Ben. A sweet guy with marriage on his mind. I'm not ready for that."

"I don't have marriage on my mind." He ran his fingers over the condensation gathering on the glass of ice water in front of him.

"Pshhh." Angie waved a hand at him and downed the rest of her beer. "Sure, you don't. You are Mr. Responsible, Always-Do-The-Right-Thing, Put-A-Ring-On-It. Maybe if you'd been more impulsive or spontaneous, we'd still be together."

Ben tipped his head to one side, the corner of his mouth quirking in doubt. "That wasn't the reason we split up."

"I know, I know. I guess Colby cheating on me is karma for what I did to you." Angie rolled her eyes, and reached for his hand, giving it a quick squeeze. "Trust me, I wish I could have made myself feel that way about you. But you're like a brother to me."

"And I'm totally okay with that." It was funny how Angie cheating on him and dumping him for another man had led them to this point of their odd but working friendship. He lifted his glass in a toast. "To making better decisions in the future."

"You drink to that. I'm drinking to misbehaving tonight." Angie clinked her beer bottle against his glass, her gaze shooting toward the door of the bar as it opened. Ben didn't miss the instant interest there just before she tossed back what little was left of her beer. She rose and dragged her hand over his shoulder. "Head home, McQuaid. I just found my ride for the night."

He watched as she strolled over to where Ryan and Kevin, the two probies in the department, including the one he'd knocked around a bit, made their way to the bar to order drinks. Sliding one arm around each, Angie's body language would be difficult to mistake. She wasn't going home alone and she could take her pick of which man she wanted, or both, which left him free to head home.

"I'm going to kill that fucking bitch the next time I see her." Jake's voice carried across the pool tables and the televisions tuned to some sports talk show. "Please, tell me that's her truck."

"Where?" Brandon tried to pull his brother away from the windows that ran the length of the wall.

"Right there, and if she so much as sets foot in here—"

Ben saw Emma's truck parked a few spots from the front doors and heard the chirp of her car alarm. Jake was already staggering toward the front doors, ready to meet her at the entrance. As much as Ben had wanted to reconcile with Emma, it looked like he was going to have to rescue her first.

Now, he had to figure out how to rescue a woman who didn't even understand she needed saving?

Chapter Sixteen

IT WAS TIME to celebrate.

Emma had let Monica and Sadie know that Jake and Brandon were both gone and, assuring them that Jake wouldn't be setting foot on the property again.

After everyone had left for the night, Emma had big plans to do nothing more than soak in a bubble bath with a glass of Merlot but she couldn't quite shake her restlessness. But unlike poor Buster, she had a new-found grip on her freedom and she was going to make the most of it, even if it meant braving the people from town who weren't exactly fans right now. She was tired of holing up on the property. She had nothing to hide. Between that realization and shedding the millstone Jake had been around her neck, Emma felt like nothing was going to bring her down tonight.

Emma even had a little skip in her step as she jogged

up the stairs to the front door of Know Place, Hidden Falls' solitary sports bar. Tonight she was going to have a beer or two, play a game of pool and show the people in this town that this was her home, just as much as theirs. She hadn't felt this carefree since coming back to town and it felt good.

The door was tugged open from inside as she reached for it. "Nope, not tonight, turn around."

Standing in front of her, as solid a barrier as any brick wall, was Ben in cargo pants and a navy t-shirt with a Hidden Falls Fire Department emblem on it. His broad shoulders blocked some of the noise and nearly all of the light from inside. Her body broke out in goose bumps. She might not be able to see his face, but she knew it was him.

"Excuse me?" She tried to take a step forward, expecting him to back up. Instead, he moved toward her, pulling the door shut behind him and forcing her to take a step backward. "Kindly move."

"You're not going in there, Emma."

"Oh, yes I am." She planted her fists on her hips. *Just who did he think he was?* "You don't get to—"

"Trust me, I'm doing you a favor." He frowned and glanced backward at the closed door and the commotion coming from inside, growing louder by the moment. "Turn around and get back in your truck."

"Who the hell do you think you—Hey!" she yelled as she was suddenly flipped upside down over his shoulder and lifted from the ground. *How freaking tall was he anyway?* She felt like she was twenty feet off the ground. Emma wrapped her arms around his waist to keep from falling. "Put me down!"

"Not until you agree to go home."

The concrete blurred with every long stride he took across the parking lot, his shoulder jabbing into her diaphragm, his amazing ass just inches away from her face. If she wasn't so distracted with possibility of tumbling headfirst to the ground, she might appreciate the view more.

"McQuaid, you'd better put me down this instant," she ordered, doing her best to force authority into her voice when her palms were itching to cup his rounded bottom.

"Or what?" She could hear it in his voice. He didn't think she'd do anything.

"Last time I'm asking," Emma warned.

As exhilarating as it was frightening, Emma couldn't help but be slightly turned on by his caveman approach. Ben made her feel like she was stepping off a cliff and free-falling, but she trusted him to catch her, even if she couldn't explain why. She kicked her feet slightly, letting them connect with his abs, but not hard enough to cause any pain, but with enough pressure to make him realize that she wasn't going to be manhandled, not even if his manhandling was actually gentle.

When he didn't react, she kicked her foot against his stomach again and his arm tightened around her legs behind her knees, locking her legs in place. He slapped one hand against her butt, making it sting slightly and causing her to yelp with surprise. It might have been unexpected, but it certainly wasn't painful or unpleasant. Her body instantly responded to his hand on her rear, growing warm and tingly. Unfortunately, her mind reacted the way she'd learned in self-defense class. Clasping her hands, she brought them down against his lower back.

Ben grunted and dropped her onto her feet under a light in the parking lot. Trying to regain her bearings, she shook her head and took a step back, bumping her hip against the vehicle beside her. "Ow! Damn it!"

"Shit, Emma." He bent over, reaching one hand to his lower back, massaging where she'd caught him in the kidney.

"I told you to put me down," she pointed out. "I'm not some fire hose for you to throw around."

"Damn, you make it hard to be nice to you." He looked up and the light bathed his face. One cheek had a monstrous goose egg already forming near a cut beside his eye, his lower lip was split and swollen and she could see several bruises already forming.

"What happened?" All thoughts of him trying to force her to leave against her will fled as two new ones took their place—he was hurt and she'd just added to his injuries.

She reached her fingers to the split at the corner of his lower lip, spinning to locate her truck only to realize they were already beside it. Lifting the back hatch of the cover over the bed, Emma flipped the tailgate down. "Here, sit."

Digging for her keys in her pocket, she unlocked the vehicle and pulled the first aid kit from under her backseat, setting it beside him at the back of the truck. "Talk."

"About what?" He pressed his thumb against his bloody lip and eyed the front of the bar again. "The fact that we should leave?"

She arched a brow. "I'm not going anywhere until you tell me what happened and how you ended up looking like . . . well, this." She waved a hand at his battered face.

The front door of the bar opened and his gaze immediately shot toward it. He sighed when no one exited. "Jake's inside."

He acted like that explained everything. It didn't tell her anything at all. She took a step back and crossed her arms, waiting for him to explain.

"You fired him?"

"Not that it's any of your business but, yes."

She opened a bottle of water from the case she kept in the back of her truck and dug some sterile gauze pads from her gear, tearing open the packaging and wetting the cotton. She moved closer to him, looking at the various cuts on his face to determine which was in most dire need of treatment. Dabbing the wet pad at the cut on his cheek, she cleaned away the coagulating blood.

"He's not happy about it."

She lifted her brows. "Would you expect him to be? I just fired him after five years working with my father."

His fingers closed over her wrist, making her stomach tumble and her pulse throb. "Why?"

She met his intense gaze with one of her own. "For the same reason I asked you to leave. It's time I surround myself with people who trust in me, and people whom I can trust."

"You don't trust me?" She could hear the disenchantment in his voice as she slid her wrist from his gentle grip.

His dark gaze continued to bore into hers. "I'm not sure," she answered honestly.

Ben snapped his attention back to the front of the bar where some sort of commotion had begun at the door, breaking the connection between them. He hopped off the back of her truck, lifting the tailgate and slamming her vet box closed. "You're going to have trust me now. Get in and drive."

"What?" A *ping* hit the side of her truck and she looked up in time to see Jake squatting to pick up another of the small river rocks that decorated the flower beds near the front of the bar.

"You bitch, I told you'd regret—"

Ben shoved her toward the open driver's side door and into the truck, following her inside and slamming the door closed. "Keys?"

Without questioning him, she handed them over, just as another rock bounced off the car parked beside her. Jake stumbled down the steps, obviously drunk, with two guys groping for him, trying to reach for his arms which, luckily for her, kept him from getting off a well-aimed shot. Brandon stood behind his brother watching the situation unfold. It seemed like every time she was anywhere near Ben, trouble wasn't far behind.

"Damn, looks like I didn't hit him as hard as I thought I did." Ben drove out of town and pulled her truck onto the main highway.

"You hit him?"

He shot her an incredulous look. "The guy just chucked rocks at you and you're going to give me a hard time for knocking his ass out?"

"No. I'm mad you didn't give me the opportunity to hit him myself."

"I mean, the least you could have done was hold him and let me take a shot."

Emma never failed to surprise him. She actually sounded disappointed.

He'd realized from the start that Emma had a temper but he'd never thought she'd be such a firecracker. He'd expected her to be outraged that he'd gotten into a fight, to be upset that he'd sunk to using brute force, but it had never crossed his mind that she'd be jealous that she hadn't had a chance to throw a punch at the guy.

"Please tell me you're joking."

"Uh, no, and if there's a dent in my truck, I'm driving back and putting a dent in *him*."

"Emma, you can't go around slugging guys."

"I can if they dent my truck." She arched a brow at

him. "You seem to be forgetting that you hit him, Boy Scout. What makes you think it's okay for you to do it defending my honor but I can't?"

"I did that to keep him from coming out to find you."

"Yeah, well, you should have hit him harder." She glanced toward the window. "I'm so sick of the double standard you men have. Why is it okay for you but not me?"

"Because he'd hit you back. That guy isn't exactly a gentleman."

She snorted with an unladylike laugh as she turned back to him. "And you, McQuaid, are too much a gentleman for your own good."

Ben couldn't help but recall the last time she'd accused him of being "gentlemanly," straddling him, just before they'd made love. He felt himself instantly grow hard at the memory and bit back a groan.

"Look, I have wrestled alligators, been charged twice by a brown bear and been bitten by a tiger. Do you really think Jake could do anything that would actually scare me?"

Ben slowly turned toward her. "You're kidding, right?"

"It comes with the job when you're working with exotic animals. There are just some inherent dangers you have to accept."

Ben stared at her in awe.

"What?"

"You're a pretty tough chick," he admitted. She shrugged a shoulder then appeared sorry she'd mentioned it. "Must make it hard for a guy to impress you when you have more balls then they do."

She gave him a wary look. "For all your bravado, men generally have extremely sensitive egos, I have yet to meet a guy okay with dating a woman who is stronger, tougher or more courageous. I'm not going to *girl* it up just so a guy can feel macho."

Is that what they were doing? Dating?

"Sounds like you're speaking from experience." She rolled her eyes at him. "A two-year relationship down the tubes. Said he didn't want to bury me in pieces."

She fell silent and Ben knew she wouldn't elaborate, but it explained why she was still alone. She'd been rejected, because of her job, by a man who felt weakened by her strength. He didn't push her for more details and turned off the main highway, down the road leading to her place.

"You're taking me home?" Surprise and what sounded like disappointment colored her voice.

"Yes. Is that a problem?"

"It is when I was hoping to escape for the night. I've been cooped up on this ranch for months."

Ben could recognize a hint when he heard one but he didn't have much choice. Try as he might to convince himself differently, Ben knew that if given the choice between Emma in his bed or sleeping alone, he'd choose her without thinking twice. This woman drew him like a moth. He knew the danger but simply couldn't resist the flame.

"I'll tell you what," she began, her voice dangerously

seductive as her hand reached over to lay on his forearm. "We can head back to your place and I promise to doctor up the rest of your wounds." She met his gaze with her siren smile. "And anything else that might ail you."

She reached up, her fingers careful as she tipped his face to one side to inspect a cut on his jaw. A sizzle of heat exploded in his chest. He wanted her, in a bad way, but he also knew it was a horrible idea. They were different, too different.

He reached for her hand, turning his head to press a kiss to her palm. Her eyes lit up like jewels. "As great as that idea sounds, it's Game Night at my place and all my brothers are there starting their all-night poker game."

"Great." She spun in the seat. "I'm in."

"What do you mean, 'you're in'?"

"I mean, I was going to the bar tonight to relax, have fun and blow off some steam. What's the difference if I have fun at the bar or somewhere else?"

Ben looked over at her. He couldn't blame her for wanting to have some time away from the recent troubles at the animal sanctuary. Between the constant, backbreaking work, the backlash from the articles and dealing with Jake, a night out might be exactly what she needed to come back with fresh eyes and a new perspective. He couldn't imagine living at the fire station 24/7 or the stress it could potentially cause. Everyone deserved a night off.

"You might be sorry. They're sort of a rowdy bunch, but I guess you're in luck. Only four of them will be there tonight."

"As long as there's beer and food, I can take whatever they throw at me."

Ben had no doubt she could.

EMMA HADN'T BEEN sure what to expect when they pulled up in front of the old bunkhouse. Ben hadn't mentioned that he still lived at home, now that she was here, there was no doubt that was his situation. Well, technically his parents lived in the house across the driveway, but he was still living on their property, just across a gravel road.

She bit back a smile when she realized he was worried about her judging him for it. Why would she? She been planning on moving back as well, a woman in her late twenties returning to stay with her father. Nothing said success that way that did. Instead, she was living on his ranch which, thanks to his will, now belonged to Sierra Tracks and her, since he'd never gotten around to naming anyone else in his trust.

Laughter spilled out from the open windows as someone yelled.

"That would be Andrew." Ben rolled his eyes. "Sounds like he's hot again tonight. He's killed us the past three weeks."

She shot him a confident grin. Emma knew she should probably keep her mouth shut since she and Lady Luck hadn't exactly been on good speaking terms lately but she couldn't resist. "That means he'll have plenty for me to take from him tonight."

"You think you're that good, huh?"

"The park I worked at had some animals doing a show in Vegas for two weeks. I went along and picked up a few tricks while I was there." She wagged a finger at him. "But don't you dare say anything."

"Your secret is safe with me." Ben laughed. "It'll be fun to watch you take him down."

Opening the door for her, Ben led her into the living room where furniture was shoved aside to make room for a game table and several folding chairs. Food was scattered across the bar that separated the kitchen and living room and the spicy scent of pepperoni and grease made her stomach growl. As they made their way into the main room, five heads swiveled their direction and the laughter immediately gave way to curiosity.

"You guys up for two more?" Ben grabbed two more chairs and slid them closer to the table.

"I thought you were having drinks with Angie?"

Emma recognized Andrew, even without his uniform, and tried not to acknowledge the stab of jealousy at the mention of Ben out with another woman.

"She had a ride home." Ben glared at him. "Emma, you remember my brother, Andrew. This is Grant, and the twins, Jackson and Jefferson."

"I'm Maddie, and so excited that I'm not the only girl here tonight." She rose and shook Emma's hand. "We need a little less testosterone in this room."

"My sister," Ben clarified when she looked his direction. "This is Emma. She's taken over for Conrad at Sierra Tracks."

"Jefferson," one of the twins said, holding out his hand. "We were all really sorry to hear about your father, Emma. He was a good guy," one of the twins said.

Emma immediately liked him. "Thank you. I really appreciate that."

"Are you two playing?" Maddie asked. "Did you at least warn her about Andrew's cheating?" She shot her brother a dirty look.

"I don't cheat. I'm a cop; I uphold the law," he insisted.

"And I raise cattle. Doesn't mean I won't barbecue one of those suckers. You always were the best liar of us all growing up," Jackson said with a laugh.

"Not to mention the biggest troublemaker," Grant pointed out. "How many times did I nearly have to bail you out of jail in high school?"

Andrew waved them off. "Kid stuff. I make up for it by following all the rules now."

"Hmm." Maddie gave a snort and rolled her eyes. "Forgive me for not believing you, liar."

"I can't help it if you guys suck at poker."

"You really sure you want to subject yourself to this tonight?" Ben asked, laying a hand at her lower back and directing her toward the kitchen. He pulled open the refrigerator and she could see what looked like several cases of beer bottles but without labels. "This is mild compared to what it will look like after they get a few more of Andrew's stash in them. I doubt this is what you had in mind when you headed into town to escape."

He passed her a bottle and she stared at it, curious about the contents. "Home brew?"

"I know it seems a little weird but he's actually pretty good at it. Just don't tell him I said so. He's already way too cocky." Ben chuckled as he slid pizza onto two plates, passing her one before popping the top from the bottles and tossing them into the trash. "Make yourself at home, eat whatever you want. Just stack the bottles on the sink. Andrew washes and reuses them."

She took a long draw from the bottle, surprised at the citrus-pine flavor that burst on her tongue just before the bitter hops kicked in.

"He makes a good IPA."

Ben's brows shot up in surprise.

"What? A girl can't know her beer? Don't even get me started on Scotch." She tipped the bottle toward him.

"I see your father raised you right."

"Damn straight."

Chapter Seventeen

"No FUCKING WAY," Andrew muttered, throwing his cards on the table as Emma gathered the pot and stacked it in front of her with a victorious smile. "What the hell did you even bring her here for, Ben?"

"Vengeance," Maddie supplied.

Andrew pursed his lips, trying not to look pissed but Ben knew better. He was pouting like a baby after losing six hands straight to Emma. "I saw her hand. How the hell did you pull that off?"

"I thought you said you didn't cheat, *Officer*."

Guffaws and cat calls sounded from the table as Emma called Andrew out on his slipup.

"At least now we know how he does it." Ben laughed as he rose. "Anyone want another round?"

"Nope, I'm heading home." Grant rose from the table. "I promised Bethany I wouldn't be too late and

I'm taking James out fishing in the morning so she can get some wedding planning accomplished."

"Soon you'll be a shackled man." Jackson laughed as he rocked back in the chair, dangerously close to tipping it. He slowly began to whistle "Taps."

"Well, I'm headed to a warm bed with a woman who loves me. You're headed to a bunkbed with your twin brother," Grant pointed out. "Not sure you have any room to talk shit, baby bro."

Ben laughed. "Need a ride?"

"No, I stopped a while back." He held up his can of soda. "Besides, Emma's going to need an escort. These guys may jump her on the way out to get their money back."

"What is it with you guys and your outdated chivalry?" Emma shook her head and finished off what was left in the bottle in front of her. "I'll bet that my overweight black bear at home has better wrestling moves than any of you, and his signature move is to lie down."

Jackson laughed and Jefferson's eyes lit up at her challenge. No way in hell was Ben letting either of those two get their hands on her. Jealousy shot through him, even as he reminded himself that none of his brothers would break the unspoken code they'd always had. *No screwing with another guy's woman.*

"We'll leave the wrestling to Ben." Jackson slapped Ben on the shoulder. "But next time, warn me before you bring the cardsharp, you dick. I won't bring so much money." He took his bottle to the counter and grabbed one Ben had just taken from the refrigerator. "She cleaned me out."

"I'm tapped too." Maddie rose and headed into the kitchen to put away the food. Emma rushed in to help but Maddie shooed her away. "You're a guest and, judging from those sour faces, you may not be welcome again," she teased. "However, as far as I'm concerned, you're welcome anytime, even if it's only to help me terrorize those guys."

Ben watched Emma laughing with his siblings. She fit in with them as if she'd been born part of his family. He'd assumed that being an only child wouldn't have prepared her for the chaotic party that made up his family. He adored them, but he also knew they could be a lot to handle all at once. They were too loud, too rambunctious and too obnoxious at times. But Emma had taken it all in stride.

"So, Emma," Jefferson sidled up beside her and looped an arm over her shoulders, a little too wobbly on his feet to still be sober, and jabbed a thumb in Ben's direction. "Please tell me you're going to get this guy to loosen up. Him and Andrew are so straight-laced, the rest of us never get to have any fun."

"You have no room to talk, so stop complaining," Maddie said as she plucked the half-empty beer bottle from his hands. "Try being the only girl and the youngest." She grabbed Jefferson's arm and shoved him toward his room. "You need to go to bed before you embarrass yourself."

Ben shot his sister a look of pure gratitude. He owed her big-time for that one.

Jackson came into the kitchen with a groan. "I can't believe it's two a.m. Dad is going to be in here in three hours." He slid his half-empty bottle onto the counter. "I would just like one day, just one, to sleep past six."

"Lightweight," Emma shot at him.

"Watch yourself, Red. Those are fighting words," Jackson laughed. "But, because you've got balls, you're welcome here any time. As long as we're not playing cards," he amended.

"Chicken," Ben said with a laugh.

"No, just smart. I can beat you guys. She's a different story."

Maddie tossed the washcloth at Andrew. "I've put all the food away and sent the youngins to bed. You can finish cleaning."

"Hey! I thought the winner cleaned."

Emma patted his shoulder as she moved closer to Ben, a fact his body responded to instantly as his pulse kicked up a notch. "Not when the winner is a guest. Suck it up, buttercup. You'll live."

Maddie's eyes met Ben's, bright with humor. "I like her."

"I had no doubt you would." He put an arm around his sister, rubbing his knuckles on the top of her head the way he had when they were younger.

"Knock it off." Maddie slapped at his hand before turning back to Emma. "We need to hang out some time. I could give you the lowdown on this guy. You might want to turn and run while you still can."

"Aw, he's a teddy bear."

Emma patted his chest and Ben felt heat sear him, circling lower until it settled in his groin. Maddie looked from Emma back to his face and a slow, knowing grin spread over her lips as if she knew something he didn't.

"We should totally hang out. You have your phone on you?"

"It's in the other room."

Maddie led the way out as Emma followed her. Ben couldn't take his eyes off her until Andrew's quiet laughter drew his attention.

"Man, I knew you were going to do this. You just keep screwing yourself. One of these days, you might learn."

Ben clenched his jaw, forcing himself to remain silent. Andrew would just turn anything he said into a debate and he didn't want to deal with him.

Andrew shook his head sympathetically. "She's not your type, Ben. This one is not right for you."

"No?" It was all he could manage through his gritted teeth.

"The twins', maybe. Or mine, but not yours. You're like Grant. You're the level-headed guy, the guy women want to have a family with, the guy they bring home or marry. White picket fence, two point three kids and a dog. I get the feeling Emma wants no part of a relationship. I saw what happened to you after Angie, then Laura. Why are you so ready to get your heart broken again?"

Ben wanted to prove his brother wrong, wanted to assure him that he could be with a woman and not end up in a relationship or falling in love. She'd made it clear she didn't want any sort of serious or permanent relationships in her life. So, there really wasn't even a "him and Emma" at this point.

"It's not like that this time."

"Sure it's not."

"This is a casual thing. We're . . ." Ben paused, trying to find any word that might describe what he and Emma had, or how he felt when they were together. *Lovers? Friends?*

Andrew shook his head. "Give it up, Ben. Casual just isn't who you are."

"You might be surprised."

Emma came back into the kitchen with her phone in her hand and smiled at the pair. "Your sister said she'd talk to you both tomorrow. I should probably get back to the ranch too. Monique texted me that she fed Kit but I have to be up early to do it in the morning."

Ben pulled her keys from his pocket. "I'll drive you."

Her brows lifted in question. Since he'd left his car at the bar, if he drove her back to the ranch, it would leave him stranded for the night. Andrew glanced her way, arching a brow expectantly. Then back to Ben, his eyes widening as if he'd come to the same realization. While he had no plans of taking advantage of Emma, there was no denying he wanted her. He also wanted to wipe that arrogant smirk off Andrew's face.

Emma looked at Andrew curiously, taking in his

grin, before turning her gaze back to Ben. As if she were able to read his mind, she smiled up at him. "You sure you're okay to drive?"

He held his glass of water aloft. "I switched over a while back too."

"Good, because I didn't," she admitted, trailing her hand over his bicep with a sly wink. Ben immediately felt himself grow hard. Andrew choked on the last of the beer he'd just swallowed as she held her empty bottle out to Andrew. "This is really good."

"I'll have another batch ready next weekend. Come over." As Andrew's gaze slid over her, Ben felt every muscle in his body clench with tension.

"I'd like that." Emma cast his brother a dazzling smile as she tucked her hand into the crook of Ben's arm and he felt his patience snap. He was going to punch his brother, or throw her over his shoulder again.

"We should go."

Andrew chuckled as they headed for the front door. "You do realize, you're just proving my point, right, bro?" he yelled as they headed outside.

EMMA HAD SEEN the rage in Ben's eyes at Andrew's invitation. Maybe she'd had one beer too many and it dulled her senses, but she suspected Ben was angry at her as well and she hadn't done anything but flirt with him.

Let him be angry.

At first, she'd decided it was best to give him some time to settle down, but he just seemed to get angrier with every mile that passed between their ranches and, now, she was second-guessing her decision.

"You want to tell me what that was about?"

"Nothing."

"Oh, I see. Being a child must just be part of your boyish charm." Ben simply clenched his jaw again. "You know, if you keep doing that, the muscle in your jaw might just stay that way."

She saw him relax his jaw slightly but he still didn't look her direction.

"It's good to see you hold fast to tradition, that you perpetuate the cliché."

He turned to look at her, slowly, his eyes dark, daring her to say more. But luck had been on her side tonight playing poker and she'd firmly believed in pushing it as far as it would go.

"You know, the strong, silent type."

"I know the cliché." He pulled into the driveway and punched the security code she'd given him into the keypad at the gate. "I thought Andrew told you to change this."

"I will, when I'm ready."

"How about now since you've pissed off an employee and someone is vandalizing your property."

"Don't go getting all caveman on me again, McQuaid. I'll do it when I'm ready."

"I see you're not bucking the stubborn Irishman cliché."

She gave him a tentative grin. "You know I'm Scottish but touché. Maybe some clichés are based more on reality than we like to think," she offered. "I will change it in the morning when I have light." He tipped his chin down in disbelief. "I cross my heart. You want to tell me what sparked your temper?"

He looked back out the front window and she could see him shutting down on her again. "Andrew." He took a deep breath. "And you."

"About him offering for me to come try his new beer?" He couldn't possibly be serious.

He parked the truck in front of the house and turned it off. There was no sound but the slight ticking of the engine as it began to cool from the short trip. The muscle in his jaw ticked in time with the sound and she could see he was trying to work up his nerve to answer.

"Look, if you want to hook up with Andrew, I'm cool with that—"

"Are you? Because this," she said as she circled her open hand in front of her, "tells me that you're *not* cool with it." She flipped the console up between them and slid across the seat so that her thigh pressed against his. "And, for the record, I don't want to 'hook up' with your brother."

Emma slid her hand down his bicep. There was only one McQuaid brother she wanted to hook up with and she was finding it increasingly hard to remember that this was supposed to be a one-time, no pressure thing, that she was supposed to keep her distance from him emotionally because she couldn't do serious. She had enough trouble in her life without adding a relationship to the mix, or burdening him with her drama.

But Ben McQuaid had a way of worming himself into her thoughts when she least wanted him there. When she was working, it was all she could do not to call and ask him to volunteer again so she could watch him work. It wasn't just the sexual attraction to him—hell, she'd have to be dead not to be attracted to him. But she wanted to be the one to give him new experiences. He made her laugh, even if it was due to his discomfort around the animals. More than anything, she liked that he'd been willing to take a beating, or give one, for her. No one had ever stood up for her like that, and it made her feel guilty for her previous accusations about the articles in the newspaper.

"Emma, we still need to talk about this . . . thing, with us."

He reached for her hand but instead of removing it, he simply curled his fingers between hers. It was tender, sweet and comforting.

And exactly what she didn't want from Ben.

She had to find a way to stop these feeling for him, this emotional longing, from developing. This was supposed to remain completely physical. It *had* to, or she had to walk away now. She didn't have the emotional stamina for anything more permanent than a few nights.

"If you don't want this, McQuaid, all you have to do is say so. We could call it quits right now." She prayed he wouldn't stop her as her hand dropped to his firm thigh. Ben sucked in a breath as her fingers trailed upward, brushing over his zipper where his erection strained against the material.

"No, we can't," he admitted, his voice strained.

She laughed, surprising herself with the huskiness of the sound. Ben made her feel things she shouldn't, didn't want to, too. "So I see."

Emma swung one leg over his, and settled herself into his lap, leaning back against the steering wheel and pressing both hands against his chest. "You know, you're not *really* the strong, silent type. Your mouth might be silent, but the rest of you gets the message across loud and clear."

"Is this all you want, Emma?" His face was shadowed and she couldn't quite read his expression, lit only by the stars in the sky and the small sliver of a moon outside. There were no lights on, except those within the animal compound across the driveway. "Do you even know what you want?"

His hands found her hips, his fingers dug into the flesh slightly, as if he was trying to maintain control of himself.

She almost laughed at his question. She wanted him, this. She didn't need to talk about it. She wanted Ben to lose control, to stop thinking. But she understood he was trying to protect her from herself, to give her an opportunity to change her mind or back out but it wasn't going to happen. In spite of her earlier comment, she *did* trust him, had from the moment she'd met him. Maybe not completely, but as much as she could trust anyone.

There was a quiet confidence in Ben, a fortitude that assured her that she was safe with him, protected. She wasn't sure how she knew it, he'd almost shot her with a dart gun, after all, but she had no doubt he'd have thrown himself between her and Buster if it had come down to it. Ben didn't just look like a superhero, he was one. He was a guardian, a protector. Not because it was his job but because it was in his DNA. It was who he was in every thought he had and he'd simply chosen a profession which let him be what he was inside.

She'd seen it when he was with her and when he was with his family. He was a good man, too good for her. He was going to make someone a good husband, a father. If she had half a shred of decency, she'd walk away from him now and let him find a woman who could love him the way he deserved, instead of a woman who could only offer him a little fun.

His hands moved up her sides to cup her face and she reveled in his touch, leaning into it. She cursed her own weakness. She didn't want to admit it but she needed him. Far more than she wanted to.

Needed the way he helped her forget her fears, the way he made her feel desirous, the way he made her feel like she could be a good person too. She needed to keep feeling like she could be the woman he believed she was, even if she knew it wasn't true.

Chapter Eighteen

BEN STARED INTO Emma's eyes and could see the indecision raging within. There was a battle going on inside her but she wasn't willing to open up to him. Andrew's words circled in his mind, like vipers, striking out, reminding him that he was falling for Emma, hard and fast, and that he just didn't have it in him to *not* get involved.

He closed his eyes, trying to figure out how Andrew could be with a woman like Emma and not care what was going on behind the eyes that had suddenly taken on the appearance of the ocean in a storm. It was impossible.

But he also knew Andrew was right, Emma didn't want a relationship. She wanted something without strings, no commitments. As much as he wanted to ask what was going on in her head, he didn't. He would stick to letting her set their pace, somehow.

Ben drew her closer and Emma leaned in willingly, sighing as his mouth covered hers. Desire surged through him, hot and bold, but he kept their kiss gentle, sweet, almost languorous. Emma's hands slid from his chest to the nape of his neck as his tongue swept against hers, dancing with eager strokes. His hands slid down her back, pulling her against him and sending his body straining against the tight rein he kept on his self-control.

She moved over him, trying to get even closer, but there were too many clothes separating them. Emma's hands moved down the front of his chest, tugging his Henley from the waistband of his jeans when he stopped her. She whimpered a protest but he laughed quietly.

"This isn't exactly the most comfortable place to . . ." Ben let his words trail off and gave her a slight shrug. "You know."

"Get busy?" she offered, flashing him a brilliant smile. "Where's your sense of adventure?"

"I can be far more adventurous when I'm not worried about you leaning back on the horn and waking your neighbors."

Emma pressed her lips to the edge of his jaw. "My neighbors are almost two miles away on either side. I could sit on this horn and they wouldn't hear it." She gave him a flirty smile, letting her lips brush over his. "But now you have me intrigued to see this adventurous side you claim to have."

Before he could say anything, Emma opened the door. He groaned as she seductively slid off his lap and stood at the door, waiting for him. Ben dropped his head against the back window, closing his eyes for a moment, trying to calm the ravenous hunger raging through him. Whenever Emma was involved, all of his good intentions and control seemed to disappear.

He opened his eyes and reached for her hand when two small flashes of light behind her caught his attention. Ben narrowed his eyes, trying to see it again, but now it was gone.

"What's over there?" He reached for her shoulder and pointed toward the front of her house. "I saw light that way."

"What light? Where?"

A faint low growl carried to where they stood. Ben instinctively moved to Emma's left side, protecting the only vulnerable side of her, when he saw the faint yellow light again. Only it wasn't light. It was the reflection of light from the eyes of an animal, walking straight toward them. From the loud snarl, it didn't sound friendly.

"Shit," he muttered, staring ahead in the darkness, unable to make out anything but a large shape and immediately wondered if Buster hadn't somehow gotten out again. "Can you tell what that is?"

"No." Emma leaned into the truck and flipped the headlights on. The front of the house was bathed in yellow light as what appeared to be a wolf froze, mid-step, as if confused how to react.

Emma pushed her way past him much to his dismay. "Get back here," he called, reaching for her arm.

He'd just missed her as she moved toward the front of the truck. "Cana?"

Ben moved to flank her and the animal immediately sank on its haunches, teeth bared again. It snapped once, taking a step backward. Emma took a step forward, away from the protection of the truck and squatted on the balls of her feet.

"Cana, it's okay. It's me."

"Emma?" Ben reached for her, determined to pull her back to safety but she shook him off. "Emma, get back here. That wolf is going to kill you."

The wolf's amber eyes flicked at him and the snarls turned more violent as the animal lashed out.

"No, he won't." Her gaze never left the animal as she waited, looking far more relaxed than she should. "This is a wolf-dog, but a very high concentration."

"How can you tell?"

"Because I know him. Do me a favor and sit in the truck. Just leave the parking lights on."

"No way." Ben was not about to leave her vulnerable, in the dark, with this wild animal while he sat and watched her get attacked.

"Ben," she repeated, her voice more adamant, "he's not growling at me. He's growling at you. Now, get in the truck."

Ben realized she was right as the animal met his gaze, each growl louder than the last, before the beast's gaze looked at Emma warily. He took a hesitant step back and the hair on the scruff of the wolf's neck seemed to lie flatter.

"Are you sure?" If she was wrong, the consequences could be disastrous. However, he wasn't doing her much good right now, aggravating the beast. He was going to have to trust that she could take care of herself with the animal.

"Yes."

Ben took a few steps back, never taking his eyes off Emma, prepared to rush back to her side, even if it meant putting himself between her and the wolf. Instead, the wolf looked back at her, his lip dropping back over his teeth and his entire demeanor taking on a more relaxed stance.

"Cana, sit." Emma stood slowly, watching the animal for any signs of attack, but he responded the way any well-trained dog would, by plopping his rear to the ground. "Just stay there for a minute, Ben."

"Cana, come on."

The wolf jumped up, trotting toward her as she walked to the porch, but not before shooting a wary glance back at the truck.

"I'm going to get him settled into a kennel. Head inside after I get Cana to the barn."

She opened the back gate and Ben felt his pulse race as she disappeared from sight. There wasn't a muscle in his body that wasn't tensed, ready to charge into the barn, to jump between her and that animal but he could hear her talking to him the entire way, even though he couldn't quite make out her words. He relaxed slightly. As long as he could hear her voice, he knew she was okay.

It was the only thread of hope he could grasp onto since she'd insisted he head into the house, like a child being put in time-out. Ben moved one of the curtains aside in time to see her walking the wolf on a leash out to the building housing her kennels. He'd seen them during his brief volunteer stint, although they'd been empty at the time and he'd wondered at their purpose.

This woman floored him, intriguing him with the few moments of vulnerability he saw, only to be awed by the courage she displayed. She was an open book in so many ways, yet a complete mystery in others. He dropped the curtain and waited for her to return, wandering into the living room.

She hadn't moved many of her father's things from here since her arrival. His tastes still permeated the room with leather furniture, animal portraits and hundreds of books along a case that took up an entire wall, but there were a few new pictures. Ben picked one up off a shelf and studied it. It was easy to recognize a much younger Emma standing beside Conrad with a red-tailed hawk held on her arm. She was staring at the bird but her father was staring at her, pride beaming clearly from his face. He set it down and picked up one that was much more recent, showing Emma with her father again, but this time, he held the chain of a tiger and Emma was wearing a polo shirt for the animal park she'd worked at. While Conrad looked awed by the experience, Ben couldn't help but notice the sadness in his expression.

"He didn't actually want me working there, but insisted I needed more experience than what vet school or growing up here had given me. However, he said he felt like he'd convinced me to sell my soul to a glorified zoo." She sighed as she looked around his shoulder at the picture. "It's a fine line between sanctuaries and zoos, really. In truth, I guess it comes down to how the money comes in."

"What do you mean?" He settled the frame back on the bookshelf and turned toward her, wanting to reach for her but seeing a hesitancy in her eyes.

Emma shrugged. "A lot of zoos breed and sell offspring which, while maintaining the population of some species, can hurt it as well and can promote black market sales. Some sanctuaries do the same. A true sanctuary will rescue animals, keeping and caring for them until they can be released, or for their lifetime if they can't be returned to their habitat. This particular animal park fell into the middle. They did both but Dad was against the breeding program as well as the training and performance aspect."

"But he trained some of the animals here," Ben pointed out.

"He didn't see it that way. He believed there was a big difference between training an animal to perform for a show, even using methods that mimicked their natural tendencies, and training them to tolerate human contact."

"You disagree."

She shrugged again. "Whether I agreed or not didn't really matter. This was Dad's place and his rules."

"Yet, he walked wolves on a leash?"

She arched a brow at him and he realized he may have just crossed a line with her. He hadn't meant to sound judgmental when he was actually curious what crossed her father's imaginary line.

"Like I said, Cana is a wolf-dog, just a very high concentration of wolf, and he never liked men, not even my father. But he bonded with me, which is why, when I left, he was sent to a wolf-dog rescue in Nevada. He's not supposed to be here and I have no idea why he is." A frown furrowed her brow. "I was there when he was shipped out."

"You need to call the rescue and find out what happened."

"I will," she agreed. "In the morning."

"So, is this how all of our dates are going to end? With some sort of wild animal attack? At least I didn't almost shoot you this time."

He'd intended to put a smile on her face by pointing out the irony of their situation, that this was the second time this had happened, but when she looked at him, there was no humor in her expression. In fact, it was the first time since he'd met her that she actually seemed afraid.

"This isn't a date." Her voice was tight, as if even saying the words distressed her.

She had just stood in front of a wolf that was ready to attack them, without even flinching, but calling this a date had her backing away from him. He'd didn't miss the look of panic in her eyes. It was the same one he'd seen in Buster's, just before he'd run for the woods.

EMMA FELT HER heart drop to her toes. As much as she enjoyed being with Ben, and there wasn't a part of her that didn't relish being near him, this couldn't turn into a relationship. It would take away too much time she needed to give to the sanctuary. Who was she kidding? She was more afraid of getting hurt again. She hadn't forgotten how she felt when her relationship had crumbled because of her job. And she'd watched her father pine for years, missing her mother. She swore she'd never do that again. "Dating" was the first step heading down that forbidden road.

His eyes gleamed with mischief as he shot her a grin that made the dimple in his cheek appear. "I don't know, Emma. I drove you someplace where we had drinks and food. Then I drove you home. That sounds like a date to me."

He was joking, teasing her, but knowing that didn't stop the dread from welling within her. She had to stop this or, at the very least, set some boundaries.

"We didn't arrange that meeting and neither of us paid for the food. That means it was really nothing more than a chance encounter that turned into a game of cards."

Ben took a step toward her, his hands circling her waist and drawing her close. He smiled down at her, brushing back a strand of her hair that caught in the corner of her mouth. "There's nothing wrong with us having a date, you know."

"And there's nothing wrong with us *not* having a date," she countered. Her hands had come to rest against his broad chest and she could feel his heart pounding beneath her fingers, strong and steady. Just like the man, himself. "This doesn't have to be more than it is. Can't we just have fun?"

She looked up at him, hoping he would agree with her. His gaze was dark, unreadable, as if he was trying to figure out a way to answer her. As if he wasn't sure of the answer he wanted to give.

"Yes, we can." His hand slid down her back to cup her rear, pressing her fully against him, and Emma gasped as her own body surged in response. "So long as you promise me one thing."

Emma felt a chill shiver down her spine in spite of the heat Ben had sparked within her.

"We make what this is clear and decide what we each want. That way, either of us can call it quits and no one gets hurt."

"You mean, set some ground rules?"

"I guess that's one way of looking at it."

He sounded unsure, as if he wished he could take his words back but she wasn't about to let him backtrack. It was a brilliant idea.

Chapter Nineteen

THIS IS A *stupid idea.*

Before Ben could even voice the thought, Emma wiggled away from him and ran into the kitchen where Ben heard her rustling around before she returned to the living room with a notepad and a pen. A saucy grin curved her lips.

"Rule number one, no calling this 'dating.'" She gave him a mock shiver as she wrinkled her nose.

Ben tipped his chin down and sighed. "You seriously want to do this now?"

"Ground rules were your idea, McQuaid." She pointed the pen at him. "What else?"

Ben wanted to ask Emma what she had against dating. Why was the one word enough to send her into a panic when nothing else had ruffled her up to this point? And she'd had plenty of reasons to be ruffled. But she wasn't about to confess her fears, or even admit that she had them. It would serve him better to let her follow this rabbit trail, at least for now, until she was willing to let her guard down with him. *If* she was ever willing to fully let it down.

"Rule number two," she went on. "This is only for fun. Anyone can bail at any time, for any reason."

His chest constricted at the thought of Emma turning her back on whatever this was between them. He knew he couldn't do it without feeling the loss and it annoyed him that she could talk about it as casually as if she was discussing the weather.

He hadn't wanted to play along with her little game but her blasé attitude about their relationship, whatever it was, irked him, overruling his common sense. "Rule number three," he ground out. "Until then, there's no one else."

She eyed him cautiously but surprised him by writing it down. "I am safe you know."

"Safe?"

"On the pill, have condoms, tested. Safe."

Ben cringed. This was probably something he should have considered before. Maybe his brother was right. Maybe he wasn't cut out for this casual relationship thing. "I am too," he offered. "My last girlfriend—"

"Good," she said, cutting him off. "Which leads us to rule number four, no other personal questions."

Emma had just backed him into a corner and left him with nothing more than sex in their relationship. Amazing sex, some serious physical attraction he couldn't even begin to deny, but she was taking anything beyond that off the table. The glint of her eyes said she knew it too. She'd gotten her way and his option was to take it, or leave it and walk away.

Ben wasn't about to give up without a fight. It wasn't in his nature to walk away, not from anything, and he never turned his back on someone needing his help, and Emma needed it more than anyone he'd ever met.

"Rule number five, you have to always tell the truth."

She rolled her eyes. "Really? Have I lied to you yet?"

Ben reached for her hand and tugged her toward him, winding his arms around her waist and moving his hands up her spine. He dipped his head, brushing his lips against hers ever-so-slightly and catching her gasp of surprise.

"I wouldn't know, would I?" His gaze remained steady as it flicked down to meet hers. "But I'm going to trust that you'll follow all these rules, the same way I have to."

She gave him a sly smile even though, with her chest pressed against his, he could feel her heart racing. "No problem."

He narrowed his eyes and nipped at her lower lip. "Don't be so sure, Emma."

She slid her hands over his chest and walked him backward, until he felt the couch at the back of his calves. Emma gave him a slight shove, and he dropped onto the cushion. Sliding into his lap, straddling him, gripping his thighs with her own, a wicked smile lit her eyes as she yanked his shirt over his head.

"Oh, I'm sure. I know exactly what I'm capable of."

She pulled her shirt over her head and tossed it aside, leaving the curve of her breasts partially exposed for his view and nearly at eye level.

His hands glided up her sides to cup them and he felt her nipples bead under the thin material of her bra. Ben couldn't help but smile at her body's reaction to his touch. There was an honest vulnerability in it, as if it wanted something completely different from what Emma claimed. As if her body wasn't afraid of letting go, of recognizing the connection that sparked between them at a mere touch.

Reaching behind her, she unclasped her bra and it disappeared with her shirt. Ben didn't waste a moment, leaning forward to take her into his mouth. Emma reached for his shoulders and he wrapped his arms around her back, letting her body arch into him. Desire, white hot and frantic, shot through him, like lightning.

This woman had proven to be his polar opposite yet she seemed to match his every desire. Where he would have backed off, she urged him for more. Where he led with caution, she rushed in headfirst. Where he was hard, she was soft. His hand cupped her breast . . . *oh, so very soft.*

Emma tugged at the button of his jeans unsuccessfully, grunting slightly when it didn't cooperate. He laughed at her impatience. "Do you need some help?"

"What is this? Fort Knox? Some kind of medieval male chastity belt?"

Ben slid his hands under her rear and stood up, effortlessly lifting her with him, and carrying her down the hall toward her room. "Maybe it's just a sign that you shouldn't be in such a rush. Sometimes slow is even better."

"And sometimes it's not." She nipped at his neck before pressing soothing kisses over the flesh.

Every touch of her lips against his neck sent bittersweet yearning through his veins. This was fun, but he couldn't help feeling like something was missing, that there was more, just beyond his reach when it came to Emma. He just wasn't sure how to break through the wall to find the treasure he knew was in her, that she was so desperate to keep hidden.

Letting her down onto her feet, Ben dropped to his knees in front of her, first removing her shoes and socks, then letting his hands slide up her calves. She might be trying to keep this lighthearted, but he was going to show her that he could be more than just *fun*.

EMMA THOUGHT HER legs might buckle beneath her as Ben ran his hands up her thighs. A quiver of heated desire shook her, spreading up from where his palms ran over the rough denim to pool at her core, leaving her quaking as his thumbs brushed over where she burned the hottest. If not for his hands at her hips, she would have dropped into his lap on her bedroom floor.

Ben looked up at her through long eyelashes most women would covet and gave her a sinful smile. "You're about to see how fun going slow can be."

She wasn't sure if it was a threat or a promise but Emma shivered at the husky rasp of his voice, just as his mouth pressed against her bared stomach. One hand slid between her thighs, stroking her over her clothing, as the other unbuttoned her pants. With his lips against her lower belly, nipping and laving away the pain, he slid his hands into the back of her pants and over her butt, pulling her even closer. With nothing to hold her up, nothing to help her balance, she could only lean into him, her hands on his shoulders.

In one sweep of his hands, he pulled her jeans and underwear down her legs, helping her step out of them before shoving them aside. His hand crept up the back of her leg, with aching slowness, his fingers trailing over every sensitive crevice and dip, running them over the curve of her rear and to her hip. She waited for him to stand but Ben hadn't moved from his position in front of her.

"You're so beautiful, Emma."

He brushed his thumb over the curls at the apex of her thighs, finding her aching and ready for him. Even that slight touch made her gasp sharply, unable to stop the flood of pleasure that rushed through her.

"Ben."

His name was barely a breath of sound since she couldn't remember how to inhale. She could barely remember her own name. When his mouth replaced his fingers, her legs did give way but Ben was there to catch her, to lift her to the edge of the bed without changing his position.

His tongue flicked over her once quickly, setting off fireworks in her, igniting every inch of her flesh, then circled her slowly. The groan that slid past her lips was one of pained ecstasy. Ben took his time, touching, tasting, teasing her until she could no longer remain still beneath his onslaught of pleasure. The callouses on his hands were rough against her skin, even as his kisses were devastatingly gentle. His touch was giving but she could feel the tension building in her as he demanded her release.

And she was more than willing to comply as the first tremors washed over her, nearly drowning her in wave after wave of pleasure. But Ben didn't stop. He slid a finger inside of her. Emma bucked against him, unable to control any part of her body as it was his completely, to do with as he chose, as she succumbed to the passion he wrought.

Ben rose finally, a smug, sexy-as-sin smile on his face and his eyes practically gleaming with hunger. He reached one hand down and flipped the button of his jeans effortlessly as she fought to catch her breath, even as it stalled in her chest at the sight of him. Every rock-hard muscle gleamed as they flexed with his movements. Emma was dying to get her hands on him, if she could convince her limbs to move again.

With one quick movement, he stepped out of his jeans, freeing his entire body for her viewing pleasure. Or maybe it was simply more torture because suddenly, she ached. Every part of her body wanted him. But he was moving so damn slowly it was killing her.

BEN COULD SEE the desire in Emma's eyes, in the way her gaze slid over him, and when her tongue snuck out to moisten her pouting lips, he nearly gave himself over to the hunger raging through him like a wild beast, clawing to be released. But he wasn't ready to give her what she wanted; he wanted this to be so much more than just a quick romp before she retreated again into that cave she was trying to hermit herself away in.

He eased himself onto the bed beside her, letting his fingers trail over her skin. Emma sighed in contentment, turning toward him, reaching down to cup him. Ben caught her hand before she could.

"Oh, no, I'm not finished with you yet." Ben dropped his head, tasting the sweetness of her skin as his tongue swirled over one breast before moving to the other.

"I don't know how much more I can take," she whimpered in feeble protest.

Ben laughed against her. "Do you want me to stop?"

"God, no!"

"I told you that I'd prove why slow is better."

She slid her hands over his back to grip his ass and pull him against her, hooking one leg over his hip and cradling him against the heat of her. It took every ounce of his control to hold back the groan of need and stop himself from plunging into her. "If you move any slower, you'll be going backward."

"Maybe we'll try that later." He slid his hand up her thigh and moved away from her, brushing his fingers over her again, grinning as her body bucked beneath him, craving more of his touch. "It's going to be a long night for you, Emma, but I'm pretty sure I can convince you to join me over here on the dark side."

EMMA WOKE TO Ben's body cradling her own in the still darkness before the light of dawn trickled in. His knees were tucked perfectly into the back of hers, with one arm under her head and the other draped over her. She was completely enveloped by him, as if he'd been afraid to let her go, even in sleep.

They'd made love last night.

She wished she could call it sex, wished she could relegate it to the recesses of even friendly sex. But it was, without a doubt, making love. At least it had been for her.

She needed to fix this, needed to somehow repair the wall he'd torn down around her heart last night. What she needed was to walk away. But as much as her mind warned her it was the only logical option, she couldn't convince herself to actually *do it*. There mere idea made her heart feel like it was being torn from her. Because she liked him. She really, *really* liked him.

Damn it!

Ben was sweet and kind, gentle and patient. Both with her and the animals. The man had already tried to protect her from a mountain lion and a wolf, had spent an afternoon cleaning up shitty pens for her, and the fire he ignited in her was unparalleled. What more could she possibly ask for?

But Ben wasn't lacking. She was. He deserved more, better than what she could offer him.

Even now, knowing that this was wrong for her with all of the craziness she was facing, knowing that getting involved with Ben would only hurt him in the long run, she found herself scooting backward into his embrace. She couldn't give in to it—this fantasy of a white picket fence and a man who could understand her at her innermost level—but she wanted to and was finding it harder to remember why it couldn't be hers.

Emma could have one or the other, but even her father, as good a husband as he'd tried to be, hadn't been able to manage both. This life of dangerous beasts and long nights, of emergencies and travel, had chased her mother away and Emma had seen the toll it had taken on her father. He hadn't wanted to, but her mother had made him choose between his two passions. Ultimately, she knew from experience how this would end, from the start. Emma would make the same choice her father had. She had to keep the sanctuary running because failing couldn't be an option either. She had to believe that she and her father had made the right decisions.

No one wants to love someone they might have to bury in pieces.

Ben's lips brushed over her bare shoulder, his breath warm over her skin as he swept her hair back from her face. Goose bumps chased one another over her skin. "Penny for your thoughts."

"Hmm, wouldn't that be considered a personal question?" She leaned her head to one side, giving his mouth better access to her skin, savoring his kiss.

She felt his shrug against her back. "More of a statement than a question." His hand moved to cup her breast, his thumb brushing over the nipple that immediately pebbled in response.

She turned in his arms to face him, feeling his erection pressing against her, sending a surge of yearning through her yet again. "I was thinking about last night," she lied. "I'm almost convinced that you were right about slow being better."

He gave her a satisfied smirk. "I told you—"

"But not quite," she finished, pushing the thoughts of her parents, her past and the weight of her responsibilities aside. "I do believe that another experiment might be in order. I may need a little more convincing."

"I'd love to, but I have to get to the station."

"What if I call in a fire?"

He laughed quietly. "Then you'd end up with an engine, at least four firemen, an ambulance and probably a police car or two. Not sure that's what you had in mind."

"Probably not," she agreed, wrapping her leg around his hip.

Ben growled and pressed himself against her. "You're making this really hard."

"That's exactly my intention." She brushed her lips against his. As long as she could keep this on a physical plane, she could pretend to ignore the emotional attachment she was feeling toward Ben. She had to, because he was the only thing keeping her grounded and sane right now.

Chapter Twenty

BEN WATCHED AS Emma moved around the kitchen, preparing several bowls of food for various animals. She moved with a quiet grace, the confidence of a woman who knew exactly what she was doing and that she did it well. They didn't speak but she cast him a curious glance every few minutes, as if she was waiting for him to pry, to try to force himself beyond what she was comfortable with, to break one of her "ground rules."

Rising from her table, he poured himself a cup of coffee and glanced at hers. "You want more?"

"Not just yet. I'll get it when I come back inside after feeding."

"You want me to fix you breakfast before I go? I make a mean omelet."

She paused, putting a hand on one hip and cocking it to the side. "You're going to make *me* breakfast in my own house?"

"Sure." His gaze slid over her curves, kept trim he suspected because she was too distracted to even eat most days. "You're so busy taking care of animals, I get the feeling you haven't had someone to take care of you in a long time."

She narrowed her eyes at him suspiciously. "I don't need anyone to take care of me," she muttered, grabbing for the food bowls and hitting the back door open with her hip.

"I didn't say you needed someone to do it. I said I wanted to do it."

She stopped, halfway across the driveway, heading toward the animal compound. "Let's get something straight," she began.

The theme song for *Cops* sounded from his back pocket, breaking her train of thought. "Hang on, it's Andrew." He swiped a finger across the screen but didn't even get a chance to answer.

"Get your ass back to Mom and Dad's and bring that woman with you. She better be able to answer a few questions or there's a good chance she's going to find herself in a big mess today."

"What now?"

"I've got two dead calves here and looks like some wild animal did it."

Ben glanced at Emma, careful not to say anything that might worry her. "What makes you think that?"

"They're pretty torn apart, but not like usual when it's coyotes or dogs," he added before Ben could even suggest it. "Whatever this was, it was big."

"How recent?" Buster had been caught days ago and hadn't left his cage. The entire compound had echoed with his complaining since, but that wolf had been out and they had no idea how long before they'd arrived to find him.

"Twelve hours, maybe a little more."

"I'm supposed to be at the station this morning. Let me call them and we'll be right over."

"We're in the south pasture, about three hundred yards from the water hole."

Ben thanked his brother and hung up, quickly texting his captain to explain why he'd be late this morning.

Emma used the radio to call Monique to come relieve her for the feedings and turned back toward the house. "What are you doing?" he asked.

"We've got trouble, right?"

"Are you asking or telling me?" Ben didn't like the resignation he saw in her face.

Emma shook her head. "Telling. Because with me, it's always trouble. Haven't you discovered that yet?"

EMMA COULD EASILY read the concern in Ben's eyes. He watched her warily, driving through the pasture to where his brother and parents waited. She felt the dread coil in her stomach, settling in. Damn it, he was still trying to protect her and refused to say where they were going or what to expect, only that Andrew wanted her input. But she knew enough to decipher the issue from what he wasn't saying. She'd been dealing with this for weeks now.

They suspected one of her animals of something. There was no other reason to need her presence, or her expertise, unless there was another animal on the loose or, worse, damages from one. Either way, it likely meant even more trouble for the sanctuary, whether or not she was to blame.

Ben parked the truck near a tree and they walked the short distance to a small watering hole where she could see the form of what appeared to be at least two carcasses. She really couldn't tell without inspecting them closer because the body parts were strewn at least fifteen feet over the field, with blood still seeping into the grass at the water's edge. Flies buzzed, lazily moving from one area to the next, sluggish in the morning chill but not willing to forgo the feast. The metallic smell of blood hit her as they drew closer and the dread she'd felt earlier turned to deep-seated fear as she took in the grim faces at the scene of the carnage.

"What happened?" She should have known Ben would be the one to break the silence, facing things head on.

"I don't know," his father answered. "We came out to dump the hay this morning and saw the buzzards." He looked around him, shaking his head. "I've never seen anything like this before. It looks like they were butchered."

Emma moved closer, tugging latex gloves from her pocket and squatting to inspect the gore surrounding her. The bones were, in fact, scattered but, from the size and number of them, she could confirm it was at least two calves. Several of them had teeth marks ground into the surface. A few of the smaller ones were splintered where they'd been chewed on by animals attracted by the smell of blood. Most of the entrails were missing.

"Ms. Jordan?" Andrew began.

She looked back at him over her shoulder. "Why all the formality, Andrew? You didn't mind calling me Emma when I was taking your money."

"Because this is a formal investigation that may result in a claim against the sanctuary."

"Andrew," his mother scolded. "Emma, I'm sorry for my son being rude. He's just trying to do his job."

Emma immediately took a liking to Ben's mother. She seemed friendly, in spite of the fact that there appeared to be plenty of evidence that Emma was responsible for the loss of two of their calves. Not exactly the best circumstances to meet his parents.

Andrew pressed on, ignoring his mother. "Have you had any other animals loose in the past few days?"

"You don't have to say anything," Ben said, jumping to her defense.

She loved that he was so ready to stand up for her, even taking on his own family in the process, knowing there was a possibility that Cana caused this.

"It's fine if I do." She stood up and waved over the small group of people she knew had already judged her guilty. "Because this wasn't one of my animals."

"You think it's another mountain lion that's coming down into the area?"

"No. You see this?" Emma pointed at what was left of one of the calves' head and neck, torn from the rest of the body.

"What exactly am I looking at?" Andrew sounded confused so Emma squatted down and pointed directly under the jaw of the animal.

"Here. An animal couldn't sever a head this cleanly. This was a knife. This calf's jugular was cut and he bled out, which attracted scavengers. I'm guessing from the teeth marks, and the blood that I saw on Cana, that he was here, but he didn't kill these calves. They were already dead."

"Why would someone sneak onto my property, all the way out here, to kill a couple of calves and leave them?" It wasn't difficult to hear the dubiousness in Ben's father's tone.

Emma looked at each one of the McQuaids in turn, wondering if any of them would believe the truth. As it turned out, she didn't have to voice her suspicions. Ben did it for her.

"Because someone is trying to sabotage Emma and get her shut down."

BEN CALLED ANGIE and explained the details, hoping she'd take pity on him and cover his shift, even though she just ended one of her own. He was going to owe her for it but he didn't want to leave Emma alone with Andrew when they returned to the sanctuary to inspect Cana. If Andrew found anything suspicious, Ben doubted anything would stop him from closing her down immediately.

"I have to warn you," Emma began, "Cana isn't fond

of men and I'm not sure why he's even here." She explained how Cana had been sent to the rescue.

Andrew cocked his head at her. "Can you tell whether it's blood on him or not?"

"Would you trust me to tell you the truth?" Andrew's brows lifted, daring her to test him. She met his gaze with a challenging one of her own. "I can tell whether it's blood, but I can't tell what kind without running some testing. I doubt he'll let me get close enough to even try to get a sample if you're with me."

"So, either way, you're telling me I just have to trust you."

Emma's hands hit her hips and Ben could see the frustration building in her, tension bunching her shoulders, and he longed to massage them, to do something to help. He also knew it was the last thing she'd want from him right now.

"Well, unless you're qualified to run the blood test yourself and want to chance being attacked by a dog that is ninety percent wolf just to clip some hair from him, then yes, you'll have to trust me. Think you can manage to do that?"

The muscle in Andrew's jaw pulsed and Ben knew he was considering his options. It wasn't in his nature to trust anyone quickly. That was Ben's MO and what usually got him into these kinds of messes.

"You can't sedate him so we can go in?"

She dropped her chin, somehow managing to look down at him, in spite of the fact that Andrew was at least a foot taller than she was. "You seriously want me to give an animal drugs, not knowing his physical well-being or his tolerance, rather than trust me to do my job?"

"Give me a break. We don't run blood work on animals in the wild before we dart them. Don't act like it'll kill him to do it."

"Just because you're willing to take that risk, doesn't mean I am. If that's the route you're going to insist on—which I find ridiculous, by the way—I'm going to have to insist that I get in touch with the rescue to find out his history first."

"I could just call in Animal Control and let them confiscate him."

"You could," she agreed. "But then you'd have to wait for your tests because I'd call every rescue in the area to pick him up and you'd be back at square one."

"I don't have time for that."

Emma folded her arms over her chest and stared at Andrew defiantly. Ben had a hard time not grinning as she stood her ground against a man who had at least one hundred pounds and eight inches on her.

"You think this is all I have to do today?"

She shrugged. "Probably not, but that isn't my problem."

"It's about to be. I could just shut you down pending my investigation."

"Go ahead and how will you explain that to the press? Animals left to die in cages with no one to take care of them, until another rescue steps in. Do you have time to handle that mess, or the paperwork and bad press? Because I promise you, there *will* be bad press. I'll make sure of it."

Andrew looked to Ben for assistance, throwing up a hand. "Will you explain to her—"

"I'm not an idiot," she interrupted. "I understand the situation, as well as the gravity of it. However, you have nothing but circumstantial evidence that I am housing the animal that actually attacked those calves. You know, as well as I do, that even if it was Cana, he didn't kill them, he just . . . chewed on them."

Andrew looked from Emma back to Ben, shooting him a glare that clearly warned him to deal with her, to convince her to go along with Andrew's demands. Ben gave his brother an almost imperceptible shake of his head. If he thought Ben could convince Emma of anything, he didn't know her at all.

Andrew let loose a growl of frustration. "Fine, you go. Do your damn test and call me with the results. But, if I think for one second that you're lying, I'll shut you down."

Emma smiled sweetly. "I have no doubt you'll be leading the town charge with a pitchfork in one hand and a torch in the other."

Ben snorted and Andrew glared at him, storming back to his patrol car. "I expect a call."

"As soon as I have any answers but, by all means, Officer McQuaid, feel free to hold your breath," she yelled back.

EMMA WATCHED AS Cana romped playfully in the enclosure, coming back to her to flop into her lap, almost making her forget he was far more wolf than he was dog. He'd always held a special place in her heart, much like Buster, and it had physically pained her to send him to the rescue but she hadn't been able to take him with her when she'd left for her job at the park and he couldn't stay here with her father where he endangered both Cana and the staff.

Lindsay returned her call quickly, relieved to hear recent news of Cana, but the information she imparted wasn't what Emma had been prepared to hear. Cana had been brought back, a year ago, apparently at her father's request.

Emma had no clue where Cana had been for the last year because she'd been to the sanctuary several times to visit and had never seen him. Why hadn't her father told her he'd brought him back? He'd known how much the animal meant to Emma.

Her questions only seemed to lead to more, making her mind race and her suspicions take root even deeper. Emma rubbed her hands in the salt-and-pepper–colored fur at his shoulder as he tried to lick at the side of her hand, a sign of affection and submissiveness, when her fingers felt a ridge of marred flesh under the skin. Parting the hair carefully, she could see what looked like a deep cut that had healed over, leaving a thick scar. She didn't remember him having that when he was last with her but it was possible he'd gotten hurt at the rescue facility.

Or worse, after his return here. Her mind filled in the logical answer she didn't want to consider.

Emma ran her hands over Cana examining him for more wounds while he yipped in delight at what he saw as bonding. Relaxing into her touch, Cana rolled to his side where she found several more thick scars, as well as one recent open wound near his hind end that was going to require a few stitches. It wasn't an emergency, but she needed to get it cleaned and taken care of.

Since she was going to have to sedate Cana after all, Emma figured she might as well have Andrew there in case he needed anything else for his investigation. Not that it would actually matter much now. She'd already tested the blood that had matted much of the fur on his chest. As they'd suspected, it was bovine and, most likely, from the calves. But, allowing the cop to be there might earn her at least a little sympathy, although she doubted Andrew was much for sympathy.

Cana rolled onto his back, stretching his legs into the air and whining playfully for attention. She rubbed his chest and felt him tense, just before he jumped to his feet, growling at something beyond her sight. The hair on his neck stood straight up and he backed, moving so that a large boulder provided him a place to hide, snarling and snapping. Emma searched around but couldn't see anything.

"Cana, stop. Down."

His eyes barely flicked in her direction as he focused on something only he could see. Emma's heart sped up. She scanned the area he watched closely. He was obviously afraid of something but she had no idea what might have triggered his fear since she saw nothing. Even if there was something outside the enclosure, it couldn't get inside. She was in a precarious position.

If she couldn't get Cana to mind her commands, she was at risk of being attacked. She needed to calm him, for both of their safety. If she couldn't, there was a high probability that he might turn on her.

"Cana, down," she repeated. This time, his yellow gaze met hers and he let his head lower as he edged closer to her and moved his body behind hers. It was a sign of submission as well as one that solidified the fact that he believed she was his pack leader. "Down."

Cana sat, keeping his shoulder pressed against her knee, growling quietly at whatever had spooked him. She would allow him to growl because his stance made it clear she was no longer in jeopardy from him but she strained to see anything that might have him riled. Emma squinted at the foliage that dotted the landscape surrounding the enclosure. She felt the hair on the back of her neck rise as goose bumps broke out over her arms. Near a pine tree she could just make out an odd shadow that seemed slightly out of place, moving when others didn't. Taking a step closer, Cana moved with her. His deep growl rumbled louder but he stayed in step with her, offering protection to his female as wolves were prone to do.

The shadow shifted slightly, despite the fact that there was no other movement, and Emma knew something—or someone—was out there.

"Hey, are you okay?" Ben's voice surprised both of them and Cana leapt to one side with a yip, shocked to find a "threat" coming at him from a different direction. He bared his teeth at Ben.

Emma's focus had been torn from the shadowed area in the trees and when she looked back, whatever she'd seen was gone. She glanced at Ben and back to the trees, trying to find where the shadow had been.

"What? Oh, Cana, down." The wolf immediately settled, sitting at her feet, the hair falling back into place, and stopped growling. She looked back at the trees, narrowing her eyes. "There was something out there."

Ben followed her gaze. "Where?"

"There." She pointed.

He looked back at her but instead of doubt, she could see concern. He ran to the area she pointed out, without a thought to what, or who, might be out there or the danger he could be running into.

"Ben!"

He held up a hand to silence her but, instinctively, she knew whatever had been there was now gone.

And something *had* been there.

After several minutes, Ben returned to the enclosure, slightly out of breath. "We need to call Andrew."

"I need to call him anyway, but why?" She moved toward him and Cana followed.

"I think whoever is trying to sabotage you was watching you." He looked down at the wolf warily. "Or him."

Emma lay a hand on Cana's back and he jumped slightly, even as he leaned forward toward the fence, cautiously trying to sniff at Ben.

"Ben, don't move. Don't look him in the eye, but don't move, okay?"

"Why?"

Her gaze flicked to his face for a quick glance before dropping back to watch the wolf. "Because you're the first man I've ever seen him interested in knowing and we're going to take full advantage of this moment."

"But we need to call Andrew, now. Before whoever that was gets too far."

"This is more important."

Emma realized that sentiment encompassed exactly how she felt about this sanctuary and the animals it housed. It was the same way her father had felt about it. She would protect these animals, do what was best for them, even if it meant putting herself in danger, which was exactly what it had done.

Chapter Twenty-One

EMMA LEANED AGAINST the bricked wall of the kennel room, waiting for Cana to wake from his sedation. She'd felt sick to her stomach at what she'd found on the poor wolf but couldn't help wanting to rejoice in the progress he'd made today. He had allowed Ben to pet him, had actively sought out Ben's touch and licked his hand. It was a first, as far as she was aware, for the animal to connect with any man.

"He's going to be okay?" Ben's quiet voice drew her from her thoughts.

"Physically." She looked back at the doorway where he waited. "Why would anyone be so cruel?" The images of the crudely healed puncture wounds that had scarred Cana's skin rose up in her mind again. "Lindsay, the woman who runs the rescue, said he'd never left the property until my dad requested him back. Why would he bring him here? He couldn't control him."

"You don't really believe your father did this to him?"

She shook her head. "No. Dad would never harm an animal." She looked back at the wolf-dog. "If he'd known about it, he'd have been more likely to hurt the person doing it. But he did some things over the past year that I didn't understand. Like canceling all of his educational programs. We'd always planned on building that aspect of the facility together." She shook her head, trying to figure out the motives of the man she'd thought she understood and was now finding out she might not have known as well as she thought she did. Emma glanced back at Ben. "Thank you for your help with him today. That was a huge step, especially if he was abused the way it appears."

"Emma, I'm happy to help you. All you need to do is ask."

His voice was husky and she knew he wasn't just talking about Cana now, or the sanctuary. There was far more to Ben's offer than simply protection from someone targeting her, or her ranch. His words held a note of a future beyond this moment, or the next.

And she wanted to take him up on it.

Emma closed the distance between them, her hands landing on his stomach as she rose on her toes to kiss him. This wasn't the same as their previous kisses, this one was tentative, seeking, asking for so much more than just sex, more than she dared voice.

Ben answered. His large hands cupped her face as his mouth met hers, making a promise neither dared speak. A promise of a deeper relationship, of friendship and understanding and intimacy. Even as it made her stomach twist in knots of fear, Emma felt the wall around her heart splinter, letting the barrier fall away as she opened herself to Ben completely. As if feeling the change in her, Ben pulled back.

"Emma?"

She didn't want to think about how she was breaking her own rules, crossing the boundaries she'd set. She didn't want to think about the risk she was taking, or putting him in. Emma only knew she couldn't lie any longer, trying to convince herself that she didn't feel something more than a casual attraction for this man. She couldn't pretend that they were just having fun, that this was nothing more than a fling. This was so much more than that, she wanted so much more than that from him.

Ben tipped her face up, looking into her eyes where she knew she'd bared her soul for him, as he tried to ascertain the desire she hadn't realized was written on her heart.

"Ben, I'm asking."

Mouths fused, passions ignited and walls crashed to the ground.

BEN WASN'T SURE he was hearing her correctly, but looking into the depths of Emma's eyes clarified everything. She needed him. Not just his assistance with the animals or with the trouble at the sanctuary, not just for some fun to help her blow off steam, she needed him emotionally.

She was afraid, he could see it in her tear-filled eyes. She had the same look he'd seen in the wolf's as it took the first wary steps toward him this morning, not yet sure but unable to hold back any longer. He'd earned Emma's trust the same way he had the wolf's—by remaining steady.

"I told you. I will be whatever you need me to be for you."

"You have no idea what you're even promising." She shook her head and a tear slid down her cheek.

Ben brushed his thumb over her cheek, stopping it. "Yes, I do." Her eyes pleaded with him to walk away, to be the one to stop this but he couldn't understand why. "Emma, what has you so afraid? What possible harm could come from you letting someone in?"

"You have no idea the cost this job has demanded. My parents' marriage, my past relationships, now my dad."

"Your dad had a stroke. It had nothing to do with the sanctuary."

She gave him a sad, bitter laugh. "You don't think trying to manage this place could cause one?"

Ben wasn't about to argue with her. Maybe the stress of running the sanctuary *had* been at the root of his stroke. But there was just as much likelihood it had been something else. Conrad hadn't exactly been known for his healthy living habits. He'd enjoyed his Scotch and his cigars too much. But he got the feeling the sanctuary wasn't the root of the sudden change in her.

He brushed her hair back from where it had fallen over her face. "Then why are you here? Why take on this headache?"

Fierce pride flashed in her eyes. "Because I thought it was what Dad wanted, for us to do it together. Now I come back to find out he wanted someone else to run it? That he didn't think I could do it alone, and there is someone trying to shut me down. It's just too much."

Warning bells sounded in him at her admission. Why would her father choose to have Jake run this place with her? Between the mysterious return of Cana, the articles and now the slaughter of the calves, this was taking a dangerous turn, not that she would ever walk away. Unless that was exactly what she was telling him—that she was choosing to leave.

"And what about what you, Emma?" Ben ran his thumb over her cheekbone. "What do you want? This is your opportunity to live your own life, your way."

She pulled back, putting distance between them. "I know that."

He didn't push but he could see the lie in her, even if she didn't yet realize it. "What does this have to do with letting someone close to you?"

"My life isn't exactly conducive to a serious relationship."

"Why not? We've done fine so far."

"I . . ." Emma looked confused, like she'd never really had to explain her reservations before. "I've tried. It just . . . doesn't work. I'm on call all hours, ready to leave at a moment's notice and my needs are usually the last to be met. You've seen how dangerous my job can be, what sort of caution is needed at all times."

Ben nodded. "So, a lot like being a fireman."

"What? No."

He tugged Emma forward so that she slid back into his arms and he wound them around her. "Would you ask me to give up firefighting?"

She looked up at him, confused. "No. It's your job."

"And what I love to do. It's part of who I am." Ben brushed his thumb over her jaw. "The way this place is with you. Maybe you've dated guys in the past who didn't get it, but I do, Emma."

"It's just that my job, this life, has to take priority over everything."

"Relax. I understand." He smiled down at her. "I can't change the decisions other people made in the past, but don't let their mistakes keep you from finding your future."

He could see the apprehension in her eyes. "I can't help it." Her hands splayed over his chest but she didn't move away from his embrace. "I don't want anyone to get hurt again, not because of me."

Ben tucked her head under his chin, holding her while he willed her to finally release the death grip she had on her fears. "It's okay, Emma. I'll help you. We'll figure this out together."

BEN MET HIS brother at the front door of Emma's house, ignoring Andrew's cagey grin. "Let me guess. She's got some sort of fire emergency?"

"Shut up." He opened the door wider for his brother to come in.

"Does she have a Dalmatian she needs your help with? Another kitten in a tree? Or did she just want to add a hose monkey to the sanctuary animals?"

"Shut up," Emma repeated as she entered the living room.

Ben grinned slightly at the shocked look on Andrew's face. "I'd have thought you'd be a little more appreciative for someone giving you a real case for a change. Or would you rather chill down at the doughnut shop like you usually do."

"Says the guy with the second most famous job using a pole."

"Will the two of you stop?" Emma moved to stand between them, her back braced against Ben's chest, and he immediately felt his pulse quicken at her body pressed against his. "We have enough here to deal with, without the two of you bickering like bullies on the playground."

She glared at Ben over her shoulder. "Why don't you get your brother some coffee and bring him—"

"A doughnut?" Ben offered.

She shoved against his chest and threw her hands into the air. "Just take him into the kitchen while I go get the pictures."

Ben watched her head down the hall to the room that had once been her father's office, now hers.

"Oh, you've got it bad." Andrew shook his head. "Told ya this would happen."

Ben glared at him. "She needs our help."

"What you're really saying is that she's not putting out now and you're so hung up on her that you're hoping helping her will help *you*."

"No, what I'm saying is that if you don't shut the fuck up, I'm going to kick your ass."

"Yeah? Let's see you try it. Why do you always pick the projects? Laura said she needed your help and that ended up with her cuffed in the back of my car and spending several nights in jail after cleaning out your apartment, remember?"

"Don't be a dick."

"I'm a dick? This may not be what you want to hear but you have a type, Ben. We can all pick her out from a mile away. We just look for the woman who's in the most trouble. You're a typical fireman, Ben. You can't stand not to be the hero."

"Shut up, Andrew." Ben felt the rage boiling up from deep within. Emma wasn't some kind of a project to him and he certainly wasn't attracted to her because he wanted to save her.

Andrew laughed. "Dude, can you even name one woman you've ever dated that didn't need your help with something? Face it, you go for the damsel in distress."

"I may be a damsel in distress, officer, but unless I'm mistaken, you're the one needing *my* help." Emma shoved the digital photos she'd taken of Cana's wounds as well as the blood on his chest. "Take the pictures and get out. Why don't you figure out a way to solve this one on your own? Don't come back until you've got a warrant."

"Excuse me?" Andrew took a step back, catching the pictures as they started to feather to the floor. "Emma, I didn't mean—"

"I don't really care what you meant. I've been more than cooperative with you but you are just acting like a bully with a badge. This is my property and—"

Ben reached for her shoulder. "Emma, you need him. He's here to help, even if he doesn't have the most winsome bedside manner."

Andrew glared at him but at least he knew when to keep his mouth shut. Ben turned back to his brother. "Remember those tire tracks I told you about? There were more near the back of the property yesterday and someone was watching Emma while she was with Cana."

Andrew glanced at Emma for confirmation. "You're sure?"

"He left a calling card. The choke collar he'd been using on Cana." She tapped the photo of the disgusting item that had been left behind the pine tree yesterday where she'd seen the shadow. She could only assume that collar was what had caused several of the punctures around his neck. She couldn't even begin to speculate what else had been used on Cana. "I think someone was coming to try to steal him back."

"Steal him back?" Ben hadn't filled Andrew in on this part yet and could see the confusion in his brother's face.

"According to Lindsay at Wild Dogs Rescue, where Cana was supposed to be, he was brought back at my father's request about twelve months ago. However, I've been here several times over the past year and I've never seen him."

"And you don't think your father just forget to mention it?"

"I doubt it. He knew I was one of the only people Cana would respond to. He would have wanted my help. He never mentioned Cana after he was transferred to Nevada."

"What about someone else?"

Emma shrugged her shoulders. "You've met everyone who stayed after my father died. Jake was the only one who had an issue with me personally but he would have wanted Cana released, not hidden for a year."

"Are you sure he didn't bring him back and turn him loose? Because this would seem to be a perfect way to make this happen." Andrew tugged a newspaper from his pocket and opened it for them to see the headline:

A Big Bad Wolf Loose in Hidden Falls

SON OF A bitch!

Emma stared at the headline wondering how this reporter kept finding out their information. She was tired of feeling like she was hiding.

"You think this reporter was on the property yesterday?" Ben asked.

"It's definitely possible." Andrew looked at her pointedly. "You still haven't changed the code for the front gate. Anyone could get in if they tried just a little."

"But why me? And why would a reporter spray-paint my front gate? Or plant a bobcat kitten in a tree?"

None of this made sense. How would a reporter have gotten his hands on Cana? Lindsey had said her father requested his return and that someone from the sanctuary staff had picked him up, although she couldn't remember who. Emma had her suspicions that Jake was behind this but there were just as many factors that pointed elsewhere and nothing concrete that directed Andrew to view him as a suspect.

Andrew shrugged and headed for the porch. "I have to get back to the station but I think this is our best lead right now. Whatever the reason, whoever this is, he's getting more ballsy. It's escalating and, the fact is, I don't have the manpower to watch the entire ranch. Or the nearby ranches either."

Ben slid a hand to her shoulder and, for a change, she soaked up the strength he offered. He was willing to share her burden, regardless of the danger, without asking her to give up a career that was as much a part of Emma as her red hair or her temper.

"So, what should we do?" Andrew spun to look at him. Ben saw his raised brow but appreciated that he didn't comment on Ben's collective term.

"I'd like Emma to stay at the ranch with us. We know our place is safe and the twins will help keep an eye on her there."

"No." She didn't even care to hear his reasons. They honestly didn't even matter to her. There was no way she was leaving her home. Or leaving her animals to fend for themselves with some crazy person on the loose. Someone had abused Cana. She wasn't going to leave him unprotected, to be taken by that person again.

"Emma," Ben protested. "I know it's—"

"No, this is what we talked about. These animals need someone here around the clock. I can't leave them. They come first." She followed Andrew down the porch steps toward his car. "Your parents' place isn't any safer than it is here. They've had two calves killed. I'll keep Cana with me at the house when I'm not working."

"I have some vacation time coming. I'll stay here with you," Ben insisted.

She should have realized he'd offer. It would have actually been out of character for him not to but she couldn't let him risk his position at the fire department. What if this lasted longer than a few days, or a week? It had already been a month. She couldn't let him put his life on hold, and she wouldn't let him put himself in danger.

"I appreciate that, I really do, but it's fine. Cana will protect me if anyone comes around and I can call you," she said, pointedly looking at Andrew. Ben frowned and she hated the uncertainty that flickered in his eyes. Letting him stay would only put her heart more at risk for falling for him.

"He was hiding behind you when I arrived," Ben pointed out. "I'm not sure how much *protection* that will give you."

"We'll be fine. Really," she assured them both. "I'll call the paper. Maybe if I offer to do an interview, or invite a group to come for a tour, they'll see there is nothing here threatening the town, and its livestock."

"No!"

"That's a great idea!"

Ben glared at his brother when they answered in unison. Emma knew Ben wouldn't like the idea but it would be a great way for people to see that there was nothing at the sanctuary for them to be afraid of. She might not be ready to open it back to the public yet but it would also prove she was just as able to run the place, perhaps even more qualified, as her father. It was also a way to lure this anonymous reporter into their midst and put a face to the ass writing these hyped-up stories.

"Emma, if this reporter is the one after you, the last thing you need to do is to invite him in."

Andrew jammed his hands into his pockets. "Or maybe it's the best way to lull someone into thinking they have you fooled, that they are completely safe."

Ben ate up the distance between him and his brother with quick strides. The pair stood only inches apart but Ben looked down at Andrew, taller by several inches. "He *is* safe. You have no clue who this person is and yet you want Emma to roll out the red carpet. Have you forgotten that this person already mutilated two calves? Who knows what his next move is?"

Andrew shot his brother a warning look and Ben could read the dare. It wouldn't be the first time they'd come to blows. "I haven't forgotten anything. But it's not like we'd leave her here alone." He shoved his brother to one side. "If you have a program, or a tour, or whatever, you need help right?"

"It depends on the size of the group but, usually, yes."

"You set it up and the two of us can come act as your assistants."

"What do you know about wild animals?" Ben scoffed.

"I know as much as you do. Plus I know how to shoot one if need be." He quickly glanced at Emma. "Not that I'd have to. I'm just saying that we can be here to protect you."

Emma looked at Ben. It was clear he didn't want her to do this. Worry colored his eyes and she could easily see the tension bunching his muscles. The side of his jaw twitched as his mouth pinched into a thin line. She bit the corner of her lip and looked back toward the enclosure where the animals were starting to make noise, reminding her that mealtime was nearing.

"What day are you off, Ben?" She shouldn't put him in this position to feel responsible for her, shouldn't give her heart any more opportunities to fall for this man.

He threw his hands into the air and turned in a circle, talking to no one in particular. "This is absurd. Do you really think no one will recognize us?" Ben shoved his hand into Andrew's shoulder. "This is a small town, you jackass. Everyone here has grown up with us, they know our family. You're going to put her in even more danger."

"So, we'll just say we both volunteer here a few days a week. We do it for the animals." Andrew gave him a smirk. "It wouldn't exactly be untrue, unless *you* volunteered for other reasons."

Before Emma realized what was happening, Ben had drawn back his fist and knocked his brother to the ground.

Andrew pushed himself up on one elbow and held his jaw, moving it from side to side. "Are you fucking kidding me?" He drew himself up onto one knee, preparing to stand. "I'm on duty, you son of a bitch. I could arrest you."

"Go ahead." Ben sucked in a shaky breath as he tried to calm himself. Emma had never seen him so angry. "I won't let you do this, Emma. Ignore whatever this prick says. He just wants his own headlines since he can't seem to get them any other way."

Andrew laughed bitterly. "Oh, Ben, there you go again. Getting yourself all worked up for a woman who isn't emotionally available." He pressed the back of his hand against the corner of his mouth, dabbing at the blood Ben had drawn. "Have you told Emma about your tendency to look for women in trouble? How you so desperately want to be a hero?" Andrew shot her a pained glance. "It's sad really."

"Shut up, Andrew."

"Or how I had to arrest your last fiancée for selling half of your apartment and stealing your car?"

"Last fiancée?" Emma's eyes widened as her gaze swung toward Ben. "How many . . ."

"Oh, there have been a few over the years." Andrew laughed sadistically as he rose, only to be knocked back to the ground when Ben tackled him.

Emma wasn't sure what was happening, or why the

pair were even fighting, but she couldn't just let them go at it like two kids in a playground fight. However, she wasn't about to get in between two brothers any more than she was about to get into the middle of a dogfight. She looked around from something—anything—that might distract them. She ran down the stairs and jerked the hose from the flowerbed, twisting the spigot and turning the water onto the men wrestling in front of her house. They jumped apart as she'd hoped they would, sputtering, trying to block the water from their faces with their hands raised.

"Knock it off, both of you!" The two men glared at one another, looking like they were sizing each other up for round two. "You," she said, pointing at Andrew. "Go. I'll call you after I talk to the newspaper."

Andrew nodded as he bent over and collected the pictures that had scattered over the porch stairs when he fell. As he headed toward his patrol car, he muttered something colorful about where Ben could put a hose. Ben started to go after him again but Emma reached for his arm, pressing her hand into the middle of his back to direct him toward the house.

"Inside, now."

He shot another glare at his brother as he climbed up to her porch. "Don't use her to prove to this town you can get your shit together, Andrew."

"Maybe you should take your own advice, big brother."

Andrew slammed the car door shut and headed

down the driveway without a backward glance. But Emma knew the damage was already done. Andrew had accomplished exactly what he'd intended. She now had her doubts about Ben. In addition to those she already had about herself.

Chapter Twenty-Two

_____

EMMA FOUND BEN in the guest bathroom, where he was using a hand towel to wipe the dirt from his face. There were three scratches on his cheek and several running the length of his bicep but they weren't deep. She leaned against the doorframe.

"So, you want to tell me what that was about?"

"This is a bad idea. It's too dangerous. This person has gone from spray-painting to slaughtering animals. It's insane that you want to invite trouble right in your front door."

Emma arched a brow. "Insane?"

He dropped his hands to the counter and bowed his head forward for a moment before turning to pin her with a pointed look. "Yes, Emma, insane. As in you're deliberately putting yourself in harm's way. Rational people avoid that."

She cocked her head to one side. "Um, didn't we just have this conversation? You know, the one where I told you how my job and relationships don't mix well because it's dangerous. And," she tapped a finger against her cheek, staring up at the ceiling, "weren't you the same guy who told me we'd figure it out?"

"That was about working with dangerous animals, not some crazy guy out to get you."

"Protecting *my* sanctuary from some guy trying to get it shut down is part of my job. Safeguarding this place and the animals housed here is my job. This *is* my job, Ben. This," she said, circling her hand in front of him, "is why I don't date and do relationships."

"I'm trying to protect *you*, Emma. Not some animals, not some land. You."

She took a deep breath and looked up at him. His eyes begged her to understand, to agree with him, but she didn't. She laid her hand against his cheek, feeling the stubble on his jaw, rough but seductively so.

"Ben, I've never asked you to protect me and I'm not asking for your permission. I am a grown-ass woman and this is my business to protect."

Maybe Andrew was right, even if he was acting like a dick about it. Ben wanted to save her from her troubles. He did. But the fact was, Emma didn't want to be rescued. She wanted someone to believe she could be her own savior. She'd thought Ben understood that but, apparently, he was no different than anyone else in this town. Emma knew what she had to do, had known this was a bad idea from the start, but it didn't break her heart any less to utter the words.

"You should go."

BEN COULD FEEL the sweat trickling over his skin as the late afternoon sun bore down on them and they tried to turn the grass fire back toward the pond nestled in the center of the pasture. The dry pastureland had been a perfect opportunity to give the two probies experience fighting grass fires with plenty of veterans to help out if there was any trouble. Unfortunately, as a lieutenant, Ben always ended up working behind the newbies, carrying the hose. A boring, thankless job if there ever was one on the crew.

"Hey, probie," he said. Ben tugged the hose, pulling Ryan back slightly as he corrected his trajectory and aimed at the fire he was supposed to be putting out. "Watch the flames instead of Angie. You're crossing the fire line."

"What?"

Ryan looked down at the ground where he'd stepped outside the charred grass, taking his focus off the fire ahead of him. The kid had been mooning over Angie ever since she'd gone home with him. Ben knew several of the others were already razzing him about it. He needed to get his head back on straight or they were going to have to cut him loose. Ben dreaded the talk he was going to have to have with the guy.

"This is why you don't sleep with women on the crew, kid."

"I've got this under control."

Ben heard the defensive note in Ryan's voice. He didn't have time to pander to some joker playing fireman when it was his life on the line. "Then maybe next time you should turn the hose on the fire *before* you start walking through it."

"Do you want to take this end?" Ryan sounded pissed. Ben could hear it in his voice but he really didn't care. The kid was reckless and he wasn't putting his neck on the line for reckless people anymore.

Images of Emma filled his mind. She wasn't just reckless, she was impetuous, hot-headed and irrational. Why the hell couldn't that woman recognize the fact that she needed help, whether it came from him or someone else, and stop taking risks she had no business taking?

"You coming or are you going to keep daydreaming?" Ryan jerked at the hose Ben was carrying for him, tugging him off balance.

Shit! He'd just done exactly what he scolded Ryan for doing—losing focus on the task at hand. It was something he didn't do. At least, he never had before Emma. He wasn't going to start doing it now.

They finished dousing the fire and headed back to the trucks. Angie moved closer, sliding her goggles onto the top of her helmet before tugging it off.

"What's your issue, Ben?" He shot her a sideways glance and kept walking, ignoring her question. "Hey! I'm talking to you." Angie reached up and jerked the back of his turnout coat in her gloved fist. "What the hell gives you the right to interfere in my relationships when you can't even manage your own?"

"Relationship?" He leaned over her, shadowing her with his much larger frame, hoping that it was enough to convince her to back off. This wasn't a subject that was up for discussion. "You've slept with half the guys on the crew and propositioned the other half. How is that a relationship?"

"Wow! I had no idea what a son of a bitch you could be. I thought you left that up to your brother. Good to know." She shoved him back a few steps, not intimated in the slightest by him. "Ryan is different. If you ever got your head out of your ass you'd realize that not all relationships look the same."

"He's five years younger than you."

"So? What does that have to do with anything?"

Ben looked over at Ryan laughing with one of the other guys near the engine as they cleaned up. Angie and Ryan? As in a serious relationship? She'd never had one, not even for the six months they'd been together.

She arched a brow at him, daring him to question her again. "Things aren't always the way they first appear, McQuaid. Just because we started out as a one-night stand doesn't mean it can't turn into more, or that we have to get married. Quit being such a judgmental prick."

He opened his mouth but she shook her head and slammed her helmet into his chest. "For almost screwing up my date for tonight, you can take care of my gear. No bitching either since I saved your ass last week."

She winked at him. "Oh, the joys of having you owe me favors."

Angie walked to Ryan and Ben didn't miss the way the guy's eyes lit up. It was easy to see he was head over heels for Angie. Ben had no doubt that Angie was going to tear him up and rip his poor infatuated heart to shreds. She had never been serious about anyone. Angie smiled at the kid, grabbing him by the front of his coat and tugging him close for a kiss. The look on her face as they separated suddenly made him question his own presumptions.

If that wasn't love in her eyes, he'd clean every engine at the station single-handedly.

And it was the same way Emma looked at him.

At least she had until yesterday.

EMMA WATCHED AS the crowd made their way to the gate of the main compound. She'd already been through the facility, double-checking all of the locks and making sure the animals were fed before hanging signs and rope barriers where she didn't want visitors wandering. During her last walk-through, most of the animals had been sleeping, full and happy, after breakfast. She glanced at Andrew, who walked in the lead, directing the visitors to an open area at the sanctuary gate. She almost laughed at seeing him decked out in cargo shorts and a polo shirt bearing the sanctuary's emblem.

"If everyone will come this way and gather around, we can start the tour," she instructed. "We're going to split everyone up into smaller groups. Some of you will follow Sadie." Her volunteer raised a hand and waved at the crowd. "And some of you will follow Drew."

Andrew glared at her but recovered quickly, waving at the group. They'd planned it the day before in hopes that most of the people attending wouldn't recognize him. Since each volunteer carried a clipboard with them, Emma had written him a script to use while taking his group on the tour. They had invited twenty people from the community, including a Make-a-Wish child and the reporter from the local paper who had been writing the articles. While there were several people with cameras ready, there was only one with a lens long enough to capture every individual hair on Buster. That had to be the reporter. Emma would make sure that he ended up in Andrew's group where they could keep an eye out for suspicious activity as well as his reactions to the animals.

She handed out colored slips of paper to the group, including the three children in the group. She knew the Make-a-Wish girl wanted to pet a wild animal and Sadie had been instructed to let them all pet Millie since she was tame. "Everyone with a yellow card will follow Sadie. She's going to take you to the see the cats first."

Emma glanced at Andrew as he jerked his chin toward the man she suspected was the photographer. "The rest of you are going to go with Drew and start with our aviary and the birds we house in there."

Andrew nodded as he headed for the bird enclosure, with the group following him closely. It was an easy place for them to start and for no one to be suspicious when she followed since she would be taking Winger, their red-tailed hawk out for them to see up close. She heard Andrew making small talk with the reporter as she hurried to grab the gauntlet from the trunk and meet them outside the aviary.

"Emma."

Her heart skipped a beat at the sound of Ben's voice behind her. Part of her wanted to rejoice at his presence. Part of her ached with pain at his return, knowing they could never make it work. She kept her back to him, hoping that if she didn't turn around, it would hurt less and she could maintain her restraint. Especially when her legs were twitching, wanting to turn and run into his arms.

"Why are you here? You made your thoughts about this clear the other day, Ben."

"I was wrong."

She turned hesitantly. She had no idea what had caused this change of heart and, as much as she didn't want to, she had to question his sudden backtracking.

Before she could ask him, he closed the distance between them, looking far too handsome in his jeans and a polo shirt matching Andrew's. "I'm here to do whatever you need, even if you just want me to go to hell."

He started to raise his hand, reaching for her, but she sensed the hesitation in him. She wanted to reach for him, to drag him down to her, to feel his mouth on hers, to savor the taste of him again. But nothing had changed. He was still trying to rescue her, to save her.

"You promised me once that you'd be whatever I

needed. I need a friend. Not a lover." His hand dropped back to his side and she saw the defeat flicker in the depths of his eyes. "Ben, we both know that neither one of us can go back to that."

He dropped his chin toward his chest, disappointment clear, and closed his eyes. When he looked at her again, there was something different in them. She no longer saw the softness, the gentle gaze he always seemed to have when he looked at her. There was a fierce determination in them she'd never seen before.

"You're right. This is exactly why we set up the ground rules, isn't it?"

She took a step backward, unsure how to react to the new man she saw in front of her, a man she didn't know. A man who sounded harder, more self-assured. A man who seemed more like his stubborn brother than the gentle man she'd met only a few weeks ago in this very same spot.

"I can follow them and go back." His mouth formed a thin line as he set his jaw stubbornly. "Are you saying I can do something that you can't?"

She'd never been one to turn down a challenge and she could hear it in his tone.

"If you can, I can. Let's go get Winger. You think you can keep from dropping her this time, wimp? No woman likes to be let down."

"Bring it."

It had been a joke. She'd been teasing. But instead of being funny, it sounded more like a dare. And she wasn't so sure he was talking about holding the bird.

THE GROUP WAS already waiting for them as Ben slid the gauntlet onto his arm. The hawk flew from her perch as soon as he stepped into her enclosure and he held her tether between his fingers, sliding her hood on the way Emma had shown him. He knew he should be concentrating on the bird on his arm but he couldn't help but watch Emma instead.

He was waiting for the right moment. Somehow he'd managed to lie to her face, telling her he could be just a friend. But, like Angie said, their relationship didn't have to look a certain way. It had started burning hot and, in spite of the trouble dogging her, it hadn't cooled the way others had, or the way she'd suggested it would. If anything, he was burning even hotter for her, yearning for her. Not just physically. Ben wanted to be with Emma, to be a part of her life, for her to be part of his. Even if it meant watching her put herself in danger on a daily basis. She was trying, exciting, challenging and sexy as hell. A life with her would be a never-ending game of tug-of-war, but it would also never be boring or predictable. He'd thought that was what he'd wanted. Maybe it was, until he'd met Emma.

If that meant telling her he'd be nothing more than a friend, for now, then that's what he'd be. He had no doubt that, somehow, they'd work their way full circle. He'd make sure of it and this was merely the first step. Any other answer would have ended with her pushing him away permanently.

Ben stood where Emma directed, waiting for her to indicate he should take the bird's hood off.

"This is Winger, a red-tailed Hawk. As you can see, she's a beautiful bird with a very wide wingspan and very sharp talons."

As if understanding Emma's spiel, the hawk shifted, digging her talons into the thick leather of the glove, climbing higher on his wrist. Ben lifted his arm slightly and she shifted back toward his hand.

"Red-tailed hawks are very intelligent and have been trained to hunt for falconers since medieval times. However, they are wild animals and they can become frightened so when Ben here removes her hood, I need everyone to stay quiet and still, okay?"

A hand from the crowd raised and Emma pointed at a woman standing close to what appeared to be her husband. "Can we pet her?"

"Because most of the animals here are not tame pets, only trained personnel can handle them. The volunteers have been instructed on how to hold her and even we don't pet her. Here at Sierra Tracks, we try to keep the animals' environment as close to natural as possible, even for those like Winger, who are unable to be released back into the wild."

The woman raised her brows at Ben, as if still questioning. "That's a no," he clarified. The last thing he wanted was to have his eyes clawed out by a spooked hawk just because some woman decided to rush in.

Emma shot him a warning glance. Okay, so maybe he could have been a bit less blunt. "Go ahead and take her hood off, Ben."

He cupped his hand over the hood, lifting it up and

sliding it down the bird's beak quickly. Winger immediately looked around, curious at her surroundings and the people circling them. It wasn't hard for him to imagine the bird spreading her wings and beating at him with them as she shifted nervously. Ben raised his arm slightly and Winger spread her wings wide for a moment, eliciting an awed gasp from the group as she beat the air slightly before ruffling her feathers and settling on his arm again. Ben saw a man in front drag a massive camera to his face and take some quick pictures.

"You can see that, while she's calm right now, those wings can pack a lot of power. The red-tailed hawk uses them to rise above the air currents."

Emma continued to talk to the group about the hawk as the man shot pictures, moving quietly around the crowd capturing several angles. Ben shot his brother a warning look and caught Andrew's that mimicked his own concern. If this was the man they were looking for, he was gathering plenty of information, including how each and every cage was locked and the layout of the facility. While it may have given them a face to the anonymous reporter, they had also opened the door wide and knowingly escorted danger inside.

BEN WATCHED AS the group came back together at the end of the tour for lunch, catered by a local butcher shop and included in the price of the tickets. He had to admit that the outreach event had gone well and everyone seemed to be having a good time, however he couldn't shake the doubts about the guy with the camera. In spite of Emma's insistence that he be there as a friend and that she didn't need rescuing, Ben wasn't about to let a man who could be putting her life in jeopardy escape without a warning.

Looking around the group, Ben saw Emma chatting with a mother and her child. She'd already told him that there was a Make-a-Wish child on the tour and he had no doubt the cute little girl was who she'd meant. Standing on the outskirts of the crowd, Ben tried to get his brother's attention as he made his way toward the man who'd been far more interested in taking pictures all day than what Emma or Andrew said about the animals.

The guy just seemed suspicious. Ben had no doubts he was making a snap judgment, based on nothing more than his suspicions, but when it came to Emma's safety, he'd rather be overcautious than look back and wish he had spoken up. He slid into the chair next to the man.

"Having a good time?"

"Um," the man mumbled around a mouthful of tri-tip sandwich. Wiping his hand on the side of his pant leg, he held it out to Ben. "Sorry. I'm Charlie Sims."

"Ben McQuaid." Ben hoped this guy recognized his name. He wanted him to know Emma had people at her back. He shook the man's hand and tried to read what was going on behind Charlie's hazel eyes. "This your first time at Sierra Tracks?"

He'd hoped Charlie's reaction to the point-blank question would tell him something but the man's gaze never faltered. "Yeah, it's pretty cool. I wouldn't have expected there to be so many animals here. It's a really nice facility compared to a lot of the others I've seen."

"Oh, you've been to a few?" A niggling doubt started to circle in his gut but Ben latched onto the statement. He glanced up in time to see Emma frowning at him from across the tables she'd had set up.

"Yeah. I'm a wildlife photographer by trade so I do a lot of work with advertisers and magazines. I've even had a few pictures in *National Geographic*."

Ben nodded, trying to lull the guy into a false sense of camaraderie. "Newspapers, that sort of thing?"

Charlie laughed. "Newspapers don't have the budget for my photos. I actually came today to see if Emma would be interested in working together. I wanted to volunteer my services so she'd have photos for promo, maybe something to start with on her website."

"What's in it for you?"

Charlie shrugged. "It's philanthropy. This place is local and I can help. Between you and me," Charlie said, lowering his voice and leaning toward Ben. "I've seen the articles the paper's been running. I was concerned enough to want to see for myself. Now that I have, I think if other people could see what I've seen today, they'd realize those articles are complete B.S. She's got one of the best facilities I've ever seen."

"You're here to *help* Emma?" Ben narrowed his eyes, trying to get a better read on this guy. As much as he wanted to distrust him, Ben had the feeling that Charlie was being completely honest. But he wasn't going to bank Emma's safety on his gut. He looked around for Andrew, hoping his brother could talk to Charlie and they could compare notes.

Charlie turned back toward his lunch, obviously uncomfortable under Ben's intense scrutiny, and popped the top on a can of soda. The fizz cut through the tense lull in their conversation. "Ben, have you talked to people in town recently? Emma needs all the help she can get. There are a few who have already started a petition to get her shut down."

"A petition?"

"Yeah. Didn't you read the last article?"

Ben frowned. He'd been so wrapped up in protecting her physically that he hadn't stopped to keep his finger on the pulse of activity around town, to even listen to gossip that seemed to flow like a leaky faucet. He'd forgotten one of the most important things about living in a small town—gossip could cut as deeply as any knife. If someone couldn't scare her away, they could put pressure on her from the rest of the community until she had no other choice but to close her doors.

"Apparently some ex-employee has come forward and claims the animals are being abused."

Ben's jaw clenched tightly and he felt the muscle cramp. He looked up to see Emma standing beside him with a suspicious look in her eyes as she gazed down at him and Charlie. She wouldn't be happy with him for meddling but she had no idea that they may have been horribly wrong about the reporter being behind the vandalism and loose animals. From what Charlie said, Ben was almost positive Jake was the man set on destroying her.

"Thanks, Charlie. You've helped Emma more than you'll ever realize." He leapt from his seat, leaving Emma to wonder where he was going. Ben needed to get to Andrew. The two of them needed to find Jake and when they did, Ben was going to make him pay.

Chapter Twenty-Three

WHAT THE HELL is she doing now?

He watched Emma escort the crowd through the sanctuary. There was a reason her father had put an end to this tour nonsense. It stressed the animals and, while it was a ridiculously small source of income, it pandered to the idea that the sanctuary was more of a zoo or park than a legitimate rescue facility. Not to mention that it drove the insurance rates sky high, chipping away at any income it brought in.

His gaze fell on the wolf lying in the midst of the trees within the large enclosure. He was surprised she'd turned Cana out instead of hiding him inside one of the indoor kennels. But Emma had always had a soft spot for the beast, which made her weak. And stupid.

He'd have been able to snatch the animal yesterday if it hadn't been for that son of a bitch fireman showing up unexpectedly. But he'd made sure Emma knew he was there, leaving her a little warning. A calling card, if you will.

He slid the binoculars to his eyes again, scanning the enclosure entrance. In preparation for her little party, she'd added extra locks on the cages but he knew Emma. She might have added them to the front entrances, but she hadn't added them to the back ones. Later tonight, he'd sneak down and find out for sure. Even if she did, he doubted it was anything that would pose much of a deterrent to stealing the wolf back.

The news article had worked exactly the way he'd planned. And, now that he and his brother had been able to stir the town against Emma, forcing them to ask themselves about her ability to run Sierra Tracks, there'd been some grumbling that if Emma was forced out, that the entire facility should be shut down but both he and his brother had pointed out that Conrad had run it for years without any incidents, and that the two of them could do the same, which had been his intention all along.

Now, he just had to get his hands on that wolf again and stage another animal attack. It would be the final straw for the people in Hidden Falls. They were scared and they needed someone they could trust. Right now, that would be him and his brother.

EMMA SKIMMED THE article again. Jake's interview made his intentions clear. He was bound and determined to undermine any allies she might have left in Hidden Falls, to turn everyone in town against her, even if most of his accusations were completely false. It hurt that both he and his brother had turned on her but she wasn't about to let the rumors stop her from running the sanctuary. Nor did it actually prove he was the person sabotaging her. She had seen Jake with the animals, knew how much the sanctuary meant to him. He might not agree with her methods but she had a hard time believing he'd go as far as abusing any of the animals, letting them loose or trying to destroy the facility entirely.

She crossed her arms over her chest. "Jake is a disgruntled employee. It shouldn't come as any surprise that he'd talk shit but that doesn't mean he's the guy we're looking for."

"Don't fool yourself, Emma," Ben warned. "If Charlie Whats-his-name isn't the guy we're looking for, it's Jake."

She rolled her eyes at him. "Why would it be Jake? He was working here when this mess started. He's worked here for five years. I might not be able to work with him, but my father did and he trusted him."

"That means absolutely nothing." Ben looked to his brother for support in his argument. "What are you waiting for? You need to drag him in for questioning."

"I don't think it was Jake," Sadie offered. "Why would he try to shut down the place he talked about running with Emma?"

"What?" Sadie's comment had Andrew's full attention.

Emma sighed. "Apparently, my father had mentioned to Jake that he wanted the two of us to run the facility together," she explained. "I'm not sure I believe it since Dad had always talked about the two of us running it together but—"

"Actually, Emma," Sadie hemmed, twisting her mouth to one side. "Jake was supposed to run the place alone. Something about how Jake's vision was closer to your father's but Conrad never got the opportunity to change his will." She shot Emma an apologetic glance.

"I'm assuming this is coming from Jake?" Andrew pressed.

"Maybe. Well, actually, Brandon was the one who told me about it but I think Jake told him."

"I know Jake. I don't like the guy and how judgmental he is but he would never do something to jeopardize the animals."

Ben scowled and pinched the bridge of his nose, sighing heavily. Sadie pinched her lips together, trying to not look uncomfortable with the argument.

"The man threw a rock at your truck, Emma. I think it's safe to not make any assumptions about what he might do."

Andrew inhaled slowly and rose to his feet. "Okay, you," he said, pointing at his brother, "need to calm your tits. Emma's right."

"You don't know that," Ben growled.

"First off, Jake was here, working. Why would he spray-paint a wall he'd likely be the one to clean? As a matter of fact, he was working every time something happened. He was here, with witnesses when you picked up that kitten."

"Who would have had more opportunity to get Cana and say it was your father's request. No one would suspect him," Ben pointed out.

"No, *everyone* would suspect him. Which is another reason I don't think it was him."

"Jake is pissed right now. He had no idea I even wanted him gone, let alone, that I'd actually fire him. *If* my father ever insinuated that Jake and I could run the place together, it would be even more reason for his anger. He might be disappointed, or feeling betrayed but I don't think he's angry enough to go against his own values, killing two calves in the process, to make me look bad."

Emma saw the flash of worry in Ben's eyes. She'd better be right, because if she wasn't, she'd just left herself open for almost anything.

THE NEXT WEEK was eerily calm, like the sky just before a lightning storm. Currents crackled through the air, lighting sparks wherever she went. Emma had tried to avoid heading into town at all, letting Sadie take the business credit card to purchase any necessary items for the sanctuary while Ben made sure her cupboards and refrigerator were well stocked. After her refusal to return to his family's ranch, he'd insisted on returning to her place to stay, sleeping in one of the guest rooms and maintaining their agreement to be just friends. It was driving her nuts.

She peeked into her kitchen, praying that it was clear

and she could grab her coffee before heading out to the nursery for Kit.

"Morning, Emma."

Her pulse immediately began to race, nervous excitement twisting through her veins at the rich, husky sound of Ben's voice. He held a steaming cup of coffee out to her. This was something she could get used to.

Damn it! No, she *couldn't* get used to this because she didn't want a relationship. At least that was what she was trying to tell herself. But with Ben in the house, what should have been entertaining was turning into an exercise in avoidance. Because if she didn't stay clear of Ben, she was going to realize she was falling for this guy, hard and fast. Even worse, he'd realize it.

"You okay?" Her gaze jumped back up to meet his, the dark pools filled with concern. "I thought I lost you for a second there."

"No. Um, thanks." She slid the mug from his fingers, careful not to touch him. Ben moved back to the stove where she could see half of her refrigerator contents spread over the nearby counter. "What's with the mess?"

"I told you before I could make a mean omelet. I figured I might as well put my money where my mouth is."

Oh, I have a far better place for you to put your mouth.

Emma tried to stem her wanton desires but not quickly enough and felt her cheeks heat with the mere thought of kissing Ben again. It felt like it had been forever, even if it had only been a few days. The first three days after the tour had been torturous enough since she'd barely seen him. But now, with him having two days off, being forced to share the intimate space of her house last night, had been even harder. He looked too comfortable, too much a part of her life, and it frightened her.

But she also couldn't help the feeling that she wanted it. For the first time, letting the chance of having it slip away frightened her even more.

"I . . . uh . . . I have to go move Kit into the enclosure so it might be a while before I can get back inside."

"You want help?"

He had no idea what helping might entail, no clue what she might ask him to do, but it didn't seem to matter to him. He was willing to step up in any way for her. Just as he had been for the past few weeks since he'd first arrived at her door with Kit. It struck her suddenly, like a divine message.

Ben wasn't trying to rescue her, he wanted to *help* her save herself, and he'd been trying, in the only way he knew how to prove that. Whether it was showing up to volunteer or staying here to protect her ranch from an outside threat.

"Ben, I . . ." Emma wasn't sure what to even say, how to tell him what she wanted. Her tongue snuck out, moistening her lower lip and she heard his soft groan. His eyes shifted, turning hungry and even darker. Emma's breath caught in her lungs.

She reached out and grasped the front of his shirt, dragging him closer and winding her arm around his neck. She pulled him down to her and sealed their mouths. Like a man dying of thirst, he drank from her, taking all she would give and she wanted to give him everything.

Ben wrapped his free arm around her back and held her close, their bodies fusing in spite of their clothing. She melted into him, the explosive heat surging through her. He slid the coffee cup onto the counter and tightened his other arm around her waist, pulling her even closer.

"God, Emma," he growled as his lips trailed over her jaw to the side of her neck. "I thought that you—"

"Shh, don't ask questions," she begged. "Just . . ." She couldn't say more, couldn't tell him what she wanted because even she wasn't clear.

She wanted Ben. Not just for a fun night, not just until this fire between them burned out. She no longer cared about the danger of her job. He understood it better than anyone and was willing to not only support her but dig in and get his hands dirty. For the first time, she'd found someone who not only understood her passion but fueled the desire in her, sought it out.

"Love me, Ben." He drew back, his eyes wide with shock. "Don't say anything," she said, her cheeks flaming with embarrassment. This wasn't who she was, this needy woman begging, but Ben made her want, and yearn and need more than she ever had before.

"Are you sure you want to throw out the rule book?" He looked down at her, his gaze questioning. "You said—"

"I know what I said." She ran a hand over the back of his head and smiled up at him. "What can I say? You wore me down."

He returned her smile with his own, looking sinfully sexy and absurdly cocky. "Took long enough."

"Really?" She arched a brow and laughed quietly.

Ben shrugged and nuzzled her neck again. "But you are one stubborn Scot." The magic of his lips drove away any comeback she might have considered. Goose bumps broke out over her skin, making her shiver against him, her fingers clenching in the front of his t-shirt. "I should probably let you take care of Kit, right?"

For the first time, she wasn't looking forward to the work she had planned for her day. In reality, it was that she wasn't looking forward to leaving the sanctuary of Ben's embrace. Now that she'd finally decided what she wanted, she didn't want to wait any longer to have it. He chuckled, the sound vibrating his chest against hers, warming her.

"I'll tell you what. Let's go get whatever it is you need finished this morning done, then we'll come back in and I'll cook for you."

As if the thought of Ben standing in front of her stove wasn't attractive enough, her mind took the opportunity to picture him there naked. Emma knew that letting her imagination run wild was a bad idea but couldn't seem to help herself. It was more than enough to make her look forward to getting her work done faster.

"This might take a while," she warned.

His gaze skimmed over her, scorching every inch of her with the heated passion she could read there. "Emma, it will be worth every bit of my appetite when we get back."

She had no doubts that food was not what he was thinking about.

WATCHING THE BOBCAT kitten playing in his new home gave Ben an odd sense of satisfaction. As Kit stalked the bug crawling on the ground while the larger bobcat cast him a bored glance from the shade made his heart swell. He no longer minded the scratches he'd received dragging Kit from the tree. He was optimistic that Emma was right and Kit would be hunting live prey before long, thanks to his new housemate and the lessons he was sure to impart.

"You're sure they're going to be okay in here together?" Emma leaned into him as they watched from outside the enclosure. "I wouldn't turn him out if I wasn't. Davis has taken him under his wing, which surprised me a bit at first with him being another male."

"We males can be nurturing too, you know."

She looked up at him, her eyes bright with humor. "Did I offend your delicate ego? I'm so sorry."

"You don't sound—" His cell phone buzzed and he rolled his eyes. "Hang on. Hello?"

"Ben, it's Ryan. Angie told me to call you to see if you could make it in today."

"What's up?" It had to be big if Angie was calling in.

"I'm not supposed to say why." The probie lowered his voice. "But we're eloping. I asked her to marry me and she said yes." Ryan sounded almost giddy with excitement.

"What?" Ben didn't mean to sound so surprised but *married? Angie?* She was the last person he'd ever expected to do something like this.

"So? Can you come in and cover her shift?"

"Are you sure you want to do this?"

"What?" Ryan sounded incredulous. "Why wouldn't I be? Angie's the best."

Ben caught himself from laughing at the guy's exuberance. It wasn't his place to judge. Angie had already ripped him a new one once. "You just surprised me," he covered as best he could. "I can head in now. Tell Angie I'm happy for you both, okay?"

"Thanks Ben. We both owe you."

Ben hung up, feeling slightly awed at the change in Angie but thrilled for her all the same. She'd finally found someone who made her want to settle down. He glanced at Emma, taking in her sweet smile, the tender concern in her eyes.

"Trouble?"

"Not exactly, but I have to go in to the station." It killed him to think about what he wanted to do to Emma, to do *with* Emma, after they got back to the house. She'd finally let down those walls that he'd thought would never fall and now he had to leave.

Disappointment clouded her eyes. "Oh. I hope everything is okay?"

"It's Angie. And, trust me, if I didn't owe her, I would absolutely stay here but—"

"I get it. Duty calls."

"She covered for me when I stayed here." Someday

he was going to have to explain the weird history he and Angie had but he was in too much of a hurry to give her all the details now. "Apparently, she's decided to elope with one of our probies." Ben shrugged. "I can't leave the station shorthanded."

She dipped her chin and looked at him through her lashes, making him want to forget owing Angie and carry Emma back to the house. "Go. You don't need to stay here. I told you that before."

"I know what you said, Emma, but—"

"Seriously. Go." She waved a hand at him. "Everything has been quiet for the past three days. Everyone is over it."

Ben didn't share Emma's confidence. It had been quiet but it didn't feel over to him. He had that twisted feeling in his gut, the one that usually came just before a big fire call. The one that usually led to him facing the fire and risking his life anyway.

Chapter Twenty-Four

HE WATCHED FROM the shadows. She wouldn't see him. Emma never had paid him much attention, never given him the credit he was due for the help he'd given her. She'd never admitted that he had good ideas. Of course, he couldn't be too angry about it. She'd never agreed with anyone's ideas, including his brother's. Hell, she hadn't even listened to her own father when he'd tried to tell her about the changes he wanted to make.

And now, he was going to have to force her hand.

He stared into the enclosure where the wolf paced nervously, whining slightly. It pissed him off that he wasn't going to be able to jimmy the lock she'd placed on any of the entrances. To protect the damn animal, she'd purchased heavy-duty combination locks and he hadn't brought his cutters on his last trip into the facility. Cutting the fence wasn't an option. That wolf would attack him before he could get ten feet. Cana hadn't liked any men before he'd gone to the rescue in Nevada, but keeping him locked in a small kennel, using sedatives and the choke collar, as well as a swat when necessary, to control him over the past year, had turned the wolf's dislike to hatred and his uncertainty to fear, making him too dangerous to let loose.

So, he'd returned home to come up with a Plan B. It hadn't been easy. It wasn't even one he liked. If every detail didn't go as planned, the entire thing would crumble. But he had to take the chance. For Conrad's wishes. For the future of Sierra Tracks. For his brother.

Emma had to leave and this was the only way to make sure it happened. The doubts he'd planted around Hidden Falls weren't working quickly enough. It was time to take drastic steps to make sure she was run out.

Slipping past the enclosure, he ducked behind several trees and headed for the back field, away from any of the animals, to the acreage they used to grow alfalfa hay for livestock. What they didn't use for their own animals was sold to raise money for the sanctuary. Another of his brother's ideas.

Lighting the match, he flicked it into the grass, watching it nearly smolder. It wasn't as dry as most fields in their current drought conditions but it was dry enough. The ember caught and started to move up the stalks, reaching the leaves with a small burst of life. Just before it fizzled out, it caught another stalk, then another, moving it away from the facility, toward the foothills behind the property. He prayed the wind continued to move in that direction, carrying the flame away from the sanctuary.

He didn't want anyone injured, he just wanted Emma's future destroyed.

THEY DON'T EVEN need me here.

I need you, Emma thought as she read Ben's text, the seventeenth in the past thirty minutes. She'd barely managed to finish all of her daily chores after he'd left because of the many texts he'd sent. There were a few telling her how bored he was, a couple mentioning how much he hated cleaning but the vast majority were about how much he wanted to be with her. Those were the ones that made her body sizzle, humming with anticipation.

It was odd for her to feel this way and, while it made her slightly uncomfortable, it also excited her beyond reason. It wasn't just the newness of the feeling, it was the unique emotions flitting through her at random times. She'd enjoyed giving Ben new experiences but he was doing the same for her. She was looking forward to her first real nonsexual date with him the next day. —her couch with the movie and popcorn he was bringing back with him. While there was a good chance they would end up in her bed, there was no expectation.

A shiver of desire fluttered in her stomach and spread through her body, warming her to her toes. Okay, maybe a little expectation on her part.

She was in deep, deeper than she'd ever been with

anyone before. It still frightened her in a "what am I doing, this isn't me" kind of way but she was beginning to realize that being Emma Jordan had been lonely. She'd been on her own, shutting out everyone else, for so long that she was actually worried she didn't know how to let anyone in. Then Ben showed up, finding weaknesses in her barriers that only he seemed to be able to breach.

Hang in there. Are you coming straight back here in the morning? I'm making plans for you.

She hoped he was. Desire curled in her belly, warming her. She'd be waiting for him in the kitchen with breakfast ready and nothing else on. Her phone vibrated with his return text almost immediately.

You're a cruel woman, Emma Jordan.

Emma laughed as she slid her phone into her back pocket, hurrying toward the aviary. She had a lot to finish in the next hour, before she could quit for the night. The birds needed to be settled in and she still had to make sure each of the cages was locked tight. It had been a while since anything had happened but that lull was exactly why she double-checked every cage each night now.

The cloying scent of smoke caught her attention and she frowned, trying to figure out where it might be coming from. She scanned the horizon line, looking for even the faintest wisp but the sky was still clear, just fading to pink and orange as the sun began its rapid descent. She reached for the radio on her hip.

"Sadie, Monique?"

"Yeah, boss?" Sadie's voice crackled through.

"I smell smoke. Do either of you have a clear view of the area behind the house and the outbuildings?"

"Shit!" Monique's epithet came through clearly. "The alfalfa's on fire."

"Sadie, hit the sprinklers, drown that field. I'll call the fire department." Emma jerked her phone out of her pocket as Sadie responded, sounding out of breath, as if she was already running to do as Emma asked. The dispatch operator answered Emma's call.

"I have a fire. My alfalfa field."

"Ma'am can I have your address?" Emma provided it as the woman on the other end of the line sent her call through to the fire dispatch.

"I need you to stay away from the fire ma'am, but I also need you to answer some questions for me."

"Okay." Emma didn't have time for this. She had animals to get inside before the fire got any closer to the facility. She had evacuation procedures for several of them, to get them off the premises. "Right now there are no structures threatened but I can't see the fire from where I am."

"How do you—"

"I can smell the smoke and one of my staff informed me where the fire is. We've already opened up the irrigation valves in an effort to quench the fire in the field itself."

"I've sent out an engine. Is the fire threatening any lives?"

"Yes, my animals. I need to get everyone out. So

just get a truck out here now." Emma hung up on the dispatcher. She'd given them the information they needed. They'd arrive within minutes. She had no time to waste.

Emma ran to the house to get a clear view for herself. Thick plumes of smoke poured from the field, moving quickly as flames caught the top of the hay and jumped. She could see the irrigation spouts pouring water but it wasn't fast enough as the flames licked their way past, moving toward the mountains. It was a small blessing but would be enough to buy her some time until the fire department arrived.

Before Emma could even finish her thought, the winds changed, twisting the flames in the air, carrying them into the sky and lifting the embers back toward the house, licking the tall pines along the way. Within moments, several trees were engulfed in flames, the dry needles burning like kindling. Emma stood, transfixed for a moment, paralyzed by the sight of the massive branches being consumed quickly by flames and then slowly as the embers traveled over the bark. It was frighteningly beautiful, seductively awful. A loud pop of fire meeting with tree sap snapped her out of her hypnotic state and she ran into her office to find the numbers of the many people she had on stand-by to transport the animals in case of emergency.

She'd sent a group text message out before calling the first name on the list—a local veterinary hospital—who would then call the next name until they had all been reached. Then she called Ben.

After several rings, it went to his voice mail. Did he know? Was his crew the one heading to her place right now? She quickly texted him the only message she had time for:

I need help saving my place. Hurry!

SITTING AT THE fire station was monotonous, until a call came in from dispatch. He slid his phone back into his pocket, desperately wishing he could be back with Emma, trying to alleviate his boredom while he was stuck here by fantasizing about what she might have planned for him when he arrived back at her place in the morning. But morning was still fourteen hours away and his fantasies were only engulfing him in unsatisfied longing, leaving his entire body burning for more.

When the alarm blared, tearing him from his thoughts of Emma, Ben jumped from where he'd been stretched out in a recliner. His body reacted completely out of instinct, hurrying into the engine bay and to his locker against the wall. He slid his feet into his boots, yanking his pants up and reaching for his jacket and helmet in one swift movement. Years of being on the department had made it possible for every one of them to be out of the station only minutes from the time the alarm sounded, and the Hidden Falls Fire Department was a well-oiled machine. As he was taking Angie's place on the front line crew, he jumped into the cab of the engine, behind the driver and began settling his mind on what was to come when they arrived, listening to the information the dispatch provided over the radio.

Grass fire, ten acres, threatening structures nearby.

The captain responded that they were en route and their ETA of six minutes. Another engine would follow, due to the potential size of the fire but Ben prayed it didn't spread. Years of drought had grass drier than ever this year, making fires even more dangerously unpredictable.

"Engine 3, be advised that we have just received a call that the fire is now heading back toward the house and animal sanctuary. Evacuation is currently underway."

Ben's heart completely stopped in his chest as the dispatch relayed the information. *Emma!*

He had to focus on his job, on what he could do to not only save her ranch but to rescue her. The dispatch recited the information about current weather conditions: seventy-eight degrees, sixteen percent humidity and winds variable, gusting northwest at ten to fifteen miles per hour. It was taking the fire away from the mountains, directly toward Emma's house, the barns and his parents' house before heading toward town. With the drought conditions they'd had for the past six years, this was devastation just waiting to happen if they didn't get this under control before it hit the trees along the highway corridor. He knew his job, knew how much was at stake, but could only focus on the one thought circling his mind. Even as the sirens pierced his ears, Ben only heard two words in his mind, choking out every other sound—*Save Emma.*

"EMMA."

Spinning, she saw Jake running toward her. He was the last person she wanted to see and rage flooded her chest. "You son of a bitch! Ben was right? You *are* the one doing this, aren't you?"

"What?"

Emma threw herself at him, ready to tear him to shreds with her bare hands. "How dare you come here? Don't you realize what you've done?"

"What? No!" Jake shook his head, reaching for her wrists to keep her from killing him.

"Are you seriously trying to tell me you haven't been behind all of this? The spray paint, the animals that just keep showing up?" She twisted her arms away from his grasp and shoved against his chest, knocking him backward. "You've been out to get me from day one."

She ran for the front door. She didn't have time for vengeance; she had to get the animals safely into their enclosures and sedate the most dangerous in hopes that transportation would arrive. Trailers should be arriving any moment for several of the larger, harmless animals like the two white-tailed deer she'd planned on releasing in the coming weeks. But, with animals like Wally or Buster, she had to tranquilize them and pray their specialized transportation arrived before it was too late.

"Emma, wait for me. I'll help."

"I don't want your kind of help. You've done more than enough," she yelled back, over her shoulder.

She didn't want to hear his voice. What she wanted to hear were the sirens from the fire trucks, indicating their proximity. Instead, she only heard the eerie pop of the trees heating from the embers landing within the dry tinder and igniting.

"The sprinklers. Turn on the sprinklers around the enclosures," Jake yelled, his voice nearly drowned out as he choked on the smoke the wind was now carrying into the facility.

She skittered to a stop and Jake, on her heels, nearly ran into the back of her. "The sprinklers," she repeated, dumbly.

"Yeah, your dad installed them last year, because of the drought. The main is in the barn office." Without waiting for her, he ran toward the barn. Emma followed, sprinting to catch up. "No," he yelled back. "You go take care of the animals. I'll do this."

She looked back where the smoke now billowed from the field, creeping closer to the house. Turning on the irrigation system had helped keep the fire at bay but only until it had moved to areas the water hadn't reached yet. It was too hot, too big and, without enough water pouring on the ground, it simply turned any water to steam before consuming everything in its path. She had limited time and even fewer hands to help. She had no choice but to trust Jake, the very same man she believed had caused this.

As if reading her mind, Jake shook his head. "Damn it! It wasn't me, Emma. I wanted to run this place *with* you, not destroy it. Now go, or there'll be nothing left for either of us."

Against the voice of reason, the logic that said Jake

was to blame, she placed her trust in him. Turning away, she bolted for the nursery, intent on saving the littlest, most vulnerable creatures first. As she reached the brick building, water rained down on her from sprinklers set high in the trees, plastering her shirt to her skin within minutes, just as she heard the sirens from the road.

The gate! It was shut, sealing out the people who needed in. "Jake!" she called as he came running out from inside the barn.

"Already on it!" He slid into the driver's seat of the golf cart parked outside and headed for the front gate.

Emma ran into the nursery, glad she hadn't yet found time to change the code, and found Monique already inside, placing animals into various travel crates and carriers.

"Are you okay?" Emma asked, her heart swelling for her volunteers who were willing to stay, putting themselves in danger to help.

"I'm fine. We're good here," Sadie said as she and Monique slid two orphaned opossums into one carrier and latched the door.

"We have quite a few of the cardboard carriers, but take a few to the aviary and get the birds out before it goes up, Emma." Monique shoved two empty carriers at her.

She was right. The aviary was closer to the trees that were catching and filled with plenty of foliage that would light like a torch. Scooping up several more carriers, Emma ran to the building, heading for Winger's cage first. Her heart was heavy but she knew the female could take care of herself, at least for a short time. Sliding her hand into the gauntlet, she carried Winger outside, releasing her into the sky to find a safe place to land until the threat of the fire was gone. She watched for a moment as Winger took flight, circling the facility before rising over the air currents and letting them carry her toward the foothills.

A tear slid silently down Emma's cheek as she prayed the hawk would return, however, she couldn't keep her here and risk her being burned alive. Running back inside, Emma headed for Mama Hoot and the owlet she'd become a surrogate to. She'd barely reached for the latch on the door when something jerked her backward, slamming her against the wall and knocking the wind out of her.

"You should have left when you had the chance. I tried, Emma. I really tried to not let it come down to this."

Emma reached a hand to the back of her head and squeezed her eyes shut at the pain. Stars danced in her vision and she couldn't quite focus, but she knew that voice. "Brandon?"

"You shouldn't have come back, Emma. You're not ready for this place. Jake was supposed to take over. It's what your dad wanted."

"No," she groaned, bracing her back against the wall and forcing her body to stand. Sirens blared outside and she could hear them getting closer. "This is *my* home, my future. It always was."

She squinted, seeing the blurry image of Brandon

coming into focus slowly. She shook her head again. "You did all of this?"

"You just couldn't see the vision of this place. Jake did. I did. Your father knew that. I'm just making sure his last wishes are fulfilled."

"You did all of this so Jake could take over?"

"I had to get you to give up, to leave or be forced out." He shook his head. "I like you Emma but you just didn't know when to quit. Even with the entire town rallying against you. Not even when you almost got drugged trying to catch Buster."

"You did that. You tried to shoot me, not Ben." Pieces suddenly began to fall into place. "You were in the barn. You were watching. That dart came from your gun."

"So? You're a danger. To the animals, to this town and to yourself."

"So all of this was to get me to quit? To try to make me run away with my tail between my legs?" Hot rage started to boil up within her.

Brandon closed the distance between them, his eyes reflecting the hatred he had to feel to cause this much turmoil. "I did this for my brother. I did this to help him realize his vision for what this place *should* be, not the amusement park you want to turn it into."

Emma could hear the commotion outside as trucks parked and sirens blared. She could hear the voices of people barking orders, yelling as they tried to move frightened animals quickly. The thick acrid smoke was closing in which meant the fire was close, too close for people to remain on the premises and still be safe. She shook her head, defeat steamrolling her. In spite of the dying light of sunset, the inside of the aviary practically glowed as the fire surrounded the building. The heat making the enclosure nearly unbearable.

"You're insane. You've put your ideals before the lives of these animals, or the people of this town. How many *lives* are you risking just to make a point?" She tried to shove her way past him but Brandon caught her by her upper arm and shoved her back against the wall, pressing her shoulder against the brick.

"No, I'm getting the job done. That's what you always told me to do, remember Emma? When Jake or I would suggest something to make this place better? You'd tell us that doing it your way would get the job done. Now, I'm doing things *my* way. I'm putting Sierra Tracks first."

Her fingers curled into the front of his shirt as she shoved him away. "By burning it to the ground, you son of a bitch?" He stumbled backward, his foot catching on the carriers. Emma took the opportunity to run to Mama Hoot and the owlet, forcing the panicky animals into the carrier.

The wooden door of the aviary jerked open as a firefighter ran inside with the nozzle of a hose, followed closely by another.

"Get out!" the firefighter yelled. "The fire is just behind the building."

"No." Emma wasn't leaving without getting the rest of the birds out. The fireman reached for her arm as she saw Brandon bolt for the door. "He caused this."

One of the other men grabbed Brandon by the arm. "Sir?"

Emma barely caught a glimpse of the firefighter dragging a flailing Brandon out the door. She didn't have time to worry about him. The other man approached her.

"Ma'am, you need to get out."

"I'm not going." She could see the flames licking at one of the far walls, near where Winger had been housed. The entire air around her shimmered with heat, plumes of smoke beginning to fill the aviary. She rushed into one small room and scooped up a quail and her brood, dropping them inside. The only birds left were the two mallards that had adopted the sanctuary as their nesting place. She dropped both into the last carrier.

"Here," she said, shoving the carrier at the fireman who'd just run in. "Take them to the truck outside." She ran after him, wondering where Ben might be since all of the firemen looked the same in their turnout gear. "McQuaid, where is he?"

Several more firefighters ran along the outside of the building, illuminated by eerie orange, flickering light. Her heart pounded painfully in her chest; the fire had reached her sanctuary. While the animals were safe, this was the end of her father's legacy and there was nothing she could do to save it now.

"Near those bigger cages," the fireman said, waving toward the large animal enclosures where Buster and Cana were housed. "He's fine. You need to get that truck out or, at the very least, closer to the main gate in case we can't get this fire turned."

Emma wouldn't leave, not without Ben. And not when he was putting his life at risk. She couldn't lose anyone else because of her career again.

Chapter Twenty-Five

BEN SAW JAKE directing the rescue efforts, urging volunteers to load the various animals in trailers, trucks
and even a few in carriers into cars. Monique and Sadie
had been rushing back and forth from various buildings with animals. But, throughout it all, he had yet to
see Emma.

The second engine arrived right behind them and
they'd managed to redirect the fire back toward the area
soaked by the irrigation pipes, leaving one hose on it
in case it turned again. However, the problem now was
keeping the fire from the house and other structures.
The sprinklers Conrad installed had been a brilliant
idea and had kept the fire off the roofs of the structures;
however, it hadn't stopped it from leaping through the
trees and lighting various shrubbery and trees in the
enclosures. Since they weren't able to get inside, they

were fighting a losing battle, trying to keep the fire contained while animals cowered, frantic and wide-eyed, as far from the danger as possible.

Ben reached out and grasped Jake as he ran past, directing the volunteers who'd come to evacuate the large animals. "Where's Emma?"

"I don't know. I don't have time to keep tabs on her." Jake jerked himself free and grabbed his radio. "Monique, where's Emma?"

"Aviary," came the staticky reply.

"There," Jake said, his tone rushed as he pointed at the building, flames creeping closer, as one of the firemen dragged a thrashing man from within. "Shit, that's Brandon," he muttered.

"Your brother?" Before he could get a reply, Ben saw the flash of red from Emma's hair, reflected from the glow of the flames. She carried two cardboard carriers to the truck parked just a few feet from the entrance to the aviary and ran back inside.

"Look, I have to go," Jake said. "We have more cats to get out and that enclosure is ready to go up." He pointed at the large enclosure behind Ben. Cana's pen.

"Ben," his partner called. "I need you to circle around the far side of this enclosure. I can't get to it from this side and it's spreading fast."

Jake was gone and Ben caught a glimpse of Emma just as she ran back inside the aviary. He needed to convince her to leave, to head for safety. He wanted to remind her that her life was worth more than any animal. But

Ben knew she wouldn't leave even one behind. He had to trust her to keep herself safe. The best thing he could do for her was to help her save the animals.

"Watch yourself, Mike," Ben warned, turning back toward Cana's enclosure and jerking his chin toward the end of the enclosure where the wolf cowered behind a concrete slab made to look like a rock, teeth bared, snarling and snapping at the fire that hissed and spit back at him. The other firefighter had no way of knowing this enclosure belonged to an abused wolf-dog.

If he didn't get in there and stop this fire from spreading, it was going to kill Cana and he couldn't let Emma face that, in addition to the damage the fire had already caused. He could hear sirens, this time from the ambulance and police, responding to the call. Cana had begun to tolerate him; Emma had said so herself, although, in his gear, the wolf wouldn't know it was him. Plus Mike would have his back if the need arose. He jerked the cutters from his belt.

"Watch that wolf for me. I'm going inside to smother this. We need it out before it sparks something else."

Mike eyed the wolf for a moment. "Go. I'll get the fire from this side as best as I can."

Ben clipped the chain link, breaking off the pieces until he'd cut away a chunk large enough for him to peel back and get inside, tugging the hose behind him. He glanced at Cana, who went wild. The hair on his back stood on end, making him look twice as large as normal, which was pretty enormous to begin with. His white teeth gleamed yellow from the light of the fire and Ben cursed the fact that the wolf was smoky gray, making him almost invisible through the thick smoke and dimming light.

"Watch him," he warned Mike again before turning his back on the animal to attack what he knew was the bigger threat.

The heat was unbearable but he was able to soak the ground ahead of him, pushing back the fire line as he lifted the hose to saturate the trees. The hiss of the steam and dying fire drowned out any other sounds and he focused on getting the job done as quickly as he possibly could. Sweat poured down his arms and chest from the sheer effort as he controlled the two hundred pounds of force working against him but it was worth it as he saw the foliage darken from glowing orange to charred black. When smoke around him began to evaporate, changing from cloying thickness to a billowing cloud of white, Ben began to relax slightly. He gave the trees a final wash, trying to douse any last sparks and embers.

"Ben, watch out!"

Emma's voice barely reached his ears as he craned his neck to see her only seconds before he was knocked, face-first, to the ground. The force of the blow knocked the hose from his hands and, luckily, off to one side. He couldn't breathe, feeling like a boulder was on his back, until he felt the crushing pain as Cana bit into his shoulder, viciously shaking him.

"Back," Emma yelled, running into the enclosure. "Get back, Cana!"

Ben couldn't see anything through the mask that had sucked in, toward his face due to the lack of oxygen, suffocating him. When the wolf bit him, it must have gone through one of the airlines of his breathing apparatus. The SCBA was no longer blowing oxygen into his mask and he forced the face piece off, leaving him with his face in the charred earth. At least he could breathe. Sort of. The pain in his shoulder was excruciating and he could feel blood soaking into his clothing and the jacket.

"Cana, back. Get down." The sound of growling was still close but the weight moved off him, making it slightly easier to breathe. "Get away!" Emma's voice rose above the snarls of the wolf and he could see her, putting herself between him and the animal. Cana lunged slightly as she yelled back, reaching for the hose he'd dropped, ready to use it as a weapon if needed.

"Emma don't," he tried to warn her. "The water pressure will kill him if you turn it on."

Water misted over them both and he could only assume Mike had turned the hose onto the animal in an effort to save them.

"Come on." Emma pulled on his right arm, tugging him up and back toward the opening he'd cut, where Mike held a second hose, spraying toward the back of the enclosure where Cana had once been hiding, keeping the animal away from them as they escaped. "You have to get out of here."

She coughed as she dragged him through the smoke, still rising from the scorched earth. Ben shoved her through the opening first, following behind her and ripping the helmet from his head, tossing it aside to look at her. He'd never seen a more welcome, glorious sight than her face at this moment. The thought of her running into a fire, not to mention into the middle of a wolf attack, risking her life, infuriated him.

"What in the hell do you think you're doing? Are you trying to get yourself killed?" Dirt smudged her cheeks and he could see blood drying against her temple. "What the hell happened?" He reached a gloved hand toward her before yanking it off and reaching for her again. "You're bleeding."

"I'm fine." She gripped the front of his jacket. "Why did you go in there? You know what Cana is capable of, what he could have done to you."

"I had to or we wouldn't have gotten the fire out. It would have killed him."

She shoved against the front of him, causing a spiral of pain to radiate from his shoulder to his chest. "Better him than you!" She turned away from him, walking a few steps.

"Emma? Look at me."

When she turned back to face him, Ben could see the tears in her eyes, streaks cutting through the dirt on her cheeks, breaking his heart. She swiped at her face, smudging the dirt even more.

"You could have been killed."

"But I wasn't."

"You risked your life to save my ranch, to save my animals."

Ben shrugged and winced as pain cut through his arm. Her gaze landed on his shoulder where Cana had managed to bite through the turnout coat. Blood seeped through the jacket but most of the brunt had been taken by the SCBA harness.

"You need to have the EMTs look at that."

"Later." Ben couldn't believe she'd put herself between him and the wolf. She could have been killed. Winding his arm around her waist, Ben pulled her close, dropping his mouth to hers. Emma smelled like wood smoke and earth. She tasted like sweet honey but she felt like heaven.

"LET ME GO. I didn't do anything."

Brandon struggled against the handcuffs in the backseat of Andrew's patrol car. She'd already given her statement to Andrew so they knew Brandon had confessed to her but Emma didn't have the self-control to approach him, she couldn't even look at the man. She'd never been so disillusioned in her life. She'd trusted him, counted him a confidante, more than she ever had Jake. Where she and Jake had argued over the future of the ranch, Brandon had been a friend, a shoulder to cry on, a voice of reason when she'd felt like no one would listen. Now she knew it was all a ruse, a way for him to gain information to use against her.

She saw Jake approaching the back of the ambulance where she sat with Ben. Jake had been the one to get the animals off-site, or sedate those who had to stay, including Cana, until they could clean up the mess left behind by his brother's actions.

"Emma? Do you think we could talk for a minute?" Jake hung his head sheepishly, glancing up only briefly.

She looked at Ben. "I'll be right back, okay?"

He glared at Jake and even she didn't miss the warning note there. "Don't trust him," he muttered.

Emma squeezed his hand as she rose from where they sat at the back of the truck and followed Jake a few feet away. She'd barely approached when he held up a hand.

"Emma, I'm sorry. I didn't have any clue what Brandon was doing."

When he met her gaze, she could see the wetness in his eyes and felt her heart constrict. She might not agree with Jake's methods but he cared about these animals, almost as much as she did, but she also couldn't forget that night at the bar. She wasn't sure how to respond so she waited for him to say more.

Jake shook his head. "I just can't believe he thought he was doing this for me. That he thought this would help anything."

"How did you know to come here?"

"I didn't. Not really." He shoved his fists into his pockets. "He sent me this cryptic text that it was finally our time and that I should come say goodbye to Conrad. I was still pissed about being fired but I would have never let this happen if I'd known what he was planning. I had no clue he'd go this far."

Emma had to respect the fact that he didn't look

away even when he admitted his anger over being dismissed. "Are you sure it hasn't been him all along?"

"You mean, Brandon spray-painting the entrance?"

She raised her brows in silent answer.

"I . . . I don't know anymore. I never would have believed it but now . . ." He shook his head, looking at his feet again. "I'm just glad nothing worse happened. The fire is out and I don't think we've lost any animals."

"I lost half of my alfalfa crop. Winger is loose somewhere. People were hurt; anyone could have died. Most of these animals are going to be agitated for weeks. My ranch could have burned to the ground."

"I know." She could see the remorse in his eyes, the guilt he felt. "I came as soon as I got his text."

"But you saved it. If it hadn't been for you, I wouldn't have known about the sprinkler system. Everything would be gone," she admitted. "Thank you."

"Don't thank me. My jealousy over you running Sierra Tracks is likely the reason any of this happened." Jake shook his head. "If I'd just—"

"Brandon is responsible for his own decisions." She looked back at his brother in the patrol car, still yelling about his innocence. "Unless you encouraged it."

"I didn't," he insisted.

"Then don't take his crimes on your shoulders."

"But, I—"

"Jake, stop. You have your own faults." She twisted her mouth to one side, thoughtfully. "Look, you might be an opinionated, judgmental ass but I had a hard time believing you'd put animals in danger the way Kit was."

Jake frowned. "Thanks a lot."

She let her lips curve into a ghost of a grin. "Oh, come on. We've had plenty of differences of opinion on how this place should be run."

Emma looked around her at the trees in the darkness, charred and bare from twenty feet up, reaching into the sky, like the skeletal fingers of so many corpses. How was she ever going to come back from this? While the buildings still stood like brick sentinels, the landscaping was destroyed, both from fire, water and being trampled or driven over. Fencing was cut in order to allow the firefighters quick access but would need repairs and she knew there were bound to be animals that were traumatized by what had happened, far beyond what she could treat.

But they'd survived. She ran a hand through her tangled hair, brushing back the strands that had fallen into her face.

"Emma, how can I help?" Jake asked, as if he could read the direction of her morose thoughts.

"I don't know that you can. I hate to say it but I think your brother managed to achieve his goal."

As the sun rose, Ben watched Emma as she urged Winger back into her mew. The bird circled several times, looking for her customary place to land and finally settled on the edge of one of the artificial perches over her usual tree branches.

"I'm just glad she stuck around," Emma muttered.

Ben knew she was talking to herself but he nodded anyway. Emma picked up several feathers that fell off the raptor as she flew across the mew. "I have no idea how I'm going to convince her to hunt now. She's terrified."

Ben had no idea how she could tell but saw no reason to doubt her. "Emma, you need to get a few hours' sleep. Everyone is fed and safe, at least for now."

Several enclosures had been too damaged to release the animals back inside and the occupants had either been moved to another location on the premises or transported to a new facility temporarily.

She closed the door behind her, glancing back at the bird one last time. "I need to check on Cana."

"Okay, I'll go with you," Ben offered.

"No. He's had a rough night and you might just stir him up." She couldn't hide her disappointment. "He was doing so well too. I'm not even back to square one with him. I'm thrown back fifty."

"We'll work through it." He slid his hands to her shoulders, massaging the tension from the muscles bunched there.

"We?" Emma glanced back at him, turning to face him and letting her hands fall on his forearms as he reached for her waist, pulling her closer.

"Yeah, we. You don't think I'd let that beast take a bite out of me and run, do you?"

"Ben," she began, taking a deep breath.

"Don't Emma," he warned. "Don't even try to push me away again." He wrapped his arms around her and pulled her close, tucking her head under his chin. She wound her arms around him, leaning into his chest, pressing her cheek against his heart. He inhaled the scent of her, the smell of smoke still lingering in her mussed hair and realized again how lucky he was that she hadn't been hurt. Ben felt her smile just before she leaned backward, looking up at him.

"Push you away? I don't think so." Her eyes were bright and suspiciously damp. "I finally asked for help and you showed up. Not only did you take on the danger of your job but you took on mine too without even thinking twice." She reached up, cupping his jaw with her hand. "You're either the most hardheaded man I've ever met, or I've finally met someone even crazier than I am."

"Crazy?" Ben smiled down at her. "Don't you mean brave, daring and practically superhuman?"

Emma laughed, the sound making his pulse race and his exhausted body feel thirty pounds lighter. "No, I'm pretty sure I meant crazy."

Before she could say any more, Ben dipped his head, capturing her mouth with his. The smoke they'd both inhaled was on her breath but he could still taste Emma—sweet, honeyed, fiery, tempestuous Emma. His tongue danced with hers in familiar intimacy and he groaned at the desire that instantly ignited. Her hands slid up his chest and her fingers curled around the nape of his neck as she sighed. Emma whimpered in protest as he withdrew and pressed his forehead against hers.

"You need to get some rest. It's been a long day."

"It has," she agreed, lifting her gaze to his. "But rest isn't what I'm thinking about."

"No?"

She shook her head, still keeping their foreheads touching. "I've finally found someone who understands my need for adrenaline and wants the same, someone who feels as passionately about protecting those who can't protect themselves and is willing to risk everything to help." She brushed her lips over his. "I want you to stay. Not just for tonight. I want to fall asleep in your arms and wake with you, Ben McQuaid."

"Are you saying you want to toss out the rulebook for good?"

She wrinkled her nose and gave him a guilty grin. "We probably should. I mean I broke one of the rules."

Ben felt his chest constrict as he went down the list they'd come up with—no calling it dating, no ties, no one else . . . *Damn. Please don't let it be that one.* Ben closed his eyes, waiting for her to tell him which it was.

"I promised never to lie to you and I did."

Ben's eyes opened, meeting her gaze, even as he prayed it wasn't true.

"I love you, Ben. I think I have almost from the start but I just didn't want to believe it was possible because I was too afraid to let myself trust someone else to understand me or my passion."

Ben wound his fingers into her hair. "Are you saying I wore you down?"

She nodded, her smile beaming, her eyes alight with every bit of the emotion she professed. "But I'm glad you did." She stood on her toes, wrapping her arms around his neck. "Now, let's go take a shower because we both smell like smoke."

"Umm," he murmured against her lips. "Can I wash your back?"

"And everything else."

He grew hard just thinking about holding her as the water washed over them. They were both bone weary but he just wanted to hold her, tonight, tomorrow and forever. She reached for his hand, dragging him toward the house. "I'm feeling a little *dirty*."

He pulled her to a stop with him. He wanted to tell her, to make sure she knew exactly how much he loved her, but he wanted it to be special the first time he said it and his mind immediately went to work planning out his move. In the meantime, he didn't plan on leaving any doubt in her mind exactly how he felt. For now, he'd have to settle for showing her how much he loved her, starting with their shower.

"Well, I think I can take care of all your needs, ma'am."

"Can you wear the sexy turnout coat, too?" She shot him a wicked smile and a wink. "Because I've got a fire I need you to put out."

Chapter Twenty-Six

EMMA STARED AT the Grand Opening banner stretched across the front of the sanctuary gate. As the parking in front of her house filled up with visitors, she glanced over at Ben, standing to one side with Andrew, Sadie and Monique, all wearing their polo shirts, waiting for their assigned groups before taking the visitors around on the tour.

"Ready whenever you are." Jake's voice crackled over the radio but even the static couldn't mask the excitement in his voice for this, the first of many tours of the newly renovated Sierra Tracks Animal Sanctuary. He may not have wanted them in the beginning but he and Emma had come to a mutual understanding about the purpose of tours which would focus on the preservation of the animals, not objects trained to perform for a profit.

She'd debated for several weeks about whether or

not to bring Jake back on staff but, in the end, she'd agreed with Ben and Andrew's assessments that Brandon had acted alone in trying to sabotage her. Jake had worked hard over the past two months to clear her name in Hidden Falls, even going as far as to recruit several donors for landscaping and rebuilding the areas that had been destroyed by the fire. While he and Emma still didn't always agree on what was best, she realized he kept her focused on the big picture and would help her achieve the vision she had for Sierra Tracks. He'd become her indispensable right hand and she'd officially titled him the assistant director.

"Welcome to Sierra Tracks. I'm Emma and I'm going to introduce you to our trainers, Sadie and Monique, as well as my volunteers, Ben and Andrew. Everyone will get a colored card and that will indicate which group you'll be with." She passed out the cards to the large crowd, excitement welling in her chest. This was the first group to see the improvements since the fire.

After dividing the groups and sending them on their way, Emma followed Ben's group to the cage where Kit romped playfully for a moment before sprawling out over a log. Davis had done his job and taught Kit to be a bobcat again before Emma had released Davis back to the foothills last month, completely healed of his foot injury.

"What you'll see here is a young bobcat that was rescued from a tree a few months ago," Ben informed the group. "In fact, I was the one who climbed the tree to rescue him."

There were a few appreciative sighs from the ladies in the group. Emma couldn't help but smile at the memory of Ben showing up at her door with Kit in a box, or how sexy he'd looked at the time. So far, over the past few months of their relationship, little had changed. She still found him as sexy as ever, but now she saw those muscles up close, ran her hands over them as they made love each and every night. However, now she knew there was far more to him than just sex appeal. He was gentle and tender yet determined and just as stubborn as she was when he wanted to be. He'd shown her that he loved her in so many ways, each and every day, but he still hadn't said the words.

At first, she'd assumed he hadn't because he didn't want to pressure her. As more time passed, she wondered at his reasons. She saw the emotion in his eyes, knew about his past with his ex-girlfriends, including the one who had stolen most of his belongings and his car, but she also knew what they shared was different, and went so much deeper than anything either of them had ever had before with anyone else. She and Ben understood and appreciated every part of the other, their hopes, dreams, fears and goals. They had literally risked their lives for one another and would do it again without hesitation. They were equals.

Whispers began to sound around her and tugged her from her thoughts. She glanced around, realizing that the other three groups had come closer, circling behind their group of visitors.

"Emma, could you come up to the front please?" Ben

held out his hand. Slipping her hand into his larger palm, she let him draw her near. "We've had a winding path to get to this point, to finding one another, and we are only here because of a bobcat kitten. You know I'd risk my life for you—and *have*—but I don't think you realize how much I love you. How much you've changed my life for the better. How much was missing before you."

Ben reached into his pocket and pulled out a ring box, flipping the lid open to reveal a simple diamond solitaire, glinting in the rays of the morning sunlight, dazzling her as her eyes blurred. "What is this?"

He smiled and shot a look at Andrew who gave him a thumbs-up sign in return. "My brother knew before I did what would happen and I hate to admit it, but he was right. I've fallen for you Emma Jordan and I want it to be official. Marry me? Not because you need me to rescue you, but because you've rescued me."

Unable to speak, she lifted her hand to cover her mouth. Ben dropped to one knee, still holding her hand. "Say yes."

Emma couldn't help the sudden anxiety that rose up in her. How had she gone from never wanting a relationship, never letting anyone close, to loving one man so completely. Several women in the groups began to shout out their input.

"Say yes!"

"What are you waiting for?"

Emma looked down at Ben, eager to say the one word he needed to hear. "On one condition."

"Anything."

"I'm your last fiancée."

"As long as you don't pawn my stuff, I think I can promise that." Ben gave her a guilty grin.

"Just put him out of his misery already, Emma," Andrew shouted from one side.

"I'll clean as many pens as you want if you just say yes," Ben teased, his eyes dark and liquid, tender and expressive, giving her a glimpse into the deep wellspring of his heart.

"I love you, Ben." She bent down and cupped her free hand against his cheek, letting her hair fall to block them from the view of everyone else. "Yes," she whispered against his lips.

A cheer erupted from the group but Emma tuned it out. Nothing existed right now but the two of them. In this sanctuary, their hearts had found a place of safety and refuge, where they had not only saved one another but become whole again. This was only the beginning for their life together. They had already been through the fire, literally and figuratively, and their love had emerged pure, strong and as unending as the ring Ben slid on her finger.

Keep reading for an excerpt from the
first book in T. J.'s Hidden Falls series,

Making the Play

Grant McQuaid has dedicated his entire life to his
football career. Now an injury threatens his place on
the team and he's forced to return home to rehabilitate.
But when he meets his "biggest fan," a precocious,
blue-eyed, hearing impaired boy named James—and
his beautiful mother, Bethany—Grant begins to
question whether football is the future he still wants.

Bethany Mills has been doing just fine since her
husband walked out on them . . . and she definitely
doesn't need another man to disappoint her—or her
son. But when James runs into his hero at the park,
Bethany admits there is a void in her son's life that
she just can't fill. Her attraction to the handsome
football star is undeniable, but a man in the limelight
is the last thing she wants for herself, or James.

Grant doesn't want to subject Bethany to the chaos
of dating a professional athlete. But the more
time he spends with her and James, the harder
it is to resist making a play for her heart . . .

Chapter One

BETHANY MILLS WANTED to give in to the normally angelic cherub face in front of her that was now scrunched in anger. "Because we aren't playing football at recess today. I already explained that to you."

Like most six-year-olds, her son, James, was prone to throw temper tantrums when he didn't get his way. Unlike other kids his age, James would refuse to say anything verbally. Instead, his fingers flew in a blur of American Sign Language, letting her know just how angry he was at her explanation. Although he was perfectly capable of speaking, thanks to the cochlear implants her ex-husband's medical insurance had provided before James' first birthday, Bethany's son continued to fall back on signing when he was angry. She understood it was due to the fact that he stuttered and had a hard time pronouncing his words when he was emotional, but she was trying to teach him to continue to use both. Life wasn't easy and, in spite of what many saw as a disability, she couldn't allow her son to take the path of least resistance. It was a painful truth she'd been forced to face early on when her husband ran out on both of them twelve months after James' diagnosis at two months old, just before serving her with divorce papers.

Life as a single mother was hard enough. Life as a single mother at twenty to a child with a disability and no child support would have been impossible if not for her parents' stepping in and allowing her to move back in until she could finish college and earn her teaching degree.

"Not today, James," she reiterated. "The other kids are playing T-ball. You should go ask if you can play too."

She watched as her son pursed his lips and balled his fists before stomping across the playground to pout near the swings. Bethany sighed loudly, knowing this was something every child went through, that every *parent* went through, but wondering if it would ever get easier. She couldn't give in to James' demand but she couldn't stand the thought of her son being angry at her all day either. Not to mention, it would only cause trouble when they returned to the classroom after recess. There were definite drawbacks to being her son's kindergarten teacher.

She traced his steps to the swings, trying not to smile when she saw him turn his back on her as he continued to peek over his shoulder to see if she would come to him. Bethany squatted down beside him, her peasant skirt billowing around her, and waited for him to turn and face her.

"James, if you go play ball with the other kids, we'll go to the park after school today." She signed as she spoke. His blue eyes sparkled at the thought but he paused.

"Ice cream too?" This time he spoke and she let the smile curve her lips. *The little stinker thought he was conning her.*

"Yes, I think we can get ice cream too, but only if you are able to read all your sight words for Ms. Julie."

At least, she prayed that's what her teacher's aide had planned for the kids today. Julie was indispensable in her classroom after lunch, when most of the kids were hyper beyond belief, and she hoped they weren't going to have to change the lesson plans again today to accommodate the kids' activity level. Bethany couldn't help but wonder if her students' parents were feeding their kids straight sugar for lunch.

James pursed his lips and looked toward the sky. It was his "thinking" look and it never failed to make her want to hug him. Before she could, he threw his arms around her neck and ran off to meet up with the group of kids playing on the open lawn. Bethany stood and sighed again just as James stopped to get her attention.

I want chocolate, he signed.

She nodded and signed her approval as he spun on his heel and hurried toward the other kids. Her baby was growing up far too quickly for her liking.

She heard the quiet chuckle from behind her as

Steven Carter, the other kindergarten teacher at Hidden Falls Elementary walked toward her. "I don't know how you do it," he said with a shake of his head.

"Do what?"

"Teach him just like the other kids."

Bethany felt herself bristle. She'd dealt with people singling James out because of his disability for years. It never failed to make the mama bear in her rise to the surface. "I'll have you know, James is just as bright as any *normal* child, Mr. Carter. In fact, he's already reading at a second-grade level. Just because he has implants to help him hear doesn't make him stupid."

The other teacher took a step back, his eyes widening. "Uh, that's not what I meant," he said, holding his hands up in front of him. "I just meant that it's hard enough to keep twenty kids under control in the classroom and keep my mind on what I'm teaching without trying to sign at the same time."

"Oh!" Bethany felt the blush rise up her neck and cheeks at the way she'd immediately become defensive. "I'm sorry, I just . . ."

"No, I shouldn't have said it that way." He moved to stand at her side, slipping his hands into the pockets of his slacks and watched the kids play on the field. "Truce?"

She ducked her head, embarrassed to have jumped to conclusions. "Yes. I *am* sorry though. I have a tendency to be a bit overprotective."

He shot her a sideways glance. "And I have a tendency to speak before I think," he admitted. "Maybe

I could make it up to you over coffee?" He cleared his throat nervously. "Or dinner?"

Bethany felt blindsided. She hadn't expected him to ask her out. She'd heard several of the other women talking about the new teacher in the break room, swooning over his tall, lean physique and stormy gray eyes, but she thought it strange to want to date someone you worked with. What if it didn't go well? What if it did? It was just too much drama either way for the workplace, especially when that workplace was an elementary school in a town as small as Hidden Falls.

"Ah, I really appreciate the offer, Mr. Carter," she said, trying not to seem too callous. "But I don't think it would be a good idea."

She'd been out of the dating pool so long, the refusal slid easily from her lips without her having to struggle with what to say. It wasn't that she hadn't been asked out. She had, far too many times for her liking, but she wasn't about to introduce another man into her life, or James' life, only to be abandoned again. Her son would be forced to deal with enough adversity in his future. She didn't see the need to add an emotional tie to someone who wasn't likely to stick around. It was better that James knew her unconditional reassurance than suffer the added sting of rejection if that was something she had any control over. He'd been hurt enough. They *both* had.

Acknowledgments

FIRST, I NEED to thank Tessa Woodward, my editor extraordinaire, who always makes me dig deeper, push harder and step out of my comfort zone. Thank you for reminding me of who I can be when I think I've reached my limit.

Suzie Townsend and Sara Stricker, I adore the two of you for getting me. You two have been the best coach, cheerleader, inspiration and champions I could have ever asked for.

I have a special thank you for Captain Matt Picchi of the Roseville Fire Department for answering so many of my oddly specific questions and, to his beautiful wife, my dear, wonderful friend, Marsha, for sharing him with me.

Thank you to my writer friends for keeping me on track and constantly challenging me to work to the bar you set, especially Cody and Kristin, and not letting me use my schedule as an excuse to slow down. Thank you to my reader friends for not only wanting more from me but sharing with others. Amy, Allisia, Monique, Catherine, Elizabeth, Crystal, Misty, Rhonda, Jen and Pauline . . . you ladies make what I do even more fun than it should be.

Finally, to thank my family. There's nothing I can say that could possibly thank you enough for the encouragement you give me. Honestly, I can only continue to show you my gratitude with all the gifts I'll shower you with (just kidding!). I love each of you more than you'll ever understand—"to the moon and back again" infinity.

About the Author

T. J. KLINE was raised since the age of 14 to compete in rodeos and Rodeo Queen competitions, and she has a thorough knowledge of the sport as well as the culture involved. She writes contemporary western romance for Avon Romance, including the Rodeo series and the Healing Harts series. She has published a non-fiction health book and two inspirational fiction titles under the name Tina Klinesmith. In her very limited spare time, T. J. can be found laughing hysterically with her husband, children and their menagerie of pets in Northern California.

Discover great authors, exclusive offers and more at hc.com.